Psalm 42:2

My soul thirsts for God,
for the living God.
When can I go and meet
with God?

To Irma —

Psalm 42?

Book One in the Mended Vessels Series

For Such a Moment

Marie Wells Coutu

Marie Wells Coutu

For Such a Moment

© 2013 Marie Wells Coutu

ISBN-13: 978-1-938092-38-1

ISBN-10: 1938092384

Published by Write Integrity Press, 130 Prominence Point Pkwy. #130-330, Canton, GA 30114.

www.WriteIntegrity.com

Printed in the United States of America.

Lovingly dedicated to my mother,
Elizabeth Gray Wells (1911-2012),
who also taught me to read and
became the earliest fan of my writing

Acknowledgements

First, I want to thank my husband of 41 years, Ed Coutu, who supported my decision to write fiction even though it took away from "us time." Thank you for being my biggest fan and for showing how much you love me every single day.

I am grateful to my agent, Les Stobbe, for seeing promise in my writing in its early stages.

Thanks to Pat Smathers and Jim Ferguson, who graciously let me pick your brain about your trips to Guatemala.

My deep appreciation to early readers and others who helped with research. I've worked on this book for so many years that I'm sure I will miss someone. (I know now to keep a list in the future.) So if I forget anyone, forgive me. Your comments and assistance were just as valued as these I remember: Ashley McGuire, Crystal Allen, Diane Wells, Charlie Wells, Robin Johnston, Bendetta Wells, Ann Fuller, Sarah Howk, Gale Smith, Sandy Rea, Faith Webb, Joelle Coutu; and anonymous judges in the Genesis and Frasier contests who provided helpful feedback.

Jerri Menges, words cannot express how helpful you were in reviewing, commenting on, and editing the manuscript (several times). May God continue to bless and enhance your editing skills.

I owe endless gratitude to my publisher, Tracy Ruckman, who sponsored the Books of Hope Contest and who finally made my dream of being a published novelist come true. Thank you for believing in the power of story and the potential of this one and the Mended Vessels series.

Most of all, thank you to the One who gave me the ability to write and the inspiration for this story, who encourages me daily through His Word, and who offers hope and truth to all who seek Him—my Lord and Savior, Jesus Christ.

"In fact, if you don't speak up at this very important time, relief and rescue will appear for the Jews from another place, but you and your family will die. But who knows? Maybe it was for a moment like this that you came to be part of the royal family."

Book of Esther 4:14, CEB

Chapter One

Ellen Nielson scanned the large office, seeking a secret corner where she could escape. But the ten-foot-tall antique paneled walls and *Architectural Digest* furnishings offered no hiding place. No corner where she could curl up and pretend the doctor had made a mistake. Pretend to be three years old, not thirty.

She must have done something terribly wrong to have earned the blow her doctor had just delivered. *No children. Ever.*

Dr. Rostenberg continued the barrage of words—words as cold and biting as the sleet and snow hitting the tall, narrow windows.

Ellen squeezed her eyes shut. She had imagined rocking her babies, building snowmen with her children, pushing them on the swings at the park.

The doctor's voice broke through her clouded mind. "Mrs. Neilson, do you understand what I'm telling you?"

Ellen sat militarily tall, the way her dad had taught her, and held onto the arms of the overstuffed chair as if it were a life raft. She fought to keep her voice level. "I can never have children."

Dr. Rostenberg pressed her lips together. "I know this is difficult for you. I'm sorry that I can't give you more answers or at least provide some hope."

Ellen leaned toward the elegant desk. Slowly and softly she spoke, just above a whisper. "You said the infection I had as a child caused it."

Dr. Rostenberg looked down at the slim file that lay open

in front of her. "Your tests show that you had tuberculosis. I can only surmise that the infection progressed to genital tuberculosis, resulting in the intrauterine scar tissue we found. This has left your uterus incapable of receiving a fertilized egg."

Ellen hated the doctor's sterile voice, cold and remote, as if she were reading from a textbook. But she would not have gone to anyone else. Dr. Rostenberg was the top infertility specialist in Minnesota. Ellen leaned back and released her grip on the chair arms, moving her hands to her lap. Even though she had survived the illness that killed her mother, it had left her infertile. And she hadn't even known it. She willed her face to stay calm, expressionless, despite the turmoil swirling in her stomach. "Then it's my fault my husband and I cannot have children."

The doctor frowned and shook her head. "You shouldn't blame yourself."

"I didn't know TB could cause infertility."

Dr. Rostenberg leaned back and took off her glasses. "Usually it doesn't—if it is treated. We might be able to confirm my diagnosis if I could see your medical records from—"

"There are no medical records. As you guessed, I wasn't treated at the time." Ellen stood, gathering her coat and gloves. She saw no reason to continue the discussion. "Besides, what difference would it make? I'm incapable of having children, and there's nothing you can do."

She strode across the thick carpet to the door.

"Mrs. Neilson."

Ellen looked back, her hand already on the doorknob. "I appreciate your time." Her *mamá* had taught her to be polite, and she hadn't been today.

"If you would like me to meet with your husband, I would

be happy to explain my diagnosis to him," Dr. Rostenberg said.

"Thank you, but no, that won't be necessary. I'll … I'll tell him myself."

Somehow. She had to find the right words to tell Erik.

"Mrs. Neilson, you do have another option—"

Ellen didn't want to know about any other option. She wanted a baby. Hers and Erik's baby. A baby might rescue their relationship, bring them back together.

She closed the door and mechanically made her way through the clinic's checkout process. As soon as she reached the lobby of the elegant historic building, she slid into the restroom. Thankfully, it was empty. She locked herself into a stall and leaned against the cold granite door.

She let her tears flow and reached for the toilet paper to wipe her eyes. One thin square tore off. She plopped onto the toilet seat and pulled off a long section of paper. She leaned forward to blow her nose and the automatic flush activated, spattering water on the bottom of her pants suit.

She gulped air between sobs. "You've done it again, God." She wanted to yell, but instead she whispered. "Why can't you just leave me alone?"

After a few minutes, she ordered the tears to stop and took several deep breaths. She stepped out to a sink, ran cold water over her fingers, and dabbed at her eyes. She tugged at a paper towel and a thick stack fell out of the dispenser onto the marble counter. Any other day, she might have laughed at the mishap.

She wiped her face with the rough paper and leaned in close to the mirror. Using the makeup from her purse, she tried to hide the splotches on her long face and pointed chin. For once, she wished she had her mother's brown skin that wouldn't show the red streaks. Ellen looked like her *mamá*, with dark, almost black eyes and straight black hair. But she had the fair complexion, along with the tall, slender frame of her American father that obscured her Mayan heritage and led to the common assumption that she had been born in the United States.

Erik knew she was born in Guatemala. But he didn't know that she had lived there for ten years with her Mayan mother before moving to Kentucky to live with her father and stepmother. Perhaps he wouldn't have the same disdain for the Maya Indians that the *ladino* Guatemalans had. But she could not risk having him look at her with the disgust that she remembered seeing, even in the faces of the men who had visited her mother in their little shanty. No, as much as she wanted to, she could never tell Erik her whole story.

She inspected her face. Satisfied she had covered the evidence of her anguish, she returned to the lobby. Ordinarily, the snow and frigid wind that blew into Minneapolis overnight from the Dakotas would have kept her snug at home by a fire. But it had taken months to get the appointment with Dr. Rostenberg, and she would not have dared miss it. She should have stayed home, clinging to uncertainty and hope. Now, that hope disappeared into the snow whirling around the Nicollet Mall outside the large windows.

Ellen's best friend Diane had cautioned her that having a child might not be the right answer for her marriage. "That's a huge burden for a tiny baby," she had said. "The child will be the one to suffer most if you don't make the marriage work first." She had to concede that Diane might be right, and now it would seem that God agreed.

Ellen pulled on her suede gloves and snugged the mink-lined hood of her Armani leather coat around her face. She relished the soft touch of fur, the luxurious feeling that assured her she would never go hungry again. It reminded her of the comfort and tenderness she had always experienced in Erik's presence. Until the last year or so.

She gulped several deep breaths to store warm air and pushed on the heavy door. A gust caught the glass and jerked it all the way open. Fighting the blast, she struggled to walk out and to push the door shut again. Despite ice-slickened footing, she hustled across the pedestrian mall and turned the corner by Bruegger's Bagels. On the spur of the moment, she ducked into the shop for a few minutes to collect her thoughts and escape the bone-chilling cold. If only she could so easily evade the freeze locking up her insides.

The aroma of warm cinnamon tickled her nose. She ordered hot tea and sat at a small table in the corner. She inhaled the steam as she wrapped her hands around the paper cup, grateful for its heat. What would she say to Erik? He had changed since the responsibility of running the company had been thrust upon him four years ago. They had been happily in love for the first three years of their marriage; now all he cared about was growing, processing, and distributing fruits. Millions of dollars' worth of bananas, coconuts, oranges, and pineapples. His father had been like that—always preoccupied, always busy. Now Erik was becoming just like him: focused on meetings and business deals, increasing production and reducing expenses. Did he even want a child?

Her after-school class at the Walker Art Center had been cancelled because of the storm, so she could go see Erik right now. She worked out a speech in her head—brief and void of details. Better not to say too much. She gathered her things. On her way out, she tossed the full cup of tea in the trash can.

The tall buildings blocked some of the wind as she hurried the last two blocks to the Neilson Building at 46 South Sixth Street. She stepped inside the revolving door and relished the warm air. She let her cheek brush against the wet fur before she pushed the hood of her coat down and shook her thick shoulder-length hair back into place. Her brown knee-high boots struck a dirge across the granite squares.

A uniformed guard looked up from his newspaper.

"Morning, Miz Neilson. Cold enough for ya?"

Ellen paused to sign the guest log. She couldn't return his cheerful greeting, but she remembered her manners. "The week of Thanksgiving is too early for a storm this bad."

"I hear ya. Lived here my whole life, but some days, I'd move to Florida in a minute if I could." His mouth twisted down on one end, and Ellen heard more than the usual Minnesotan-tired-of-the-cold complaint.

"What's stopping you?"

He shook his head, rustling the fringe of gray hair that edged his high, shiny forehead. "Kids and grandkids are all here. The wife won't leave 'em, and we can't afford to be snowbirds."

A knife twisted in her middle. Everyone had children. "You can't blame her. Family's the most important thing."

"Yes, ma'am. Guess I wouldn't really want to leave 'em myself."

She nodded, moving away to escape the conversation. "Try to stay warm, Ed."

She hurried toward the bank of elevators. The doors of the left elevator opened, and she waited for a man to get off before she stepped in. She pushed the button marked *27* and leaned against the polished wall.

No one disturbed her by calling for the elevator, and she reviewed what she would say to Erik. She went over it twice before a soft "ding" announced that the carriage had reached the top floor.

She crossed the spacious reception area and approached the desk. Marcie, Erik's pleasant, gray-haired secretary, typed at her computer. She turned to greet Ellen with a smile that chased away some of the chill.

"Mrs. Neilson. I wasn't expecting you. Did Mr. Neilson know you were coming?" Marcie didn't wait for an answer. "The executive team has been meeting since nine. But they'll probably break for lunch soon if you'd like to wait."

"Thanks, Marcie. I'll just make myself some tea." She hurried down the hallway toward the kitchen area. She needed to be busy, not sitting in the outer office waiting. She always felt out of place there, despite Marcie's friendliness. She decided to fix tea for Marcie, too.

She returned in minutes carrying two mugs of chai just as the double doors to Erik's office opened. She set one cup in front of Marcie and then turned to speak to the executives leaving her husband's office.

The first pair of men checked their iPhones as they walked past her, looking up just long enough to return her greeting.

She smiled at the next group, a woman and two men debating lunch plans. Ellen watched the final group move toward the office door. She recognized two of the men, but not the third one.

Erik must have finally filled the vacant managing director's position. The short, muscular man shook hands with Erik, and Ellen noted his prominent, well-shaped nose and high forehead. His cropped black hair and golden brown skin told her he might be Latino—maybe even Mayan, though that would be a rarity here in Minneapolis.

When he turned and came through the doorway, Ellen looked into his dark eyes and stopped smiling.

Chapter Two

Ellen could never forget the boy with the razor-sharp nose, the full lips, and the coffee-brown eyes who had challenged other kids when they made fun of her, who had comforted her after her *mamá* died.

But her cousin Manuel couldn't be here, now, after all these years. Could he?

"Ellen, are you all right?" Warren Stubbs stood in front of her, invading her space. Long-forgotten images faded, and she focused on the familiar flabby face. Erik's senior vice president, slightly shorter than her own five foot nine inches, rose on his toes as if trying to compensate for his size.

"I'm fine, Warren. I just, uh, felt a little dizzy for a minute."

"Good. Good." He nodded as if he hadn't heard the last part. "We can't have you getting sick just before the holidays, can we?"

Before she could think of an appropriate answer, Warren scurried after the other two men.

Ellen watched as the three men got on the elevator. She found the one who looked like Manuel, and his gaze met hers. She turned away as the elevator doors closed.

The chances of him being Manuel were impossibly thin.

"Ellen." Erik came through the doors. Her six foot two husband bent his fair head toward hers and let his lips brush her cheek. "I didn't know you were coming." He put his hand on her arm and steered her into his spacious office. Inside, he pushed the doors closed, let go of her arm, and gave her a brief kiss on the lips.

He broke away and hurried to his massive mahogany desk where he grabbed the computer mouse and made several quick clicks while he peered at the monitor without sitting down. "Were we having lunch today? I don't have it on my calendar." He gestured to a stack of papers on his desk. "And I need to work on these board reports this afternoon."

Ellen moved to the leather sofa by the gas fireplace and sank into its welcoming cushions. She set her cup on a side table and bent to unzip her boots. "No, we hadn't made any plans for lunch. I was downtown and thought I'd stop by. I won't stay long." She wouldn't interfere with his work.

He continued to study the computer monitor and click the mouse. "What were you thinking, coming downtown on a day like this? The governor shut down the schools; surely the Walker can cancel your classes."

"Yes, they've canceled classes." She hated not seeing her students, even for one day. They might be the only children she would ever have. She breathed deeply and plunged ahead. "I had that appointment this morning."

"Appointment? Oh, with that Doctor Roster ... whatever?" He looked up, took a look at her, reached the couch in two strides, and sat down facing her. He took her hands.

"So what did he say?" He acted genuinely concerned. "Can he help?"

She. The doctor's a woman. He couldn't even get that right, although they had just talked about her last night. Ellen shook her head, her hair fluttering against her cheeks. Forcing back tears, she stammered, "No. I can't—" So much for the planned speech. "When I was little, I had an infection. I can't get pregnant."

A shadow fell over his ice-blue eyes. "An infection? What kind of infection keeps you from having children?"

She couldn't answer him. He moved closer and folded her

into his arms. "If it's that important to you to have a baby, we'll get a second opinion, and a third."

That was his answer to everything—throw money at it. She sank against him, and he held her for several minutes. Like it always had, his embrace took her to a warm spot, made her feel as though she were wrapped in layers of soft blankets, surrounded by an impregnable wall.

But these were not the old days. These days, he had work to do. He patted her back and released her. "We'll figure out a way."

He moved back to his desk and shuffled papers. She didn't want to leave yet, but his attention had moved on. She followed his lead and compartmentalized her thoughts, saving the problem for a time when she could be alone. She tugged her left boot off, then the right one, and her toes grasped for comfort in the deep green richness of the lush carpet.

Searching for a change of topic, she stood and padded to the oversized windows. Snow mixed with sleet continued to fall, shrouding the city below and making the streets treacherous. "Diane called. She'll be in town week after next."

Erik focused on his computer. "Diane? Your high school friend? Will you see her?"

"Of course. I asked if she could come for dinner, but she's only here one day. We'll have lunch." She hesitated. "You can join us if you'd like."

"No, thanks. I wouldn't want to get in the way of two school chums catching up on every single detail since you last saw each other—which was, when? Her wedding? I'll pass."

Relieved that she and Diane would be able to talk privately, she settled onto the sofa again and stretched out her legs. She recalled the man in the elevator and tried to sound casual. "I saw a new face out there. Did you fill that managing director position for Latin America?"

Without looking at her, Erik nodded. "Um-hmm. Good man. Worked his way up through the company. Turned around one of our canning facilities in six months. And the workers love him. I think he'll be a good fit."

He didn't give the man's name, but it couldn't be Manuel. She hadn't seen him for twenty years; would she even recognize him now?

Erik interrupted her thoughts. "We set a date for the E-team holiday party. Friday the thirtieth." He seemed to remember his manners and turned his chair around to look at her. "Does that work for you?"

The Neilsons traditionally held a party at their mansion on Lake Harriet during the Christmas season. Good thing she and Angelica, her housekeeper and cook, had already made plans, since the selected date was just over two weeks away.

All the vice presidents and managing directors —the executive team—and their spouses would come. If the man she had seen was Manuel, would his presence force her to reveal the truth about her childhood?

Erik had reports from every division to review and summarize for the Board of Directors, and he didn't take a break until mid-afternoon. When he stretched and stood up, he caught sight of Ellen's green gloves on the sofa. Her hands must have been freezing on the way home. Why hadn't she come back for them?

He walked over, picked them up, and lifted them to his nose. Her favorite fragrance—he never could remember its name—mixed with the musky scents of wool and leather. So typical of her to leave her gloves behind. One more example of why he needed to take care of her, like a child.

She wanted a baby and couldn't have one. That problem wouldn't be as simple for him to fix as returning her gloves would be. Even if they found a solution, would a child satisfy her? She seemed to think a child would fix their marriage, as if they had problems. But they didn't. Not really. She loved him, and he loved her. She just didn't understand that he had a multi-million dollar company to run.

Crossing back to his desk, he tossed the gloves in his open briefcase. He thought of the day he first spotted Ellen in the student union at the University of Minnesota where he and several fraternity brothers had been making plans for a blood drive. He couldn't take his eyes off the young woman wearing jeans and a blue sweater that set off her light complexion and black hair. He had approached her on the pretext of asking if she would give blood.

She told him she hated needles, but he persuaded her to join him for an ice cream sundae. He learned that, like him, she was an only child but her parents were dead. They had shared conversation and laughter. They both wanted to help their community, and she volunteered to help with the blood drive. Soon their friendship grew into love, and they married following her graduation.

He moved to the bookcase against the wall and picked up a baseball that sat in a wooden holder. His first baseball, the one his father gave him for his eighth birthday. He tossed it from one hand to another, a habit he had developed when he needed to think, when he wanted a connection with his father. Sometimes it helped to recall the summer days when they had played catch together, or the few times Dad had watched him play on the high school varsity team. But today it didn't help.

He replaced the ball and returned to his chair. His eyes sought the steel-blue eyes in the gold-framed photo on his desk—the desk that had once been his father's throne. From this desk, this office, his father had governed Neilson Enterprises. Grown it from the million-dollar, regional company his own father had started into a multi-million-dollar global corporation.

"Dad," Erik whispered. "Ellen thinks we're in trouble. If she can't have children, things may just get worse. What should I do?"

The photo provided no more guidance than his father had provided when he was alive. In spite of all his efforts to make his father proud, Erik had never known if he succeeded. He didn't remember a time when his father had given him advice. Commands, yes, but advice? No. As always, he had to find his own solution.

He sat in the leather swivel chair and pressed the intercom button. "Marcie, would you come in here, please?"

Moments later, the door opened and Marcie appeared, steno pad in hand. He rarely gave her dictation, preferring to compose letters and reports on his computer. But she had started as his father's secretary before the days of computers, and she always came prepared. She would have made a good Boy Scout. He smiled at the image of her wearing the famous beige uniform.

She sat, pencil poised, and watched him.

With a wave of his hand, he dismissed her note taking. He propped his elbows on the desk and rested his chin in his hands. "What do you know about infertility treatments?"

"Sir?"

"Infertility treatments. Or surrogacy. Anything to help a woman who can't have children."

She folded her hands on top of the notebook on her lap. "Not very much. Why do you ask?"

"You're a mother and grandmother. I thought you would know about such things."

Her mouth twisted in a half-smile. "I had a friend once who was unable to conceive. But that was a long time ago."

"Okay. What did she do?"

"I remember that she and her husband went to lots of doctors. They were always taking her, um, temperature." She put a hand to her cheek, which now matched her pink fingernail polish. "Eventually they decided to adopt, and right after they got the baby, she discovered she was pregnant. It seemed like once the pressure was off, they relaxed and everything just—worked."

From what Ellen had said, their issue would not be that simple. He knew so little about these things. Like why the specialist didn't suggest surgery—unless even an operation would not fix the problem.

"Mr. Neilson?" Marcie peered at him, her forehead wrinkled.

"Hmm? Oh, sorry." He sat up straight and ran his hand through his short hair. "Would you, that is, if you wouldn't mind ..." He struggled for the right words. "I would appreciate it if you would do some research for me."

Her puzzled look told him he would have to explain. "Ellen is infertile due to a childhood infection and she can't have children."

Marcie gasped. "I'm so sorry, sir. I didn't realize—"

"See if there's any surgery for that sort of thing. And then see what you can find out about surrogates. How the heck do you find one, and how does that work?"

"Of course, sir. Anything else?"

"Not right now. And, Marcie, don't mention this—not even to Ellen. I don't think she wants anyone to know. At least, not yet."

"I can understand that," she said. "It's between you and me, as always."

Erik nodded. "I know. I appreciate it."

Marcie would dig up every tidbit of information available. Then he could decide on the best option.

Chapter Three

As she climbed the steps at The Station the Wednesday after Thanksgiving, Ellen halted. She heard the clatter of the lunch crowd at the gas-station-turned-restaurant. She didn't want to deal with a host of people today, but she needed to see her best friend again.

At the top of the stairs, she spotted Diane right away. Her tall copper-haired friend was easy to find, even in the busy restaurant.

Ellen resisted the urge to run to where Diane sat alone, reading the *Star Tribune*. "Hey, you," she said as she reached the table.

Diane looked up and grinned. "Hey you, yourself," she replied, as though they saw each other every day. She dropped the newspaper on the table and unfolded her slim body from the booth to give Ellen a hug.

"It's so good to see you, Laynie." Diane used the affectionate nickname Ellen's father had given her. "You look smashing."

Ellen squeezed her, savoring her friend's nearness. She couldn't keep her emotions from leaking out in her voice. "I've really missed you, especially lately."

Diane pulled back and wrinkled her brow. "Let's order lunch, and then you can tell me all about it."

Ellen settled into the booth opposite Diane and watched her survey the funky neighborhood hangout. Hubcaps and old license plates from all over the U.S. filled the walls. The restaurant had been their favorite after they graduated from the U of M.

Last year, Diane had moved back home to Kentucky to get married, and she hadn't been back until now. She nodded. "It's perfect. Just like I remember it."

A waitress wearing a gray mechanic's shirt with "Kira" embroidered above the pocket took their orders.

Diane pushed her bright green wool coat further into the corner of the booth and squared herself opposite Ellen. "So, what's up? Things haven't improved between you and Erik?"

"Not really. And now—" Ellen waited while a young man wearing blue coveralls set their beverages in front of them. When he was out of earshot, she took a deep breath. The pain still pierced her, and she hadn't told her news to anyone but Erik. "I had an appointment with the fertility specialist last week."

"And? Can she help you?"

Ellen gnawed her bottom lip. "She said that—" Fighting the snuffle in the back of her throat, she tried again. She picked up the spoon in front of her and made it tap dance on the table. "I can't have children. Not even with in vitro fertilization. My uterus is damaged. The doctor thinks I had tuberculosis before I came to live with my dad. And it caused scarring."

Diane reached across the table with both hands and covered Ellen's right hand, interrupting the tap-tap of the spoon. "I'm so sorry, Laynie," she said. "I'll be praying."

Ellen's ears heated up, and her pulse quickened. She jerked her hand away. "Don't bother. There's nothing else they can do. I can't get pregnant; I can't have children."

"I meant I'll pray for you and Erik. That you'll both trust God to get you through this."

A meat tenderizer had just pulverized Ellen's sore heart. God wouldn't help with her problems. He had caused them. She would find her own solution, not wait for a faceless God to come to her rescue.

Kira arrived with their food, and Ellen twisted the napkin in her lap with both hands. After the waitress left, she lowered her voice. "I don't get you, Di. You know what I've been through. After everything God's done to me, why would I trust him for anything?"

"Before I answer that, do you mind if I pray for the food?"

Ellen pressed her lips together and kept her eyes wide open while Diane gave thanks for the food and their friendship. She said "amen," and they picked up their forks.

Diane tasted the smashed potatoes. "Ummm. Just as good as ever." She sipped her strawberry lemonade. "Laynie, God isn't to blame for the things that happened to you. He loves you, and He wants the best—"

"If God loves me so much, why did he let my mother die? And my stepmother and then my father? And now this." Ellen hovered on the brink of shouting. "If he's such a great God, he could have prevented all those things. So either he hates me and is punishing me, or he doesn't have any power."

To calm herself, she grabbed her glass and gulped the kiwi lemonade. "Either way, I don't want anything to do with Him. I'll figure out what to do without any help from Him." She leaned back and her shoulders wilted. "I was hoping we could just have an enjoyable visit like old times. I'd rather not hear about your God."

Diane paused her fork in midair. She moved it back to her plate and stabbed a bite-sized piece of grilled chicken. "I'm sorry. I know we've been over this subject before. I didn't mean to upset you. But I'm worried about you."

For several minutes, they ate without talking, letting the sounds of clanking silverware and laughter of the other diners fill the awkward space. Ellen knew how passionate Diane felt about her relationship with Jesus. It had been the only sore spot between them in their twenty-year friendship. When she had first come to the U.S. to live with her father, out of all the girls in her fifth-grade class, Diane had been the first one to befriend her.

She regretted her outburst, but she wouldn't change her mind.

Diane broke the stalemate. "What does Erik have to say—about the doctor's verdict, I mean?"

Ellen picked up a breadstick and tugged it in half. "All he said was that we could see other specialists, or find a surrogate. I'm not sure he cares whether we have a child or not."

"Laynie, I'm sure you're wrong about that."

The waitress removed their empty plates and asked if they wanted dessert. The two women grinned at each other.

"Cheesecake," they said in unison and laughed. The double-decker dessert had always been their shared indulgence.

When the server left, Diane reached for her glass and sipped the lemonade. "Erik's always taken an interest in orphans in the countries where the company owns facilities, hasn't he? You could look into international adoption." She hesitated. "But like I said before, you need to be sure you have a solid marriage before you and Erik have a family. Otherwise, you may be setting yourselves up for failure."

"You're probably right. But I don't know what else I can do."

Diane's face turned serious. "For starters, isn't it time you told him about your childhood? Especially in light of the doctor's diagnosis?"

Ellen pointed her fork at Diane. "No, Di. I can't tell him. Ever."

"I have to say it again. A relationship that isn't completely honest will never have the solid footing that a strong marriage needs."

Heat rose to Ellen's face again. "Diane, you know I'd like

to tell him everything. But I just can't. Things would never be the same between us if he knew all that I went through as a child."

They remained silent as the waitress delivered their dessert. The sight of the four-inch-high slices lightened the tension. Diane dug into hers and, closing her eyes, smiled a crooked smile.

"What? Are you that starved for cheesecake?" Ellen took a bite of her own piece.

"No. Just thinking about us. Sisters forever, right?"

"Right." They clicked their forks together, repeating a ritual from their teen years.

"It's ironic, huh?" Diane reloaded her fork. "We both married men who inherited their family's business, and now, if you and Erik should adopt, we'll both be mothers to children who are not biologically ours."

"Speaking of that, how's the home schooling going?"

Diane's face lit up, as it always did when she talked about eight-year-old Michael and six-year-old Doreen, her husband's children from his first marriage. "It's great. The kids have really taken to it, and I love it. Forgive me, but I have to show you this picture." She pulled out her smartphone and handed it over, revealing a photo of herself with two children—and an elephant in the background. "Mike took a day off for a field trip to the zoo. Our home school association planned it."

A spasm of jealousy surged through Ellen. She swallowed that thought along with the last bite of her cheesecake.

Diane dabbed at her face with her napkin. "So what else is happening, Laynie?"

"You remember I told you how Manuel used to watch after me?"

"Your cousin. Yes, I remember. Did you ever get in touch with him?"

"No."

"I know you wanted to forget that part of your life, but he's family." She laid her napkin over her empty plate. "Have you decided to try to find him now?"

Ellen shook her head. "I saw someone who looks like him. At least, what I think he'd look like now."

"Here? In Minnesota?"

Nodding, Ellen sipped her lemonade. "In Erik's office, of all places. It can't be him, of course, but I can't stop thinking about him."

"Why couldn't it be him? Did you ask Erik?"

"No!" Ellen shifted in her seat. "I mean, he did say he's the new Latin America managing director, but I didn't dare ask his name. I ... I can't risk Erik even suspecting that I might know him."

"Where's he from? Did Erik say if he's from Guatemala? How did he wind up working for Neilson Enterprises? What's the chance? Oh, Laynie. You have to find out. I mean, if it is Manuel, aren't you excited to see him after all these years? Did he recognize you? What a reunion you could have." Diane's reporter's instincts had kicked in, the questions coming faster than Ellen could think.

She waited until Diane wound down. "This guy will probably come to our holiday party. I'll find out then. But if it is him ... I hope he doesn't recognize me. He could ruin everything."

Diane locked eyes with Ellen. "Why don't you tell Erik? Then you won't have to worry anymore. What's the worst that could happen?"

"He wouldn't understand." Her words escaped as a whisper. "If it is Manuel, and he recognizes me, I'll just have to pretend he's mistaken."

"You know I think you're wrong, Laynie. Erik loves you.

Your past wouldn't bother him any more than it does me."

Even her best friend didn't understand. She fanned her warm face with her hand. "You married a guy you've known all your life—good for you. But I'll handle my marriage the way I think best."

She grabbed her coat and gloves, needing to escape while she could still breathe. "I've got to go. I'll take care of the bill on my way out."

She hurried down the winding metal stairs before Diane could say another word.

Chapter Four

Overhead fluorescent lights only amplified the shadows in Ellen's classroom at the Walker Art Center. Beyond the vast windows along one wall, heavy gray clouds threatened more snow. Even her afterschool art students seemed to have abandoned their usual enthusiasm and replaced it with gloom.

Why had she left Diane so abruptly after lunch? It would be months before she would see her again.

Sixteen pairs of small fists hammered and patted at red lumps of clay. With their heads bent over low tables, the children poked and pushed the lumps into shapes that resembled owls.

Ellen leaned over a little girl whose curly black hair was pulled back into a bushy ponytail. Her bright yellow sweater contrasted with her ebony skin. "Lateesha, I like the way you've made the head." She reached for the mass of clay. "May I?" The girl nodded, and she picked up the formation and lifted it high for the class to see.

Table Four, where Lateesha sat, had only two occupants today. Tyrone Barnette was absent. The boy considered this class as important as air. Knowing that only serious trouble would keep him away, Ellen's insides felt as misshapen as the children's sculptures. "Now, boys and girls, don't make your owl's nose stick out, because it will break. You want to give just the impression of a nose."

The nine and ten-year-olds all attended Loring Park Elementary School, just two blocks away. They would know if Tyrone had been in school. She should ask. But did she want to know? The family seemed to attract bad luck the same way she did. Tyrone's mother had died a few months ago, and no one knew what had happened to his father. His seventy-five-year-old paternal grandmother had taken in Tyrone and his younger sister.

Ellen set Lateesha's sculpture on top of the Wal-Mart bag spread out on the table and moved around the room, stopping to check progress on the different owls. She took one boy's hands and helped him to form a hole in the base, being careful not to get clay on the too-big, gray Minnesota Twins sweatshirt he wore. She showed him how to press the sides together, making the inside of the figure hollow.

As she released his hands, she gave him a gentle squeeze with her forearms. She enjoyed all the classes she taught, but these children meant more to her than those from middle and upper-class homes. Like her, they knew about wearing "found" clothing and going to bed hungry.

Mercy raised her hand. "My owl wants to fall apart."

Ellen saw that the girl's clay had started to dry out, so she went to the sink to fill a plastic cup with water. As she headed back to the table, she thought again about Tyrone. She had to ask. "Was Tyrone at school today?"

Several children shook their heads, but Mercy spoke up. "Car hit him yesterday." She made it sound like an everyday occurrence.

Ellen's hands turned clammy. She dropped the plastic cup she was carrying, splattering water across the tile floor. Several children squealed. She grabbed a stack of paper towels from the counter and knelt down to wipe up the mess. "Is he—was he … hurt badly?"

"I saw the amb'lance take him," Mercy said. "Don't know nothing else."

Lateesha knelt by Ellen and began wiping the floor with the brown paper towels. "I'll help you."

"Thank you, Lateesha," Ellen whispered.

What had happened? Children in the neighborhood often played in the streets, even in winter. Tyrone's grandmother must be devastated. And his little sister. With both parents gone, would God be so cruel as to take away her brother, too? She glanced at the clock above the bulletin board. Parents and older siblings would be coming to pick up the children in ten minutes. She instructed the students to wrap up their projects and place them on the counter along the wall. After doing so, they lined up to wash their hands. Ellen handed out wet sponges, and a child at each table scrubbed the surface clean.

While waiting for the stragglers to leave, she finished cleaning the tables and counters. She wanted to find out—what? As soon as the last child had gone, she opened the file of registration forms and found Tyrone's phone number. She punched the number into her cell phone.

"Hello. Me help you?"

Ellen didn't recognize the woman's voice. She double-checked the number. She had dialed correctly. "I, uh, I was looking for Tyrone. Or his grandmother. Do you know them?"

"Yes, yes. Tyrone live here. But—" Her tone changed to a whisper. "In hospital. I stay here, watch Neeta."

Ellen struggled to understand. "Tyrone is—alive?"

"Tyrone hurt bad," the woman said. "Much bad. Alice stay hospital. Pray much."

"Tyrone's grandmother is at the hospital with him?"

"Yes, yes. Hospital."

"Which hospital?"

The woman hesitated. Ellen realized she might be worried about giving out the information. "Tyrone is in my after-school art class. I'd like to go visit him."

"Oh, Meez Neel-son? He talk about you all time."

"That's right. I'm Ellen Neilson." She watched the second hand on the wall clock. "I want to go see Tyrone. What hospital is he in?"

"Wait. I get paper." The squeaky voices of an afternoon cartoon show filtered across the line. Moments later, the woman spoke again, apparently reading from a note. "*H.C.M.C. Pe-di-a-tric. I.C.U.* You know it?"

"I do. Thank you. That helps." Not knowing what else to say, Ellen hung up and collapsed into a tiny red plastic chair.

She had avoided hospitals for the past twelve years, loathed the memories of machines and white uniforms and antiseptic smells. But she had to see Tyrone, to know for certain that he was still alive.

Chapter Five

Five o'clock—about time she showed up.

"I was expecting that report today." Warren Stubbs spoke as soon as Therese Long, Vice President for European Operations, closed the door to his office.

Her citrusy fragrance floated into the room ahead of her, tempting him to chuck everything and fly to Florida with her. But impulsive actions hadn't gotten him this far in life—and they wouldn't get him into the office on the twenty-seventh floor.

Therese shrank into one of the guest chairs in front of his desk. "I know, Warren."

She crossed her slender legs, uncrossed them, and tugged at her skirt, pulling it toward her intriguing knees. She smoothed the fabric and rested her hands in her lap. "It's taking longer than I thought to go through those files. I've only found a few pertinent documents, but I'm sure there's more information that will help us."

She had brought him the idea of going after Erik in the first place. Divorced and raising two children alone, she had ambition, intelligence, and drive, all in a well-designed package. Her division had shown a profit each of the past three years since he had hired her. But she had revealed a loyalty deficit in suggesting this scheme, and he realized that he could as easily be her target. Now she seemed to have lost her nerve.

He leaned his swivel chair as far back as it would go and focused on the speck on the ceiling over his desk, like he often did. "You're sure? You'd better be more than sure." He should report the blemish to maintenance, but they would paint over it.

Studying the dot helped him relax, reminded him that not
everything was flawless, but that he had the power to make the
flaws go away when he wanted to. When he was ready.

"Six months ago, you came to me, remember?" He righted
his chair and speared her with a keen look. "You told me Erik
was wasting company resources because of his do-gooder
policies. It would be easy to prove, you said."

She kept her gaze down, like a cat about to spring for
cover. He swiveled his chair and stared out the window. A few
blocks away, as if stretching toward the storm clouds above,
the Target headquarters towered over the other buildings.
Maybe he should have gone there after Erik's father died. But
he had put in twenty-eight years here at Neilson. He wanted the
presidency. He deserved it.

"Our friend has fronted you a lot of money, Therese." He
picked up a pen from his desk and clicked the tip in and out in
a warning rhythm. "Your new car, private school tuition for
your kids. You'd best not let us down."

That got her attention. She jerked her head up. "Don't
worry." Her voice wavered, and she cleared her throat. "I
won't. I just need more time to finish going through the files
and crunching the numbers. I'll have the figures to support our
position."

He didn't want her to forget how high the stakes had
soared. For both of them. He moved to sit in the chair next to
her and gave her a don't-screw-this-up smile. "I know you will,
Therese. After all, this was your idea. I'll get you another
week. Skip the Neilsons' holiday party if you have to. Just
finish it by a week from today so I can review it before you
deliver the report to our friend."

Chapter Six

Ellen shivered as she rode the cold, sterile elevator to the seventh floor of the Orange Building at Hennepin County Medical Center. She followed signs to Pediatric ICU down a long hallway lined with windows. The white bubble of the Metrodome glared at her through the snow-speckled darkness. Unable to recall the last time she and Erik attended a Twins game—before the team moved to the new ballpark—she trudged on.

The ICU nurse pointed to the third bed where a gap in the blue privacy curtain allowed her to see in. Tyrone's grandmother kneeled by the bed where the boy lay asleep. His lifeline scrolled across a video screen as the monitor played cadence to the rise and fall of the elderly woman's resonant voice. "Oh, Jesus, my Jesus, please help my Tyrone. Lord, we love You. Jesus, Tyrone too young to go be with You just now. I need him, Lord. Neeta need him."

Tyrone's thin body looked like a dark boat in a sea of white linens and bandages. Wires from a metal contraption held up the mast of his right leg. Tubes ran to his arm from the metal rigging that supported bags of clear fluid. Another tube coiled under his hospital gown and into one nostril.

His grandmother sounded so sincere, like she was talking to a friend who would do anything for her. "Lord, Tyrone done lost his momma. His no-good daddy gone. He and Neeta all I got left. Oh, please, Jesus, You can heal him, I know You can, and I'm asking You now to do it, God."

Ellen wanted to barge in and tell her to stop asking someone who didn't—or couldn't—answer. But instead, she stepped through the curtain and cleared her throat. From where she knelt on the floor, Mrs. Barnette turned her head and looked at Ellen then closed her eyes and again rested her forehead on the bed.

"Thank you, Lord, for what You gonna do. Amen." The elderly woman put one hand on the edge of the bed and slowly pushed herself to her feet. She turned and hobbled to Ellen, holding out both arms. Her eyes crinkled in a warm smile that didn't quite make it to her mouth. She nodded and grabbed both of Ellen's hands. "I remember you, Miz Neilson. Tyrone do love your art class. Real nice of you to come see him."

"How is he, Mrs. Barnette?" Ellen spoke softly, not sure if Tyrone could hear her.

The older woman tilted her head toward the bed. "He got a broken pelvis, leg, and arm, and his face banged up. But all that'll heal. Worst thing is, he in a coma. Doctors say he may not wake up, but they don't know my God. My God love this boy, and He gonna bring him back to me."

Ellen extracted her hands from the woman's grasp. She didn't want to get into a discussion about God. God, who let this happen to a child like Tyrone. After all this family had been through. This sweet lady had suffered enough. What could she say? She had no words of comfort. "Do you mind if I talk to him? Can he hear me?"

Mrs. Barnette grimaced. "Where my manners?" She grabbed Ellen's arm and drew her to the bed. "Course, you come to see him. I think he hear, even if he don't show it."

She let go of Ellen's arm and pulled a vinyl-covered chair close to the bed. "You sit here. Talk to him long as you want. I wanted to get me a drink, anyways. I'll be back in a while."

Before Ellen could respond, Mrs. Barnette was gone. Ellen perched on the edge of the chair and waited. She listened as the respirator supplied air to Tyrone's lungs.

"Tyrone," she whispered at last. "It's me, Mrs. Neilson."
Only the machine answered with its rhythmic beeping.

"We missed you in class today. I'd have visited you sooner, but I just heard today that you'd been hurt."

This child had found joy in her art class, in spite of the misery he had endured in his life.

"We made owl sculptures today. You would have liked playing with the clay, Tyrone."

She studied the monitor. The line jumped, straightened out, and jumped again as it scrolled across the screen, taking her back to another hospital ICU, watching another monitor.

She had just turned eighteen, and her dad lay in the bed. Four days she sat in a Kentucky hospital, holding his hand, waiting for a response that never came. She'd glanced from her dad's face to the monitor and back. The line on the monitor went flat. She screamed and struggled as someone moved her into the hallway while the medical team brought in the crash cart. After an eternity, a doctor came out, pulled off his mask, shook his head and said, "I'm sorry."

She despised the drunk driver who hit the car, who killed her father only six months after her stepmother's death. She despised God for taking away the last of her family.

Tyrone's small chest rose ever so slightly and then fell as the machine pumped. Her heartbeat kept time, pounding in her ears. She couldn't stay here, couldn't watch that line straighten out again. She knew the outcome. All the tubes and monitors and doctors and prayers couldn't change it. She had prayed for her dad in spite of her doubts. But he had died anyway. She wouldn't be here watching this time.

She jumped up and rushed out, nearly bumping into Mrs. Barnette. "I—I have to go."

Mrs. Barnette drew back, her eyes questioning. "Good you came. You come back again, hear? Tyrone would like that."

"I'll try." Ellen's dry mouth and her dry mind prevented her from saying anything more. She pulled out her business card. "Call me if there's any change. Please."

She needed fresh air. She hurried out without waiting for a reply, positive she would never again see Tyrone alive.

Chapter Seven

Warren held his breath, trying to ignore the medicine smell of the cleaning solution and the stale urine odors as he hurried down the hall of the convalescent center the next evening. He sidestepped a cart loaded with dirty linens, ignoring the half-hearted greeting of the stooped old woman who ought to be a patient, not an aide.

His mother sat on the edge of her bed, staring at the wall-mounted television. She saw him and beamed. "Hello, dearie. Have you come to visit me?"

Her nearly untouched dinner sat on the rolling tray beside her. At least he could afford a private room, so he didn't have to acknowledge a roommate. "Yes, I am here to see you." He bent and pecked her cheek. "I'm your son, Warren. Remember?"

"Of course I remember." She wrinkled her forehead. "Sit down and tell me all about college. You're studying hard, aren't you?"

At least today she didn't think of him as twelve years old. He pulled a chair close to the bed and reached for her hand. He stroked her dry skin, so thin it revealed her blue veins. "Mom, I finished college. I graduated years ago."

Her face drooped. "You did? Why didn't you invite me? I wanted to see you walk across the stage."

He sighed and patted her hand. "You came. It's been a long time. Now I'm senior vice president of Neilson Enterprises."

"Are you, now?" She blinked several times as she tried to process the statement. She nodded. "Of course you are. I'm proud of you, too. I always knew you'd have your own company someday."

He gave her a tight smile. "Thanks, Mom. It's not my company yet, but it will be soon. I'm working on something now that will give me that opportunity."

"Good, good." She put her other hand over his and gave a squeeze he could hardly feel. She was too thin, and she kept losing strength.

"Don't you want to eat the rest of your dinner?"

"No, no. I've had enough. You can have it." She reached over to the cart and pushed it toward him.

He pushed it back. He understood why she didn't eat the institutional food. "No, Mom. I don't want to take your food. You need it more than I do."

He reached around her and picked up her fork. He scooped mashed potatoes onto it and held it to her mouth. She opened her mouth and accepted the offered food.

After a few more nibbles, she darted her gaze about the room. Her fingers clutched and released the bed sheet in a continual motion. When she finally looked to him, she startled. "Where's your father?"

"He's gone, Mom. It's just you and me." He didn't remind her that his father had abandoned them when Warren was eleven. That it had been just the two of them ever since. Instead, he repeated the words she had used to reassure him forty years ago. "We'll be fine. We don't need him."

An aide stuck her head in the door. "Margaret, are you finished with your dinner? Let me get your tray out of your way." She came in and glanced at the plate and then at him. "She's still not eating much, Mr. Stubbs."

He shook his head. He came at dinnertime as often as he could to encourage her to eat, but he couldn't force her.

The aide picked up the tray and leaned closer. "I'll be

back to get you ready for bed after I get all the trays, Margaret. Okay?" She didn't wait for an answer.

Warren checked his watch. "I have a meeting tonight, so I have to go now. I'll see you tomorrow." He kissed her cheek again. "Good night, Mom."

He picked up his coat and left her staring at the television once more.

Twenty minutes later, he slid into a booth at La Paz Restaurante across from Ronald Lewis. "Is everything all set?" He disliked the dingy atmosphere and the spicy food in this joint. The owners tried to cover up the grime with bright colors and paper festoons, but it was like every other Chicano place he had been. He wanted to conclude his business with Ronald and get away from here.

"I'm ready." The man had retired from professional football seven years ago, and his bulk filled the opposite bench. "We've got two votes locked up and two more on the fence. When we get our hands on that report you've promised, they'll vote with us."

Ronald had joined the Board of Directors for Neilson Enterprises a few months before the airplane crash that killed Erik's parents. He had been the sole voice to oppose naming Erik as successor. Soon after, he asked Warren to report anything that might be used against Erik.

The waitress appeared beside the table and placed a glass of water without ice in front of Warren. She pulled a pad and pen from her pocket and waited.

Warren shook his head. He touched the glass with his forefinger and pushed it toward her. "Nothing for me."

She grabbed the untouched menu and looked at Ronald. "Your dinner will be out in a minute, sir."

As she left, Warren wiped his hands on his pants. "Therese is working on the report. She'll deliver it next

Thursday. You'll have time before the board meeting to convince the others."

"I don't understand what's taking so long. I'm beginning to wonder if you have the leadership ability I thought you did."

Warren's blood pounded in his ears. "I want to make sure Therese uncovers all of Erik's mistakes. I assure you it will be worth the wait."

"We need to get Erik out, so we can run things the way we want."

Warren nodded. The president's office would be his by the end of January. "I'm working on some strategic plans that will take us to a whole new level."

"How's the deal for those banana plantations in Guatemala coming along?"

The waitress approached with two plates piled high with steaming food. She set them down in front of Ronald. "Can I get anything else for you?"

He shook his head and motioned for her to leave.

When she disappeared into the back, Warren said, "Slower than I expected. The seller is being difficult, but I'm sure we'll convince him. He's got a gambling habit."

"Tell me again why we want these plantations."

Warren shifted, squirming to get away. "Because we can get them cheap and make them even more profitable. Use enough banana oil to grease the right palms, and the government looks the other way."

Ronald nodded. "I like the way you think. We've operated inside the lines for too long." He forked a large piece of tortilla into his mouth. "It's about time we took some chances and made some big money."

The man talked with his mouth full. Warren looked away, disgusted. "I'll be making lots of changes after the board meeting. It'll be like a different company." He took a white handkerchief from his pocket and wiped his forehead. He had stayed too long. "I've got to go. Therese will be here next week, same time."

Ronald didn't look up from his food. "She'd better have the report."

Chapter Eight

The grandfather clock chimed in the front hall of the Neilsons' home overlooking Lake Harriet. Seven thirty. The guests should start to arrive soon. The string players finished tuning up and began the first measures of "God Rest Ye Merry, Gentlemen."

Ellen inhaled the cedar fragrance of the tree in the corner of the living room. Because of Angelica's help, the decorations looked perfect, except for the slightly askew angel tree-topper that just brushed the ten-foot ceiling. The tree stood over nine feet tall, too high for either woman to reach to straighten the angel. Ellen hoped that would be the only imperfection of the evening.

She smiled as she fingered the ornaments—a beaded star made by her stepmother, the fragile, antique colored glass balls that had belonged to Erik's grandmother, and the ceramic bell she and Erik bought in Austria on their honeymoon. If only they had not lost the joy of those early days.

She wished she could enjoy the sentimental traditions. She wanted to wrap herself in the holiday warmth and settle in for a dreamless nap. But her duties called.

She stroked the chiffon skirt of her red Tadashi gown, chosen to coordinate with the decorations. Erik should be ready by now. Heading for the cantilevered stairway in the hall, she nodded to acknowledge the trio of musicians. As she reached the first step, the front doorbell rang. Instead of going up the stairs, she reached over, pressed the intercom button, and spoke into the bronze box. "Erik, our guests are here. Please hurry."

Her stomach turned somersaults. She approached the

ornately carved door where she paused and took a deep breath. She could relax with a few close friends, but this large, annual party seemed like a bad dream come to life. However, she understood Erik's need to entertain his staff, so for one evening a year, she put on her best face and pretended to be the self-assured hostess. She hoped Erik would come down before she ran out of things to say.

She pulled open the heavy door, and her heart dropped to her feet. The first guests, Warren and Rosemary Stubbs, intensified her tension. She forced a gracious smile.

Rosemary breezed into the foyer. "Ellen, my dear. It has been too, too long. How have you been?" As usual, she didn't wait for an answer. "Your decorations are just luscious. I must get the name of your florist. I was terribly disappointed with mine this year. The greenery just doesn't look very fresh, and Christmas is still three weeks away."

Warren followed his wife into the house and took Ellen's hand. "How lovely you look tonight, Ellen." He bowed formally and kissed her hand. He would probably prefer to flatter himself, not her.

She closed the door and offered to take their coats. Under her wrap, Rosemary wore a white strapless dress that reached only midway to her knees, the skirt covered with some sort of feathers. She seemed determined to dress younger than her early-forties age even though it accentuated her husband's ten additional years.

Ellen showed them to the living room. "Warren, I'm sure you won't mind pouring some wassail for Rosemary and yourself. Erik will be down any minute."

She crossed the hall and had just deposited the coats in the small parlor when the doorbell rang again. She reached the front door just as Erik came down the stairs. His black Calvin Klein tuxedo provided a sharp contrast to his Scandinavian features, and the blue tie and vest matched his eyes. Adjusting his cuff links, he crossed the floor in two strides and greeted the next guests. Erik motioned them into the small parlor and paused to touch Ellen's shoulder. "Sorry to take so long," he murmured. "The studs in the shirt didn't want to cooperate."

"You should have called me."

Before she could close the door, another couple climbed the row of steps from the street. For the next few minutes, Ellen and Erik greeted guests and took coats. Strains of violin music filled the hallway as the strings players transitioned smoothly into "Silent Night."

Ellen dropped a load of coats on the Victorian sofa in the parlor. Rosemary would be furious if her full-length silver mink coat were treated too casually, so she arranged it neatly on top. Her hands lingered, relishing the texture of the sumptuous fur.

The doorbell rang again, and she hurried back to the hall where the musicians began to play a rousing "Twelve Days of Christmas." She welcomed Philip Gibbs, Distribution Director for the United States, and his wife, Jean. Right behind them, shivering, stood the stranger from Erik's office. Her stomach felt like a rock had settled to the bottom.

"You must be the new managing director Erik mentioned." Did her voice betray her? Droplets of sweat popped out on her forehead despite the wind thrusting through the open door. "I'm Ellen Neilson." She had emphasized *Ellen* more than she intended. "Please come in out of this cold. It, uh, takes a few years to get used to."

"If you ever do," Philip chimed in. "Ellen, this is Manuel Rivas."

The live music faded, and drums thudded in her ears. She licked her lips and tried to paste her smile back in place.

"*Señora* Neilson." Manuel spoke formally, with a

Hispanic accent. "I am delighted to meet you. Your husband has been so gracious to me. I was certain you would be just as charming."

"Thank you."

Manuel shrugged off his thin black coat. "Pardon me, Señora—"

"Please call me Ellen."

"Of course." He bent slightly at the waist. "I am wondering if we have met before. You seem familiar to me."

Chapter Nine

Ellen wanted to throw up. Her ears burned, and her mouth tasted like brine. She blinked her eyes and scrabbled for a calm voice. "I don't think so. I did see you at my husband's office a couple weeks ago." She had to throw him off track, but how? "Perhaps we met at the U of M? You speak English quite well."

"Alas, no, my education was entirely in Guatemala. I was fortunate to have learned English very early from a wonderful priest and some nuns. They helped me learn to speak 'like a native,' or so they told me." He smiled. "Perhaps it will come to me later where we might have met."

"Yes, perhaps." Ellen hoped with every cell that he would drop the issue. She turned away, took a deep breath, and pointed into the living room.

She deposited the coats in the parlor and dropped into a chair. She leaned over her knees and took several deep breaths, waiting for her pulse to slow. Manuel. Rivas. Both common names in Guatemala. Coincidence, maybe?

No. Manuel was here, in her living room. She longed to greet him and hug him, tell him how much she had missed him. But she couldn't. She didn't dare. That would spoil everything.

The music from the hall changed to "Winter Wonderland," reminding her that she had guests waiting. She entered the living room and realized only a few guests held cups.

Erik had helped her greet the first few guests, but where had he disappeared? He had promised to serve the hot, spicy wassail. She rushed to the antique silver urn gracing the cherry

Chippendale sideboard. She grabbed the edge of the antique cabinet to steady her hand.

Philip stood nearby. "You need some wassail, right?" she asked.

Not waiting for an answer, Ellen picked up a crystal cup, and trembling, held it under the spigot. She handed the warm cup to Philip as Manuel joined him. "I don't know where Erik went. Do you?"

Philip shook his head. "Probably talking business with Bob and Tom. I don't see either of them."

Ellen drew another cup of wassail and handed it to Manuel with a sigh. Bob Andersen and Tom Parker, two of the other vice presidents, could easily draw Erik into a discussion about company matters. "He assured me he wouldn't do that tonight. This was supposed to be his job." She shouldn't criticize him in front of their guests. She pressed her lips together tightly as she filled two more cups and carried them to two women near the dining room door.

"Here you go." She handed one cup to Jean Gibbs and the other to Betty Andersen, Tom's wife. "I'm looking for my missing husband. Do you know where yours is?"

Taking the cup, Betty smiled but shook her head. "He disappeared right after we arrived. They're probably together."

Rosemary fidgeted close by, and Ellen reached out her hand. She wanted to find Erik but one of them had to be a good host. "I see you're ready for a refill. May I get it for you?"

Rosemary held onto her empty cup. "Thank you, darling, but what I'd really like is some hard stuff. If I remember right, you keep some in the sideboard." She tossed her dyed-blonde hair and headed across the room. She pulled out a decanter of whiskey and poured the amber liquid into her cup. She added a splash of wassail and took a big gulp. "Oh, Ellen, you should just put some of this in the wassail. It improves the flavor tremendously, you know."

Warren didn't seem to notice his wife's rudeness. He scanned the room. "I haven't seen Erik. You don't suppose he ran off with Rosemary's mink, do you?" He laughed at his own joke.

Most of the guests knew each other and were talking in small groups, so she could escape. "I'm afraid I'll have to go look for him. I suspect he's back in the office with Bob and Tom."

She knocked softly on the closed office door and waited for Erik to invite her in. He sat behind his desk, Tom and Bob facing him. "Erik, our other guests are noticing your absence. Besides, Angelica will be ready to serve dinner in about five minutes. I'd like you to get everyone seated."

"Well, gentlemen. You heard the boss, and I believe we've covered the important points. Shall we?" He gestured to the door.

Ellen stepped aside as the others filed out. She moved to face Erik, keeping him in the office until Bob and Tom were out of earshot. "I thought we had agreed." She kept her voice as restrained as she could manage. "You were not going to do this. You were going to serve the wassail."

Caressing her arms, he pecked her on the lips. "They had some important news, and I got excited. I promise I'll be the perfect host for the rest of the evening."

"Just remember this is your party. Business can wait until Monday, can't it?"

The soft holiday music from the string trio in the hall provided a pleasant backdrop throughout dinner. With six leaves in it, the Neilson heirloom table accommodated all twenty people. Red Depression glass plates and matching linen napkins contrasted with the white Chantilly lace tablecloth. Betty Andersen nodded at the empty space where Angelica had removed one place setting. "I thought someone was missing. Where's Therese?"

Ellen slid into her chair. "She called this afternoon and said her son had taken sick. She decided she'd better stay home with him."

As in previous years, only Rosemary's strident laughter kept the meal from being perfect. Conversation circled around the table as everyone caught up with events since the fall picnic. The Andersen's daughter, their youngest, had just gone off to Brown University in the fall. Mary admitted that adjusting to the empty nest had been hard.

"Oh, it won't be long 'til both kids are married, and you'll have grandkids to spoil." Betty Parker's face glowed as she talked about their new grandson, born just before Thanksgiving. "After raising four girls, it's fun to finally have a boy in the family."

Ellen lost her appetite at the discussion of babies. The familiar churning in her stomach returned. She glanced toward Erik at the other end of the table, but he was engrossed in conversation with Warren.

Neal Patrick, who had picked quietly at his food, looked up. "Neal Junior and Alicia just found out they're expecting. It'll be a July baby. Right around Marta's birthday." His smile faded. "Or the day she …"

Marta, his wife of thirty-plus years, had died just two days after her birthday following a two-year battle with stomach cancer. White-haired and now stoop-shouldered, Neal had lost at least thirty pounds and aged twenty years in five months.

Suddenly everyone became intensely interested in their food. Even Erik and Warren stopped talking. Manuel looked around the table, a puzzled look on his face, but he said nothing. Jean Gibbs reached over and touched Neal's shoulder. "We know you miss her, Neal. So do we."

Neal nodded, his face strained.

Rosemary, of all people, changed the subject. "Ellen, this salmon is positively divine." Murmurs of agreement echoed around the table. "If I can't steal—what's her name? Angel?—away from you permanently, can I at least borrow her for my next dinner party?"

Ellen attempted to smile. Rosemary's compliments always felt artificial. She was grateful when Erik turned the discussion to an upcoming business trip.

"Manuel, you're certain those plantations near Gualan can be turned around? I don't want to waste a trip if they're not a good investment."

"*Si*. With the right management, the workers at the plantations will be more productive. The current owners are, how would you say, slave drivers." Manuel's voice betrayed passion. "People do not respond well to that kind of treatment. Many of the employees are sickly, and the long hours are too much for them."

No longer the lanky teenager who hustled tourists and looked after his young cousin, Manuel seemed to still be taking care of people. The man across the table possessed the self-confidence Ellen remembered. Unafraid to do what it took to survive. But the hardness and defensive attitude had disappeared.

"Ellen, will you be joining us in Guatemala?" Rosemary's grating voice interrupted her thoughts. "I am so looking forward to lazing in the sun in the middle of January."

Ellen's ears grew warm. She avoided looking at Erik, though she could feel him staring at her. She had refused prior invitations to travel with him to Guatemala but had never explained why. She had no desire to return to the country where she had known such misery. "I haven't decided yet. I would have to miss so many classes. The children would be very disappointed."

"I can't imagine you wanting to stay here in thirty below, working with a bunch of brats, when you could be soaking up some sunrays." Rosemary shrugged. "But have it your way." She sipped her wine and turned to the man next to her. "You will be going, won't you, Alan?"

Alan was Vice President for Latin America, so of course he would be making the trip. The fact they both were married had never stopped Rosemary from flirting with him.

Crimson crept up Alan's neck and face as he avoided looking at the women on each side of him. Ria ignored the comment and leaned around her husband. "I will join you, Rosemary. We could all go to the beach one day."

Rosemary's drunken smile froze. She clamped her mouth shut and reached for her wine glass. She drained it and thrust it at Warren for a refill.

He reached for the wine bottle in the center of the table. "We need to strategize before we go down there, Alan. You're in the office Monday, right? Let's get together for lunch."

Almost as an afterthought, he added, "Not trying to leave you out, Erik, but I know how busy you are at year-end. Alan and I will develop our strategy, and I'll review it with you before we leave. How does that sound?"

"You'll want to include Manuel. He's the one who discovered this deal."

"Sure, of course. Uh, Manuel, why don't you meet us at … uh … twelve thirty Monday? How about Masa, Alan?"

Alan nodded and Warren turned to Manuel. "You should like it, Manuel. They have great Mexican food. You must know where it is."

"I'll find it," Manuel's lips tightened.

Ellen admired his restraint. She had learned to ignore Warren's subtle insults.

She suggested they move to the living room where Angelica would serve their dessert and eggnog. She nodded to Erik, hoping he recognized the cue. As the party members pushed back their chairs, he excused himself.

When all the guests had found a spot in the front room, music from the instrumental trio filtered in. Erik's baritone voice joined them. "We wish you a Merry Christmas. We wish you a Merry Christmas."

He backed through the double doors from the hallway, pulling a wooden cart laden with identical packages wrapped in red and green glossy paper and tied with silk ribbons. "My lovely wife has once again outdone herself. We want you all to know how much we appreciate your contributions to the company and, most of all, your friendship." Ellen moved across the room to help him distribute the presents she had carefully chosen and wrapped.

Erik grinned. "I trust these tokens will preclude any expectations of bonuses."

Laughter rippled throughout the room. Alan slapped Manuel on the back. "Don't worry. He's kidding. Erik gives generous year-end bonuses."

As they distributed the gifts, Ellen decided to take a chance. "Manuel, since you came alone tonight, I assume your family is not in the States. Do they live in Guatemala?"

"No, *señora*. I am single."

"You're not married?" She hastened to mask her surprise. "Does your job require you to travel as much as Alan?"

"It will, once I know the job. But I will be here for several weeks to learn the business. I've managed plantations, but I have a lot to learn about being a regional managing director."

"Perhaps we can introduce you to some people so you don't get lonely while you're here."

"That would be most gracious of you, *señora*." Manuel

bowed.

Now why did she say such a thing? The last thing she wanted was to spend time with him. That would be too risky.

Chapter Ten

Manuel found his usual spot Thursday night toward the back of La Paz Restaurante. Within walking distance of his extended-stay hotel, the restaurant had become Manuel's favorite for dinner. The bright red and yellow décor and the *carne asada* fajitas and other Mexican foods reminded him of home. Best of all, by the time he went to dinner around eight o'clock, the family-oriented restaurant had few customers.

No one disturbed him as he ate while studying his Bible. The friendly staff, who knew he always left a generous tip, cleaned around him and left him alone.

"O Lord, You have searched me and know me," he read in Psalms. He closed his eyes and prayed. "Lord, thank You for bringing me here to Minnesota. I know not what Your plan is for me while I am here, but I want to fulfill Your purpose, whatever it may be. *Señora* Neilson looks just like my aunt. She must be my cousin. Help me understand why she pretended to not know me."

He opened his eyes. The high-backed bench he sat on shifted as someone entered the booth behind him. A man ordered coffee and said he was expecting someone else.

Manuel concentrated on the 139th Psalm and reveled in the goodness of God, ignoring the rustling sounds and low voices when the man's companion arrived. Gradually, however, he became aware of an intense discussion behind him. When he heard the name "Neilson," he couldn't resist eavesdropping.

"Don't worry about Neilson." The man used a stage whisper. "He'll be out after the board meeting, and he can't fire you. We'll be able to run this company the way it ought to be."

The woman made no attempt to keep her voice down. "But are you sure you've got the votes?"

Manuel's chest thundered as if he had been hit with a football. The voice was familiar. One of the secretaries from the office, perhaps. He sat without moving.

"Yeah, yeah. We'll have them." A metal spoon clinked against a cup. "We've got two locked up, mine and one other. Two more on the fence. After they see the report you were supposed to bring tonight, they'll both be with us. Neilson won't know what hit him."

A deep sigh. "I'll just be glad when this is all over." Manuel identified the voice. Not a secretary, but a vice president. Therese Long. "I wish I'd never started this. Erik is a good guy, even if he's not a good businessman. I don't like stabbing him in the back this way."

The response was swift and abrupt. "You didn't like sending your children to a public school either. Or having to drive your BMW for two years instead of one. If I don't get that report you were supposed to bring tonight, you'll be paying it all back. With penalties."

Menace in the voice made Manuel shudder. He shot up a silent prayer. *"What should I do, Lord?"*

The booth rumbled as the man got up. "I want that report. You've got two weeks. Right here. Eight o'clock. And don't be late."

Manuel remained immobile, stunned that anyone would betray Mr. Neilson, but he had heard it clearly.

A minute later, Therese exited. Still he waited, allowing time for her to leave the parking lot. He searched his mind for a solution, a way to thwart this devious scheme.

He could confront Therese tomorrow, tell her what he had heard. But wouldn't she deny it? She had more years, and thus credibility, with the corporation than he did.

Perhaps Alan, who had hired him, would believe him if he took the information to him first. But it seemed unlikely Therese was the only one involved. And who had she been meeting with? Manuel did not know who had such power to get rid of the company president.

His fingers flipped through his well-used Bible where it lay on the table. He acquired the habit during college when something troubled him or he needed to make a decision. He paused in Proverbs, hoping King Solomon, the wisest man who ever lived, would provide some insight.

He considered going directly to Erik. But Manuel was new to the company. Erik would think he had misunderstood or, worse, sought to advance himself by concocting an outrageous conspiracy story.

He continued to turn pages, scanning the words. He stopped when he came to the book of Esther, the queen who had risked her life to save her people. This wasn't a matter of life and death, but he could see the parallels. Perhaps Ellen could warn her husband of this suspicious plan.

"Is that it, Lord?" he said aloud. "Should I tell *Señora* Neilson?" He had no reason to think she would listen to him. She had already erected an invisible shield between them. And if he pushed the idea that they knew each other, she might resist even more.

But he felt certain they were cousins. Surely she would know what to do.

At the Christmas party, she had invited him to visit the Walker Museum. Alone in the city, he had nothing else to do Saturday morning.

Chapter Eleven

"Boys and girls, no matter what your age, welcome to the Walker's exhibit of Santa Clauses."

Beginning her third tour Saturday morning, Ellen smiled wearily at the parents and children crowding the art center lobby. With only two weeks left until Christmas, visitors poured into the Walker Center for the annual exhibit of Santa Claus art. The guides wore red pants and vests over crisp white shirts so they would look like Santa's elves.

The floppy red hat, trimmed in fake white fur, threatened to slide over Ellen's eyes, and she pushed it back. "We'll see lots of pictures of Santa Claus, some of them from a long time ago. And if you're very, very good, we might even see the jolly fellow in person before we're done. Are you ready?"

Several small children jumped up and down and clapped their hands. Ellen opened the double doors and led the group into the main exhibit hall. As she gave a brief history of how Saint Nicholas evolved into Santa Claus, she spotted Manuel on the edge of the crowd. Her heart roared in her ears. He looked right at her, and she tipped her head in silent greeting.

Fifteen minutes later, she concluded her talk and invited the group to take a closer look at various works of art. She moved among the families and stopped several times to answer questions or to ask children which Santa they liked best. She noticed Manuel alone, gazing at a Norman Rockwell painting for a Christmas 1927 *Saturday Evening Post* cover. She edged up to him. "Do you have any questions about this one?"

He shook his head. "Could I talk to you—alone?"

Her face warmed. Surely he hadn't identified her. "All

right. I have a lunch break after this tour. It's not so cold today. I'll meet you across the street in the sculpture garden, by the Spoonbridge and Cherry. It's easy to find."

Bells jingled and a side door opened. "Ho, ho, ho. Merry Christmas!" A jolly old man in a red suit drew shrieks of joy from the children. "All good little boys and girls, come this way." Ellen whispered to Manuel that she'd be out in a few minutes. She herded everyone else into a smaller room where the children would receive candy canes and have their pictures taken with Santa.

Five minutes later, bundled head to toe, she crunched through the frozen garden, wishing she had worn her sunglasses against the glare from the snow. She found Manuel underneath the bowl of the spoon examining the giant sculpture. "Makes you wonder what the artist was thinking, doesn't it?"

"*Si*. Does it mean something?" He knocked on the underside of the fifty-foot spoon. "It is quite a feat of engineering, to balance the cherry so." He wasn't wearing gloves, but he did have on a hooded blue parka. Better than the lightweight coat he had worn the night of the party. He rubbed his hands together and stuck them in his pockets.

"What did you want to talk to me about?"

"I overheard something very disturbing that affects your husband."

She realized she had been holding her breath, waiting for him to accuse her of lying to him. She exhaled. "If this is about business, you'll need to talk to Erik. You work for him; I don't."

"I understand your feelings. But this kind of information … he may not believe me. I am new to the company. He does not know that he can trust me. You are the only one I know who would believe me, and I can trust. You must tell Erik about this."

Ellen stared at him, her ears warming in spite of the cold. Snowflakes settled on the fur framing her face. She pointed to another sculpture, Hare on Bell, and walked toward it. "What on earth are you talking about? And what makes you think I would believe you or that you can trust me?"

"I am not certain what it means. I do not know the legalities of U.S. corporations. But I do not think it is good for Erik." He related the conversation he had overheard at the restaurant. "Is it possible that someone could—what is the word—oust him as president of his own company?"

"I'm not sure. Erik insists I stay out of the business. I entertain, and sometimes I travel with him. But he never discusses business with me." She laughed. "If I didn't know better, I'd think he was the godfather."

Seeing Manuel's puzzled face, she shook her head. "Sorry. It's a very old movie about organized crime. Erik's not mixed up in anything like that. Some people say he is honest to a fault, just as his father and grandfather were. But he believes one person working in the family business is enough. He tells me about staff changes if it's someone I know, but that's the extent of it." She moved through an opening in the hedge walls, and he followed her. They approached a huge iron structure with a wood platform suspended from it, and she looked at him. "Tell me again what you heard, word for word."

Manuel repeated the restaurant conversation. She stopped him twice and asked him to repeat a phrase. When he finished, she turned away and moved underneath the sculpture framework. He waited.

She looked back at him. "I know there are six people on the Board of Directors, plus Erik, who is chairman, president, and CEO. It would take four votes to force him out. But …" She gestured with one hand. "They're all handpicked by his father. What could convince them to turn against Erik? And why?"

They continued their stroll through the garden. The only sounds were the crusted snow under their feet and the muffled noise of traffic from the nearby highway. "You said they mentioned the board meeting. I think there's one in early January. But I don't know what you expect me to do with this information."

"You must warn him. There must be a way to prevent this treachery."

She stopped in front of a sculpture of a horseman. "This seems like some spy novel. I don't know why you want to get me involved. Isn't there someone else you can tell? You report to Alan Monroe, don't you?"

"I do not know who else may be involved. It would be too risky."

She shook her head. "I can't believe Alan would—"

"Therese is supposed to bring a report."

Ellen faced him. "I will think about it." They climbed the steps toward the street. "But I don't understand. Why did you come to me?"

He hunched his shoulders. "Because I am certain I knew you many years ago. In Guatemala." He took one hand out of his coat pocket and touched her sleeve. "You are my cousin, are you not?"

A gust of wind blew around her. Icy snow pelted her cheeks. She feared the panic showed on her face. "You are mistaken." She allowed the chill to spread to her voice. "That is not possible. Before the party, I had never met you. I must go now."

She ran across the street and into the building without looking back.

Chapter Twelve

The security Ellen felt when she married Erik seemed now to be no more permanent than the flames from the white candles on the dinner table that evening. She could not imagine Erik losing the company. But she didn't see any way she could help. He had shut her out of the business. To protect her, he said. Because of her artistic nature, he didn't think she cared about the complexities of a big corporation.

She had no idea how to warn him without revealing her relationship to Manuel. Pull that thread, and the entire fabric of her life would unravel, just like the loose thread creating that hole in the lace tablecloth. She should ask Angelica to repair it. Another Neilson heirloom she needed to handle with care.

Neither she nor Erik spoke much during the meal, and her thoughts raced into a future without Neilson Enterprises. She had just taken a bite of chicken when Erik said, "We can find a gestational carrier."

She swallowed before she finished chewing. The meat stuck in her throat, and she started coughing. Erik jumped up, moved behind her, and thumped her on the back. She grabbed her glass and gulped water until she could swallow normally. "A what?" She coughed again.

He rubbed her back. "Are you okay?" He sounded worried.

She nodded and sipped water again. "What are you talking about?"

Erik returned to his seat and inspected her face. "A gestational carrier. A surrogate. You want a child. We'll find a woman who would carry our baby to delivery."

A sick feeling swirled in her stomach. She could not think about someone else giving birth to her baby. Bad enough she couldn't get pregnant herself, but she could never rely on someone else, a stranger. What if the woman wanted to keep the baby? "I don't think so, Erik. It sounds risky."

He cleared his throat and launched into corporate-presentation mode. "I checked into it. There's a center here in Minneapolis where they have done over a hundred. It's almost fifty percent successful."

"You checked into it?" She stared into the candle flame, watched the shimmering light rise and multiply into a sluggish Ferris wheel. "Without talking to me first?"

Erik held up both hands, trying to calm her. "I asked Marcie to do the research."

She pushed away from the table. "You told her?"

"We need a solution." He reached out and touched her arm. "If a baby will help ... I asked her to find out about options."

She jerked her arm away. She wanted to shake off his authoritarian attitude as well. Benevolent, but controlling. Once, she had appreciated his concern. But now he had strutted over the line. "This wasn't your secret to tell, Erik. If I wanted to know the options, I would find out myself."

She saw his jaw tighten. She rarely opposed him. She glared at him, felt the tears spill onto her cheeks, and fled upstairs.

The third-floor studio was her refuge. In the daytime, sunlight warmed the airy room and cheered her. Its sloped ceilings hugged her in a safe embrace, and the large arched window allowed her to watch the lake and the world beyond.

Tonight, though, the darkness penetrated the large windows and filled the room with wintry clamminess. Ellen ignored the wall switch and headed for a table lamp near the window.

Two wingback chairs were arranged on each side of the marble-topped Eastlake table. In the dim light, she tripped on the curved leg of one of the chairs. Thrown off balance, she fell over the chair and, as one hand flailed, she hit the ornate lamp and toppled it off the table. The other upholstered chair cushioned its fall. She set the lamp back in place and straightened the shade. Disaster averted. At least Grandma Neilson's lamp survived.

She switched on the lamp and sank into the chair, sitting on her feet. She pulled her favorite throw from the back of the chair and scrunched beneath it. Her heart gradually resumed a regular pace, but she veered between the desire to shriek and the desire to sob. She did neither. She merely leaned her head against the chair wing and closed her eyes.

She pulled the coverlet tighter, grasping comfort from the soft lamb's wool. She had argued with Erik. Recently they had disagreed on minor issues, but in the seven years they had been married, they had never fought like this. He had shared her diagnosis with Marcie and hadn't even asked her permission.

Her fingernails bit into the palm of her hand. Did he think he was God, moving chess pieces around, knocking down her pieces without caring how she felt? Bad enough that God kept doing that to her. She wanted a husband who would pick up those pieces for her.

Her feet tingled and she unfolded her body and stood. Wearing the throw like a cape, she paced across the room, working out the numbness. Maybe he wanted to take care of her, and this was his way of trying. He had inherited an oversupply of protectiveness from his father. But he had no right to take action without discussing it with her.

She plopped into the chair once more. Her past had reached her here, and the truth threatened to escape from the box where she kept it locked away. In spite of her anger, her future was with Erik. At least, for as long as he would have her. If he learned of her secrets, that future might disintegrate before her eyes.

In spite of the risk, she wanted to see Manuel again. She had lived with her secrets for so long, she needed to talk to someone who understood. Surely he would also see the need to keep the truth buried.

She burrowed deeper into the chair and rested her head on the padded arm, searching for answers in the darkness behind her closed eyelids.

Chapter Thirteen

Manuel looked at the ringing telephone on his desk Monday morning and cocked his eyebrow in surprise. The display showed an outside call. Everyone he knew locally worked for Neilson Enterprises.

He lifted the receiver. "Manuel Rivas here."

"Manuel." The woman's voice was deep but soft, not quite a whisper, vaguely familiar. "I think you will know who this is. But please don't say my name."

He recognized the distinct accent of Ellen Neilson—a mixture of Minnesota, the South, and, he suspected, the remnants of Guatemalan Spanish. "*Si, señora.*"

"I would like to talk to you again. In private. Can I trust you not to tell anyone?"

Manuel's heart chased his thoughts around a racetrack. Perhaps she had decided to talk to Erik about what he had heard. Or was there some other reason she was calling? He ran his free hand through his hair and cleared his throat.

"I just want to talk," she said. "In a public place, but where we won't be seen together. Would you meet me tomorrow morning at six thirty?"

Curious, he exhaled. "*Si,* I could do that. Where?"

"By any chance, are you a runner? Or at least a fast walker?"

"I run sometimes."

"Good. Wear your workout clothes but dress warm. You remember where we live, on Lake Harriet? There's a band shell at the north end. Park near there and go west on the paved trail around the lake. They clear the snow off the trail. I'll wait for you at the first park bench."

She gave him driving directions and hung up abruptly. He placed the handset on its cradle and stared at it for several minutes.

Her directions were easy to follow, and few commuters were heading south on I-35 just past six Tuesday morning. When Manuel pulled his white Honda Accord rental into a parking space near the band shell, a dozen other cars were already there. He shut off the engine and pulled off his leather gloves. He put on the black stocking cap and matching mittens he had bought at a sports store the evening before and tightened the laces on the new blue and white running shoes.

He locked the car and slipped the key into his front pocket. He straightened his right leg and put his foot on the rear bumper to stretch his muscles. Craning his neck, he admired the castle-like band shell. The Christmas lights edging the roof of the green and white building brightened the morning blackness.

He checked his watch and then loped across the parking lot to where the jogging trail started. As *Señora* Neilson had promised, most of the snow was cleared from the path. He had never run in a freezer before. Hoping the run would warm him, he picked up his pace and followed the glowing circles pooling from the lamps along the trail.

Minutes later, he spotted two park benches set back from the trail. A woman in a dark jogging suit stretched against a tree opposite the benches. It had to be her, though it was hard to tell. Her hair was hidden beneath a navy stocking cap pulled low over her forehead and ears. As he drew near her, she looked up at him. Only her eyes and nose showed between the folds of a long red scarf enveloping her neck and face.

Manuel slowed and stopped beside her. "Keep running," Ellen mumbled through the scarf. "We'll talk as we go. Just a couple of people who happen to be running together." She fell into step next to him.

Despite his curiosity, he waited for her to explain. Points of light peeked at them from the other side of the frozen lake. They ran steadily for a few minutes with only the sound of their shoes squeaking where the snow had blown across the path. His questions pounded in his ears, and his feet tried to keep up.

Finally, she pulled down the scarf, now white with frost. "You're fast. Let's slow up a little so we can talk, okay?"

"Sorry. I was cold." He slowed to a jog. "How's this?"

"You grew up in Guatemala. Where?"

"The capital, Guatemala City. Have you been there?"

She didn't answer the question. "I know you're not married. Other family?"

"I was an only child. My mother disappeared when I was small, and my father died a few years later. I mostly raised myself—on the streets."

He told the common back story with no emotion. He had given up his anger and bitterness long ago. They served no aim, only prevented him from finding his purpose in life. He looked at her but couldn't see any reaction.

"How did a street kid manage to go to college and wind up … here?"

He smiled. "By the grace of God." After a few paces, he added, "God worked through an American missionary. He and the women who ran the mission orphanage taught me English. They took me in and encouraged me. After I went to live with them, I was able to find jobs and save money to pay for college. They would not let me pay them, even for food."

He slowed his pace to allow *Señora* Neilson to move ahead of him as they passed a woman walking a fluffy white dog. Then he caught up to her. "After I graduated from college and started working, I was able to make a generous contribution to their mission. But by then, Papa Thomas had gone home."

Her head turned sharply toward him. "He's here in the U.S.?"

"No, he went home to heaven."

"Oh." She ran in silence for a couple of minutes. "And you've never married?"

Manuel shook his head. "I came close once. But the Lord showed me that she was not the right mate for me. So I will wait until He sends the one."

"You sound like my friend Diane. God did this and God did that. Wait for God to do something."

He tipped his head. "You do not like this talk about God?"

"No, I don't. Let's change the subject."

"As you wish, *señora*. I am puzzled why you asked me to meet you like this."

Ellen stopped and took several deep breaths. She looked over her shoulder then up to the street that paralleled the lake. "You asked if I was your cousin. What was your cousin's name?"

His heart picked up its pace. "Elena."

"My birth name was Elena. Elena Rivas. I am your cousin."

He blinked, and suddenly he was fourteen again, waving good-bye to the fragile girl boarding an airplane. Afterward, he had wandered the streets for weeks, alone and aimless. Every day, he checked with the missionaries at the orphanage to see if a letter had come for him, but one never came.

Now, after twenty years, she stood in front of him. His

eyes watered. "Elena? I knew it. God be praised!"

He grabbed her and hugged her. "You never wrote. I thought you were lost to me forever. I tried to find you. On the Internet. Last year. I learned your father died, but you seemed to have disappeared." He laughed. "God is so good. He has answered my prayers. To see you again. And you are well and happy. This was my prayer."

Pulling away, she looked around. "We'd better keep running. I don't want anyone to see us together."

She took off, leaving him staring after her. It took him only seconds to catch up. "But Elena, I have so many questions. I feared for what might have happened to you. Then I saw you at the Christmas party, and later realized how much you looked like your *mamá*. Why did you lie to me?"

"My husband does not know I am half Mayan. He knows I was born in Guatemala, but he would never have married me if he had known the whole truth."

"*Señora*, I do not think *Señor* Neilson would care—"

"Listen, Manuel. I am happy to see you again and to know you are successful." They reached the parking lot, and he followed her behind the band shell. She put both hands on the wall and began to stretch her hamstrings, but she kept her eyes on him. "It's important that you not say anything—not to anyone. I don't want Erik to know we are cousins. Things are … not good between us right now, and if he knew the truth about my past ..."

He joined her in stretching against the building. *Señor* Neilson had shown respect and affection toward her at the party. Surely, her past would not change his attitude.

She peered at him. "Promise me you will keep my secret."

He nodded. "If you insist. As long as no one knows we talked, I will not need to lie. But I do not understand."

"You don't know him like I do." She stretched her right arm over her head and bent toward her left side.

He mirrored her movement. "But you will tell him about the meeting I overheard, will you not?" He sent up a silent prayer that she would understand the importance.

"I don't know how I can." She jogged in place. "I run several times a week. I'll be here again Thursday, same time, if you want to come. Perhaps then I'll answer your questions."

"I'll look forward to it, dear Elena."

"No, you must not call me that. Anyway, Elena no longer exists."

"Very well. *Señora* Neilson, then." He gave her a half bow and a lopsided grin. "It has been an enlightening run. Until we meet again, may God bless you."

He turned and jogged to his car. When he reached it, he looked back, but she was already heading up the snow-covered embankment to the street. She looked both ways and picked her way through the slush to the sidewalk on the other side. He watched prayerfully as his mysterious cousin trotted toward the lavish mansion she shared with her husband—his boss.

Chapter Fourteen

By Thursday, Ellen needed to make up for the twenty years of silence since she had left Manuel and Guatemala City.

An early morning snow carpeted the path when he joined her at the same spot as before. They padded through the white fluff, the world around them eerily quiet except for their muffled breathing. Frosty trees acted as sentries as they followed the path meandering its way along the lakeshore.

The woolly odor of her scarf muted the crisp air as she inhaled. "When I came to America, I wanted to forget. Even remembering *Mamá* hurt. Any contact with you would have been too painful. I had to begin a new life."

Saying the words stirred up the memories. "Once I got settled with my father, I determined to leave behind the poverty of the garbage dump. I had plenty to eat, a real house, and new clothes to wear. Everything you and I had dreamed of, and more."

Manuel pumped his arms in rhythm with hers. "It is unfortunate that you did not hold onto the good memories, Elena—Ellen. Our childhood was not all bad. Your *mamá* loved you very much. That is a memory some people do not have."

She drew in her breath and glanced at him. Manuel's mother, her own mother's sister, had disappeared when he was a baby, and his father had died when Manuel was eight. "I'm sorry, Manuel. You never really knew your mother, did you?"

"There is no need to apologize. I have learned much about my parents since you left, and I feel as though I did know her. I simply wanted to remind you of the good times."

They met a man and woman bundled in heavy coats, walking side-by-side. Manuel held back to let Ellen go first. She waited for him to pull alongside her again. "I do remember *Mamá*, Manuel. But some of the things she did—" She forced back tears that would add to the ice already on her eyelashes. "I was ashamed, so I worked hard to put it all behind me and make people think I was, you know, American."

Realizing how absurd that sounded, she laughed. "Okay. Okay. So it wasn't 'til I got to college I could pull that off. Obviously the kids in grade school knew I couldn't speak English when I first came. They found out where I was from and called me 'Gwat' and 'watermelon.'"

"Why 'watermelon'?"

Her shoulders drooped as she recalled the taunting. "They made it sound like 'Guatemalan.' Thankfully, no one learned I was Mayan. As far as I knew, that would truly make me an outcast." She'd had no reason to think American children would have viewed her heritage any differently than other Guatemalans had. "So I worked on eliminating any trace of an accent. If I had been older, it would have been more difficult, but I did it. And once I got to college, where no one knew me—"

"Cousin, being Mayan is no disgrace. Neither is anything else that happened. Your mother had no education, no resources. She made some unfortunate choices, but they were her choices, not yours. I understand now that she repented of those things and received God's forgiveness. Perhaps it is time you forgive her as well."

She tugged off her wool stocking cap and slapped it against her leg. "I don't blame her! I know she did the best she could. It's God I blame. If He forgave her, why were things still so hard for us? Why did He let her die?"

They ran side by side, breathing hard. A few minutes

passed before Manuel spoke. "Sometimes the choices we make affect us the rest of our lives. God's forgiveness allows us to spend eternity with Him, but we have consequences in this life. Consequences that can affect those we love."

They rounded the end of the lake and fought sharp bits of icy snow blowing into their faces. It took all of Ellen's effort to focus on putting one foot ahead of the other until they reached a place where trees partially blocked the wind. "Look, believe anything you want to, but don't expect me to buy it. I'm glad all that God-stuff gave *Mamá* some peace before she died, but I'm doing just fine without it. So let's talk about something else. Tell me how you got to where you are now."

"It will be difficult to tell you my story without telling you how God has led me at every step."

"Try."

He explained how he had started doing chores around the orphanage and that the missionaries insisted he move into the main house with them since he was too old for the orphanage. He said he "found Jesus" while living there, and the missionaries had helped him to attend college.

In spite of the cold, they took extra time stretching by Manuel's Honda, the only car in the lot. She didn't want to end their time together.

"Want to run again next Tuesday?"

"That depends." He grinned at her. "Are we going to actually run next time?"

She stooped and picked up a handful of snow, packed it, and tossed it at him. "I've been going easy on you."

He sidestepped and laughed as the snowball disintegrated on his shoulder and showered his face. "You still haven't learned to throw, I see."

She reached over and brushed the flakes off his shoulder. "And you haven't learned to get out of the way."

He stamped his feet and clapped his gloved hands together. "This cold slows me down." He grinned and bowed. "I will see you again Tuesday, *Señora* Neilson. God go with you."

He got in his car and started the engine. She watched as he climbed out again and began to brush new snow off the windows. She turned and headed for home.

God has led me at every step. He sounded just like Diane. His assurance seemed just like her, too. She could understand how Diane could be happy. She'd had it easy her whole life. But Manuel—

She shook her head, clearing the thoughts from her mind. She was doing just fine without all that God nonsense. As she climbed the front steps, her eyes scanned the two-story columns and stone façade of the historic home where she lived with her wealthy and influential husband. She had all she needed. If she could just keep from losing Erik.

Chapter Fifteen

Ellen started the CD player, and Mozart filled her third-floor studio the following Tuesday afternoon.

The canvas she had prepared sat waiting on the easel. Classes were over until after the holidays, and she did not have to give any tours today. Winter light streamed through the arched window, making for a perfect day to begin the painting. The image burned in her imagination.

She picked up the summer photo of Lake Harriet and clipped it at the top of her easel. As she penciled the outline for the painting, scenes from her early years flashed across the canvas. A few were picture-book remembrances—her *mamá* laughing and loving her, Manuel teaching and teasing her, and the missionaries assuring and advising her after her *mamá* died. But painful pictures developed to replace them. Smoke from burning trash stinging her eyes and nose. Other children calling her *pocho* because of her light color. Pushing her away from the best salvage, dubbing her *perro cruzado*. Mongrel.

She tried to blink away the memories.

How could Manuel give credit to God for surviving that awful place? Couldn't he see how God failed them when they had to scrounge for food, dig through rubbish to find clothes?

She focused her thoughts on helping Erik in his business. She and Manuel had worked out the details during their run that morning. The situation reminded her of the thriller novels she read late into the night when Erik was away from home. However insignificant the whole episode might turn out to be, the idea pleased her.

She would take Erik to the restaurant for dinner on

Thursday, the day indicated for the secret meeting. "If he overhears the conversation," she had told Manuel, "I don't have to explain why we're there. And if nothing comes of it, I haven't risked anything."

Manuel had argued with her but, in the end, he conceded her plan might work. Then he had prayed for her. He and Diane insisted on relying on God for everything they did.

She grabbed her palette and slapped a glob of magenta paint on the canvas.

She was amazed that she and Manuel had found each other again after so many years. What a coincidence. She spread the paint with a knife in broad arcs.

Diane would call it a "God-incidence." She added a lump of yellow to the middle of the red half-circle.

Not a God-incidence. Erik's company just happened to have processing plants in Guatemala, and Manuel just happened to get a job at one of them.

She applied more yellow in long slashes radiating out above the arcs, just as the music reached a crescendo.

Manuel's hard work had earned him a promotion, brought him to corporate headquarters. If it hadn't been for the holiday party, they might never have crossed paths. She dabbed blue spots across the top. With quick brush strokes, she worked them into a soft background.

Yes, pure coincidence. Nothing more.

She stepped back and analyzed the sunrise over the lake taking shape on her easel.

Chapter Sixteen

Erik shot Ellen a look of curiosity as she slid into the high-backed booth next to him instead of sitting across from him. "You are certainly acting strange this evening. What's going on?"

They both faced the back of the restaurant. She turned her head and smiled at him. "What do you mean?"

"You know very well what I mean. All of this—surprising me by picking me up at work, getting Marcie to keep my schedule clear—the two of you had to have been plotting for days." He paused while the waitress set glasses of water in front of them. "And this restaurant. It's not one of our usual places. I've never even heard of it. Tell me what this is all about."

Ellen opened the oversized red menu holder. "I wanted to make up for our argument the other day. You like Mexican, and I heard this place has great food. It's time I tried eating it again. Maybe it won't bother my system like it used to." Another fib. She didn't eat spicy food because of the distasteful memories it churned up. "What are you going to have?"

Erik opened his own menu. "All right, we'll order first. But you're not going to escape." He held the menu like a privacy screen and leaned over to brush his lips against her cheek. "One thing about this place—we could neck back here, and no one would see us."

Ellen giggled. The old Erik had returned, at least for the moment. "Now, that's the idea. Let's just have an enjoyable dinner."

They studied their menus until the dark-haired, Latina waitress returned to stand by the table, pad and pen poised. She smiled at them but said nothing.

Ellen ordered soft-shell tacos, and Erik chose *arroz con pollo*. When the waitress had gone, he turned sideways to look at Ellen.

"Now, tell me. There's more to your bringing me here than you wanting to try Mexican food again."

She avoided looking at him, but she couldn't avoid giving him some explanation. "All right, Erik. There is something— maybe. But it might be nothing. I mean—"

"You're not making any sense. Will you get to the point, please?"

She filled her cheeks with air and then let it out through pursed lips. "That's just the problem. I can't tell you anything specific. It's possible something important will happen here tonight, something you need to know about. But I don't know exactly what. If nothing happens, at least we'll have a nice dinner together."

"This is crazy." He drummed his fingers on the table. "Maybe something will happen but you don't know what, and maybe nothing will happen. So you drag me to this place—and expect me to—to what?"

Ellen shushed him as the waitress approached with a basket of chips and salsa. She picked up a chip and dipped it. "I know it sounds crazy. But I can't explain it. I'm asking you to trust me. By eight o'clock, either you'll know and understand, or—if nothing happens—we'll just forget the whole thing." She placed her right hand over his left one on the table. She turned her face to him and gave him a pleading look. "Please, trust me?"

In every cell of her body, flickers of the truth struggled to escape. She had created her own prison, keeping her secrets in and Erik out. When he gazed at her as he did now, she longed to confess everything, to allow him into the darkest corner of her heart. She slammed the gate shut before making that mistake. Not tonight, when the gap between them had begun to close. Revealing too much could reverse that progress.

He turned his hand over and enveloped hers in both of his. "This is the strangest thing you've ever done, Ellen. But, fine. I'll trust you. I'll be patient for a couple of hours … But how will I know when this … whatever it is … this thing happens? And do we have to stay *here* waiting for it to happen?"

She tapped her forehead against his. "Yes, we will have to wait here. But this restaurant's not so bad, is it? If nothing happens by eight, we'll go home. In that case, you have to promise not to ask me any more questions, because there's nothing more I can tell you."

They sat for a few minutes in silence, and the strain eased when their food arrived. After eating a few bites, he began to talk about the inauguration of the new governor in January. Neilson Enterprises had been a large campaign contributor, so naturally, they had been invited to the ball.

While they sat eating and talking, several families came, had dinner, and left. Ellen's tacos tasted mild compared to the heat in her throat as she listened for the tinkle of the bell over the restaurant door. The waitress cleared their dishes, and they ordered coffee. No other customers were in the restaurant when, just before eight o'clock, someone entered. Ellen put a finger to her lips to signal that Erik should be quiet. He cocked one eyebrow at her but stopped talking and sat still, elbows on the table and both hands wrapped around his green ceramic mug.

High heels clicked across the tile floor as the waitress showed the newcomer to the booth adjacent to theirs. "Just coffee, please." The smooth honeyed voice drifted over the back of the high seat to where they sat motionless. "Someone will be joining me."

Erik's forehead crinkled into a frown. "Therese?" he mouthed to Ellen. She nodded and held up her hand in the universal "wait" signal.

Minutes passed. Erik drained his coffee mug and set it on the table without making a sound. At least he cooperated with the cloak-and-dagger scene. The tension froze Ellen's entire body. She sat with her hands clasped tightly on the table in front of her. The bell above the door signaled again. Heavy footsteps crossed purposefully to the adjoining booth.

Therese spoke first. "I was here. On time. You're late."

"You just remember who you're speaking to." The wrinkles in Erik's forehead grew deep enough to hide a boulder. The man slid into the booth behind them, shaking both sides of the double bench seat. "I am employing you. Without me, you don't have a job, much less a future in this company. Understand?"

"Yes. I understand." Therese's answer reflected a change in tone to submission.

"That's better. Now, where's the report?" They heard a sliding sound. "Good girl. Is it as damaging as you promised?"

"Paying higher than competitive wages, giving liberal benefits, and hiring and promoting locals over U.S. citizens. It shows Erik for the liberal he really is." Therese cleared her throat. "It's obvious we have compromised profits in order to coddle the workers, especially in Asia and Latin America. Not so much in Europe, of course. I've got more brains than that. I've been able to keep wages down while convincing our workers they're getting more than they're entitled to."

A snicker. "That's what I like about you, Therese. No nonsense in your division, eh?" He paused, apparently reading the report. "Uh-huh ... Hmmm ... Good, good."

Erik closed his eyes, the cords in his neck bulging. After a few minutes, a hand slapped the other table. "This should do the trick. When the other board members read this, they'll have no choice but to vote Neilson out and vote our man in."

Ellen recognized the sound of a Velcro case being ripped open. The man chuckled. "I believe our business is completed, my dear. You will get your promotion after the board meeting." The booth shuddered as he rose. "The quicker the better, to my way of thinking."

Erik pushed at Ellen and motioned for her to get up. His face had set like granite. She slid out and stepped out of his way.

He spun toward the front of the restaurant. "Not so fast, Ronald. I believe you and I have business to discuss."

Chapter Seventeen

The bulky man had almost reached the door when Erik's voice froze him. Ronald Larson, hand-picked by Erik's father for the Neilson Board of Directors, rotated his broad body a quarter turn. His head completed a half revolution as if its weight continued the momentum against his will. His jaw tightened, and his fleshy lips curled into an imitation smile. "Erik." He seemed to hunt for words to absolve himself as he lumbered toward Erik and stuck his hand out. "How fortunate you are here."

Erik wouldn't shake the hand of this traitor. "For me, yes. Not so fortunate for you."

Still digesting what he had overheard, he became aware of the waitress gaping at them from beside the cash register.

Therese hunkered in the booth, her shoulders stooped and her face averted. He gestured to the table where she sat. "Let's sit down and talk." His frosty tone turned a pleasantry into a command.

Ronald held his grizzly smile, no doubt ready to devour Erik as soon as he turned his back. "Absolutely. Therese and I have some cost-saving proposals for the board, and we want to discuss them with you first, of course."

"Save it, Ronald. Have a seat." Erik turned to Ellen, still standing next to the back table, and motioned for her to join them. He took her elbow as she sat down, then he asked the waitress to bring coffee all around and slid into the booth next to Ellen. Ronald waited for Therese to move over. Then he sat beside her.

The waitress scurried over with a pot of steaming brew

and clean cups for Erik and Ellen. Ronald pulled his cup closer to him. Therese added sugar and cream to hers and swirled her spoon in it, her eyes focused on the cup.

Erik ignored his coffee. "So your cost-saving plan begins with cutting me, Ronald?"

Ronald's voice remained steady. "Nonsense, Erik. Whatever gave you that idea? We were just discussing when we might be able to schedule a meeting with you, before the board meeting. We know how busy—"

"Do you think my father would have supported your ideas for saving money? You were his last board appointment. It's too bad you didn't spend enough time with him to understand his management philosophy." Erik had followed his father's example for running the company with integrity and compassion.

"Your father lived in a different time, Erik." Ronald tapped his first finger on the table, underscoring his points. "We're dealing with a new world now. Technology, global competition, regulations—it's all changing." Each tap grew more forceful, until the coffee sloshed in their cups. "The economic viability of this company depends on managing smarter and better than our competitors. That means practical financial decisions, not some 'feel good' philosophy that jacks up our expenses." He ended with his clenched fist hitting the table so hard the cups jumped in their saucers. He jerked back and let his right hand fall protectively to the leather case on the padded bench next to him.

Erik picked up his cup and sipped the bitter drink. "This company is not struggling financially. If anything, we are stronger than our competitors because of our philosophy. Our employees want to work for us—and work harder—because we treat them better than other companies would. These policies keep us ahead of the competition."

"Yes, of course." Ronald glowered. "But there are still ways—"

"Never mind, Ronald. I heard everything you said. Don't pretend to have the company's interests at heart. It's clear you're only interested in padding your own portfolio." Erik threw Ronald's glare back at him. "The point is we have a different approach to business." The man had fooled his father and muscled his way onto the board, but his deception ended here. Now to find out how deep the treachery went.

He turned to Therese, who scrutinized her coffee like it contained tea leaves revealing her future. "Why would you be part of this thing? You've advanced rapidly in this company. Wasn't success enough?"

She cut her eyes to look at him without tipping her head up. Her fingers tightened around the ceramic coffee cup, whitening her knuckles. "Of course it was." Her voice quivered. "I'm sorry, I don't know—"

Erik stroked his chin. "I'm sure you weren't working alone. I don't suppose you'll tell me who else is involved." He let the question hang in the air. He could entice them to answer by promising immunity, but he could find no mercy to do so. "I didn't think so. But I will find out, sooner or later."

"What—what will you do?" Therese's voice was little more than a whisper.

Erik examined his lack of pity. "Do? I'll start by taking that report." He reached his open hand toward Ronald, who tugged apart the Velcro strip of the case and pulled out a stapled document. He laid it down and reluctantly pushed it across the table.

Picking it up, Erik flicked the pages through his fingers. The edges stung, betrayal ripping his skin. His eyes skewered Therese and he steadied his voice. "You will call in sick tomorrow. I'll arrange for a security guard to accompany you while you clean out your office this weekend, and he will collect your keys when you're done. Your resignation will be on my desk the day after the holiday. Won't be much of a Christmas, but you chose your path."

He turned his focus back to Ronald, searched for signs of remorse in his face but found only defiance. He needed to be sure Ronald would be left powerless to sway other board members. "At the next board meeting, I will inform the other directors that you have resigned, effective immediately. If necessary, I'll tell them how you tried to sabotage me. I'm confident they'll back me one hundred percent, and you'll be blacklisted from any other boards in the Twin Cities.

"On the other hand, if there's no trouble, I'll tell them we had a difference in management philosophy. Still the truth. You can take your cost-saving ideas somewhere they will be—"He spat the last word—"appreciated."

He stood and pulled a money clip from his pocket. Extracting the bills, he separated a twenty from the middle of the packet and dropped it on the table. "Come, Ellen." He held out his hand to help her up. "It's time to go home."

He gathered their coats from the back booth. The frigid air that slapped him as they stepped outside broke his mechanized mood. But he still had enemies within the company. He put his arm around Ellen's shoulders and kissed her cheek. "I want to thank you for a very interesting dinner. Now will you tell me how you knew about this meeting?"

She burrowed against his body. "Does it matter? You found out what they were planning and stopped it. That's the important thing."

Chapter Eighteen

Ellen adjusted the temperature control, needing heat to warm up the air inside the car. Erik wouldn't be satisfied with her answer. But she would wait until he asked again.

It didn't take long.

As soon as he pulled the BMW onto the freeway toward downtown Minneapolis, he brought up the subject again. "Ellen, dear." His voice, smooth as cream on the surface, covered a coffee-like undertone—hot and bitter. He reached across the gray leather seat and found her hand. "What you did was smart. But it doesn't change anything. I still don't want you involved in the company."

She stared at the aging Metrodome off to their left, its roof shimmering in the frigid night. He treated her the same way his father had treated his mother. She wondered if he expected her to challenge him. She had good reasons to contest him, but she couldn't summon the effort. The entire scene at the restaurant left her worn out.

He pulled his hand away to the steering wheel and maneuvered onto the ramp that took them south onto I-35W. She shifted her gaze to the concrete wall edging the side of the highway, keeping the traffic noise away from the neighborhood and the urban blight out of view of travelers. Much like the wall separating her from Erik right now.

"I need to know everything you knew about that meeting tonight. Were you aware of what Therese was up to?"

"Just like I told you." She had told him as much as she dared. Trying to calm her rapid heartbeat, she rubbed her palm across the heated seat. "I knew she was supposed to be meeting someone at the restaurant, but I didn't know exactly what they were up to."

"But how did you know?" He hit the steering wheel hard with his right hand, causing a blast of the horn. "Someone else is involved. I need to know who."

She didn't want to fight now. In spite of her longing to tell him the truth so that he could find the answers he needed, revealing too much would lead to more questions. Questions she wanted to avoid. "I don't know who it is."

He glanced sideways at her. "Knowing how you found out could give me a clue. Or at least help me eliminate one person."

She leaned her head against the seatback. "All right. It was your new managing director—Manuel Rivas." She struggled to keep her voice from shaking. "He came to the museum a few days ago and asked if he could talk to me. He said he had overheard a conversation at this restaurant, but he wasn't sure what it meant."

"Why didn't he come to me?"

"I suggested that. He was afraid you wouldn't believe him, since he's so new. He thought you'd listen to me. I didn't know if you'd believe me either. To be honest, I thought—hoped—it was all some sort of misunderstanding. But I figured it was worth getting you to the restaurant to find out."

He eased off the gas pedal and tapped the brake as he took the exit. "So a guy's been a managing director for three months, goes to my wife with a story about a plot to get me out, and winds up saving my business."

He waited at the stop light after it turned green. "Was he in on the plan? Maybe he got cold feet, figured spilling the beans will be better for him in the long run." A horn behind them honked, and he made the right turn.

"I don't think so." She turned her head to look at him.

"He—he seemed sincerely concerned about you. He talked about how good you had been to him."

"Hmmm." They drove the last few blocks in silence. He pulled the car into their driveway, punched the button to open the garage door, and eased the car inside. "I'll find out. Sooner or later, I will know who else was involved. And heaven help them."

Chapter Nineteen

Warren stuffed papers into the shredder, forcing the machine to slice every scrap that might link him to Ronald. Chopping up his hopes of being president of Neilson Enterprises.

He had grown tired of hovering in Erik's shadow. He could run this company better, make more money, increase its market share, and maybe even take it public. Erik had done little more than maintain the status quo since his father died. By now, Warren would have expanded to more countries, ramped up the U.S. advertising, fine-tuned production, and gone nose-to-nose with their largest competitor. And beaten them. Now he found himself jamming random documents into the mouth of an already stuffed device that would devour his dreams.

Following the late-night phone call from Ronald, he had arrived at the office by six Friday morning. After an hour, he had already scoured every file folder, every desk drawer in his office, searching for correspondence or notes of phone calls between them. He thought he'd been careful, but he hadn't planned on ever being discovered.

He came to the bottom of the stack he'd made just as the shredder gave off a burning electrical odor and emitted a grinding noise, as if it might spit out every piece of the evidence.

A few more weeks and the board would have voted Erik out and made him president. Last night, he had warned both Ronald and Therese to keep quiet. He had no sympathy for either of them. They should have been more careful, made sure no one could hear them before they spoke. At least Erik had not learned of his involvement in the scheme. Better that they were caught now, before they could mess things up for him.

He deleted Ronald from his cell phone contacts and scrolled through the log of calls. There must be a way to erase the number from the record of calls. *Delete all.* That should do it.

He needed another plan. One that would not fail. If he couldn't be president, he could at least find a way to undermine Erik and make some extra profit for himself.

He shuffled papers and found Manuel's report recommending the purchase of the three Guatemala plantations. Maybe he would find his answer in bananas. He skimmed until he found a paragraph about Tex, the plantation manager.

Time to have a chat with him, to find out whether he could be useful.

The package sat waiting on the front porch when Ellen stepped out to get the mail. Wrapped in brown paper and decorated with hand-drawn stars and Christmas trees, it carried the scent of promise and love.

She bent to pick it up, knowing before she looked that it came from Kentucky. Its lightness surprised her. She hugged it with both hands as she scooted out of the cold and pushed the door shut. She set the package on the stairs and plopped down beside it. She grabbed her phone and called Diane, who answered on the second ring.

"Did it come today, Laynie?" Diane's excitement pulsed through the speaker. "Did you open it?"

"Not yet. I thought it was for Christmas." She crunched

the phone between her shoulder and her ear and traced the pattern of the star on top of the box.

"You can't wait," Diane said. "Didn't you see the 'Open Me Now' markings? The kids are jumping up and down to find out if you like it. Besides, you can use it for your Christmas dinner."

Ellen felt her heart quicken. Christmas dinner had not forced its way into her thoughts until now. She pulled at the tape holding the paper. "Okay, okay. I'm opening it now." She laughed. "Hold on. I'll put you on speaker so I can use both hands."

She set the phone on the stairs. "Shall I give you the play-by-play?"

Diane chuckled. "I'd better use the speaker, too, so the kids can hear."

Ellen removed the paper and tugged at the tape on the box. She pulled open the flaps and looked inside. Nestled among Styrofoam peanuts lay colorful yarn-wrapped figures. A shoebox formed a stable, complete with a gold star attached to its roof.

"Oh, my!" She knew immediately this creation would get a place of honor in the dining room. "This must have taken you weeks to make."

She picked up one figure and examined it. Pipe cleaners had been padded and wrapped with cotton and brown yarn to create a male figure. She guessed it to be Joseph. Another figure in blue with long hair had to be Mary. Three male characters in red, purple, and magenta "robes" wore gold crowns and held tiny gifts.

As she dug out each one, she exclaimed appropriately for the benefit of the two children listening by phone. They had made an angel, a shepherd, and even two little sheep. All crude but made chic by love, as only gifts created by children could be. She had no fondness for the Christmas story, but she could tell Diane's children had spent hours working on these pieces. Even though she had met them only once at Diane's wedding. Moisture seeped into her eyes.

She lifted out the last piece, a baby in a cardboard manger. Baby Jesus. She went mute.

"Ellen?" Diane's voice from the speaker sounded concerned.

She picked up the phone and took it off speaker mode. "I'm here. I'm speechless. I don't understand why you would make all this for me."

Doreen's little-girl voice came through the phone. "We love you, and Jesus does, too. We thought a manger set would help you 'member."

She sank onto the lower step and swallowed hard. She wanted to have sweet children like these two. But if Jesus loved her so much, why had he taken away that possibility? This whole God-thing could be so confusing.

"Thank you." She couldn't say much more or her voice would crack. "Di, I'll call you later, okay? I love the gift, kids." She clicked off. She did not deserve such a thoughtful surprise. She couldn't believe Doreen and Michael had spent so much time making it for her.

One by one, she picked up each figure and put it in the stable box. She carried the set into the dining room, blinking back tears as she moved aside an elegant flower arrangement to make room on the sideboard for the simple homemade gift.

Chapter Twenty

"Miz Neilson, this is Miz Barnette. I'm calling 'bout Tyrone."

Ellen's heart dropped to her feet. Bad enough to lose the sweet boy, but two days before Christmas? How would his family endure it? "I don't know what to say—"

"You mistook me." Tyrone's grandmother sounded like she wanted to sing. "Tyrone done woke up. He gonna be okay. God heal him, just like I knowed He would."

"What?" She must have heard wrong. "He's awake?"

"Yes, ma'am. Praise the Lord. He can't come home just yet, but we gonna take Christmas to him tomorrow."

With her free hand, Ellen groped for the arm of the couch and dropped into the seat. "That's—that's wonderful. I just can't believe it. I didn't think he would—you know, make it."

"You just don't got the faith that I got, Miz Neilson. My God's a good God, and I asked Him to heal my boy. And He did, just like He tell me He would."

Ellen tried to make sense of Mrs. Barnette's words. God didn't work like this—not in her experience. Wait. The boy would probably be paralyzed. "Is he, uh, will he be able to walk again?"

"Oh, glory, yes. They got him up today for a few steps. Doctor say he don't see no reason Tyrone won't be good as new in a few months."

Ellen listened, numb, as Mrs. Barnette raved again about the goodness of God. She had no experience with that. Why did this turn out so right when everything in her life had turned out so wrong? She hated herself for thinking that way.

"Can I tell him you'll come?"

Come? She should have been listening. "What? I missed what you said."

The woman's melodic laugh helped Ellen relax. "You still shocked, but you'll see for yourself. Tyrone said he want you to come. Tomorrow evening, anytime you can make it."

On Christmas Eve, Ellen found Tyrone's hospital room more by the music than by the number. She got off the elevator and followed the singing. She recognized his grandmother's voice—rich and resonant, like her prayers.

"The Lord has promised good to me, His Word my hope secures."

Tyrone's frail little-boy voice echoed, "My hope secures." The door stood open a crack, and she knocked.

Without stopping the song, Mrs. Barnette opened the door. Beaming at her, she reached out and grabbed Ellen's arm, pulling her into the room.

"Miz Neilson!" Tyrone stopped singing, and so did the others. He raised both arms toward her, and she went toward the bed, bent over him, and let him hug her.

She wanted to hug him back, but his bandages still shrouded him, and she feared hurting him. Instead, she placed her hand on his dark kinky hair. "Don't let me stop your singing. It's beautiful."

A woman Ellen had never seen before sat in a chair by the window holding a small girl on her lap. Mrs. Barnette introduced them as Sunita, a neighbor who watched after the children sometimes, and Tyrone's little sister, Neeta. Ellen recognized Sunita's accent as the one who answered the phone when she called.

Mrs. Barnette pointed to the chair pulled up next to the bed. "You sit there, close to Tyrone. You just in time. We was about to open our presents."

She handed Ellen a package wrapped in crumpled paper showing angels and clouds, and tied with yarn. "This from Tyrone. He wrapped it hisself." The box shape suggested it might hold a bracelet or necklace. Ellen silently congratulated herself that she had brought something for him.

"I hope you like it, teacher." Tyrone's gaze revealed his excitement. "It's real pretty, like you."

She took the package and held it on her lap like a treasure. "I'm sure I will. But you didn't need to give me a present." She smiled and dug into her shoulder bag. "I think I saw something in here with your name on it. I wonder where it went." She located the package but pretended to keep digging to heighten the boy's anticipation. "Ah, here it is."

She pulled out the rectangular box, elegantly wrapped in a blue-striped paper with matching blue ribbon. She handed it to him, and he took it as though it contained a diamond.

He glanced at his grandmother. "Can we open 'em now, Grandma?"

"Go ahead." Mrs. Barnette laughed. "Never could keep this boy from opening presents on Christmas Eve. Never mind we always waited for Chris'mas Day. He won't wait for nothin'."

Tyrone had the paper off his box and opened it. "Look, Grandma! My very own watercolor paints and brushes! Now I can paint jus' like Miz Neilson!"

The adults laughed, and Neeta slipped off Sunita's lap to come closer to the bed. Her brother showed her the paints but wouldn't let her touch them. Her eyes gleamed as she stared at the watercolor set.

Ellen made a mental note to get the girl some colored

markers.

"You gotta open your gift now." Tyrone pointed to Ellen.

She looked down at the package on her lap and pulled at the bow. The tape needed only a little coaxing to allow her to separate the paper from the box. She lifted the lid and found an ornate bracelet with links of every rainbow color. "It's beautiful," she whispered. "But I can't take this. You need the money more—"

"Hush now," Mrs. Barnette said. "You can and you will. Jus' an old trinket I had. Ain't got no use for it. Tyrone 'membered it and asked could he give it to you. I figgered you mean that much to him, weren't no point in me saying no."

Ellen blinked her eyes and put the bracelet around her wrist. She held it out for Tyrone to admire.

He grinned "See, pretty just like you."

Mrs. Barnette passed presents to Sunita and Neeta and another one to Tyrone. As they unwrapped them, Ellen envied the joy they seemed to have in these simple gifts. When the packages had all been opened, Mrs. Barnette launched into "Joy to the World," and everyone joined in. Ellen tried to sing along, though she didn't remember—or believe—all the words.

They finished the song, and Mrs. Barnette led them right into another carol. Ellen stopped singing and just watched. She'd known this kind of family bonding for a few years with her dad and stepmom. Until Mom Anne got sick.

After three more Christmas carols, Mrs. Barnette leaned over and patted Ellen on her knee. "This a wonderful way to spend Christmas Eve, ain't it? But you got your husband to git home to. We shouldn't of kept you so long."

Ellen winced. Yes, Erik would be home by now, but they had no special Christmas Eve plans. They would have dinner and go to bed, like any other night. They usually exchanged presents on Christmas morning after sleeping late. For the rest of the day, she would paint while Erik worked in his office downstairs.

Mrs. Barnette must have sensed her reluctance to leave. "You go on now, honey. Family's the most important thing they is."

The words haunted her. Hadn't she said as much to the security guard, Ed, just a few weeks ago?

Chapter Twenty-One

Ellen booted up the computer in Erik's office early Christmas morning. On this one day when he slept late, she had time to do her own research.

As she waited for the screen to come to life, Erik's oversized desk chair cushioned her with its warm leather surface and smell. The room still carried his father's influence, as if he feared disappointing his father by choosing his own furnishings. Or maybe he had been too busy to consider it. She hoped he would accept her offer to redecorate for him, since she had made that part of his Christmas present.

They had not talked about children again, but she couldn't stop thinking about his suggestion. She typed in the words he had used. *Gestational carrier.* The term sounded so impersonal.

The search engine returned seven hundred thousand results. She clicked on the first one.

The photo of a smiling couple holding an infant tugged at her heart. Just as intended. She touched her fingers to the baby's face and stroked the glass surface of the monitor. She scanned the text. "Emotionally intense, highly controversial, and legally complex."

Having another woman carry and deliver her baby seemed detached and artificial. "It's officially recognized in only a handful of states and is still illegal in others," the website stated. She clicked "print" and the printer whirred as it spat out the information.

"Finding a healthy, willing gestational carrier can take months or even years," she read. Apparently sisters and cousins sometimes agreed, but she and Erik had no relatives they could ask.

But you could use an agency. She found another site carrying classified ads for "intended parents seeking a gestational carrier" and "prospective gestational surrogates." The listings were organized by geographic region and included emotionally charged terms like *caring, loving, intelligent, healthy,* and *honest.* Another woman said she wanted "to give the precious gift of life."

Ellen felt like a shopper choosing a baby instead of shoes or a handbag. Most of the ads mentioned a desired fee. The money would not be an obstacle, of course. Erik had made that clear.

She clicked to a different page, an article about a woman in England who had been almost permanently pregnant for more than a decade, carrying some two dozen babies for other couples. She read a story about poor women in India who supported their families by serving as surrogates, getting paid ten times what their husbands could earn in a year. But the article reported, "Critics claim the clinics promoting this 'reproductive tourism' care little for the health or rights of the surrogates."

Another link caught her eye. "Forced abortions shake up wombs-for-rent industry." She closed the browser. She couldn't read any more. Instead, she checked her e-mail and found a message from Diane. The message had an attachment: the magazine article Diane had written about international adoptions. Would adoption be any better? Just as she opened the attachment, her phone rang.

Diane's voice cheered her as always. "Something told me I should call first thing to wish you a merry Christmas."

"You do have a knack for calling at the right time." She explained about Erik's suggestion to use a surrogate, and what she had been reading. She picked up the paper from the printer. "Listen to this. 'You'll have to worry about legal snags and the possibility that your carrier will change her mind.' And after all that, apparently you still have to adopt the child to make it legal. It seems, I don't know, so contrived and—so unreal."

Diane remained silent while Ellen ranted. In a gentle voice, she asked, "Did you read the article I sent you?"

"I was just about to when you called. But what makes adoption any better? Isn't it still like buying a baby?"

"For one thing, you can give a home to a baby who has already been born. It doesn't involve any artificial medical procedures."

Ellen clicked back to the search page. "Oh, yes. Assisted reproductive technologies, they call them."

"Right. Infertility treatments may be right for some couples. But thousands of kids have already been born who need parents. Why not help one of them?"

Could she love a baby she and Erik didn't conceive? "Di, adoption doesn't seem ... permanent. I mean, the baby wouldn't really be ours. Wouldn't the child know we weren't his real parents and think we didn't really love him?"

A pause. "Laynie, don't you realize how much Anne must have loved you to adopt you as her daughter? Even knowing your father had been unfaithful to her?" Ellen recalled Mom Anne's eyes shining as they celebrated their first Christmas together. She gripped the phone tighter, but she kept listening.

"You were more fortunate than most people, even though you were adopted. You were loved, not just by two parents, but by three. Your mother. Your father. And your stepmother. Each of them gave you all their love. Now you have a whole heart full of love to give to your child—whether or not the child is biologically yours."

Ellen had never considered having three different parents

a positive thing. She couldn't speak.

"Laynie?" Diane spoke quietly. "Will you at least read my article and think about it?"

"Yes, I'll think about it." They talked for a few more moments before Ellen hung up and clicked the mouse to return to Diane's story. She saw photos of a Caucasian woman surrounded by Asian children. How awkward it had been for her as a teenager with dark hair and eyes when her stepmother and father both had blond hair. Their child, even if adopted, would not have that issue, regardless of hair color. But would Erik even consider adoption?

Chapter Twenty-Two

Ellen arrived ten minutes early and found Manuel already at their meeting place on Thursday, two days after Christmas.

Gray pre-dawn skies were spitting a snow and ice mix, and Manuel looked like a little boy with his face turned up and his tongue stuck out. "Try this."

She did and tasted the cold, wet flakes. She laughed. "I bet you've never had snow cream. I should make some for you."

They stretched and prepared to run, and Manuel said, "Therese has left. Over the holiday weekend. Yesterday they sent an e-mail saying she left for personal reasons." They started to run. "It appears *Señor* Neilson believed you."

"He didn't have to. He heard it for himself, as we hoped." Her breath formed a cloud that floated up and disappeared in the frosty air. They ran side by side, slowing to a walk when they encountered a patch of shiny ice that could be treacherous. The overhead lamps lighting the path ahead glowed with halos in the morning darkness. Appropriate for the Christmas season, she supposed.

By the time she finished describing what had happened at the restaurant, they had completed one circuit of the lake.

"Good. Good. So all is well," Manuel said.

"Not exactly. There's still the matter of who else was involved. They may try again."

Manuel nodded and kept moving. Ellen stopped. He didn't understand the danger. She ran to catch up with him. "Manuel. There's more."

He turned his head toward her, eyebrows raised almost to his woolen cap.

"I had to tell him you were the one who told me." She waited for several strides. "Erik thinks you might have been part of it. The plot, I mean. That maybe you chickened out at the last minute or were trying to play both sides, you know?" He halted, and she turned to face him. "He isn't sure you can be trusted."

Manuel started running again. "That is understandable, I suppose. There is nothing I can do except to prove myself trustworthy. Such things take time."

The freezing air squeezed her chest. "Doesn't it upset you? Instead of 'thank you,' you get lumped in with the enemy."

"I suppose it would be upsetting to some people. But my motives and actions were honest and pure. I know it, and God knows it. What others think is of little importance to me. The light shall reveal what is hidden."

Across the lake, a dog barked. A car on the nearby street spun through the unplowed snow.

"Manuel, how is it you trust in this God you cannot see? He hasn't made your life easy."

"True. Life is difficult. But His yoke is easy and His burden is light."

"What are you talking about?"

"Matthew 11:30. The Lord Jesus Christ told us that He would help to carry our burdens. Just as two oxen yoked together find it easier to pull a load, so will we when we are yoked together with Jesus. God never intended that we should bear these burdens alone."

They passed a group of cedar trees weighed down by snow and ice. The trunks bent in arcs, almost touching the ground as they bowed down with the weight clinging to their branches. She reached out and brushed the branches with her gloved hand, knocking some of the heavy load to the ground.

"Why doesn't He just take away the burdens?"

"Because He wants us to depend on Him, to realize that we are weak and helpless, but in Him we are made strong."

Ellen stopped again. "I'm sorry, Manuel, but I just can't accept that God loves me. Not when He's allowed all these problems. I'm glad it works for you. But it doesn't make sense to me." His comments roiled in her head, and she couldn't handle any more right now. "I think I'll go back. I've got a busy day—"

He frowned. "Are you sick? Should I go with you?"

"No, I'll be fine. I just—See you next Tuesday?"

"New Year's Day? Of course." He grinned. "How could I turn down such an invitation?"

"Okay, then. Bye." She turned and ran at full speed in the direction of home.

She heard him call, "God bless you, Ellen."

The footprints they had made only minutes ago disappeared as big, sloppy snowflakes replaced the icy slush.

The next morning, when Ellen opened the blinds in Erik's study, she understood why some people in Minnesota suffered from winter depression. The white ground cover would stay until sometime in March. The bare trees in the backyard stretched their limbs toward the sky. Her artist's eyes searched for a radiance that would breathe life into the scene but found none. The gray snow-laden clouds hid all evidence of the sun. She turned away from the window.

A red and white airline ticket folder on the desk caught her attention. A glossy brochure peeked out from inside it, revealing the word "Guatemala." The back-and-forth hum of

Angelica's vacuuming overhead echoed as Ellen picked up the pamphlet.

She sank into the desk chair and gazed at the colorful pictures. Instead of the revulsion she had nurtured for years, she tasted desire rising from some secret place in her heart. Did she dare to go back? She didn't know if she could stand the pain of remembering. Events smoldered beneath the surface of the protective covering she had buried them under, but they threatened to blaze if she allowed herself to think about what had happened.

She pondered the brochure. "Beautiful land of lakes, volcanoes, and ancient Mayan culture." Not the Guatemala she remembered. Still, the photos of coffee plantations and the rainbow colors of the marketplace brought back the scents of coffee beans and spicy foods in the air. The lush green hillsides reminded her of her favorite days. Two, or maybe three times, before her *mamá* got sick, they had packed a lunch and taken a bus to the edge of the city. Manuel had come with them, and they had hiked to the top of a mountain. *La Cerra*. She must have been eight or nine, Manuel almost a teenager.

After a game of tag, they rested on the steep hillside, looking away from the city toward a large lake. *Mamá* had called it *Lago de Amatitlan*.

"What are you going to do when you grow up?" Manuel had asked her.

"I'm going to be a famous artist. I'll paint this." She waved her arm majestically at the colors around them—the brilliant emeralds of the grass, the crystal azure of the lake, the soft cotton clouds floating around the top of the mountain. "And my paintings will hang in the Museum of Modern Art. You'll see."

Manuel had stood and bowed. "And I—I will market your paintings all over the world. You'll be famous, and I will be rich."

Ellen laughed at the recollection of the lanky boy with the unruly hair pretending to be a gentleman. How close he had come to achieving his dream. Maybe he didn't have wealth, but he had succeeded in business. And he seemed happy, even though single.

She, on the other hand, had all the wealth she would ever need but—and she could admit this only to herself—had little joy in her life. Her art gave her pleasure, though she had never sold any of her paintings. She'd had plenty of encouragement—Diane, Erik, her art professors, even the director of the Walker Art Center. But she always refused to exhibit her paintings or offer them for sale. She feared getting negative comments. If she never showed her work, she would not have to deal with rejection. Or success.

For the first time, she began to see her life clearly. She had believed all these years God would take away any success or happiness she might find. If she didn't try to accomplish anything, she could not fail. There would be nothing for God to steal from her. And if she didn't disclose her Mayan heritage, Erik would not condemn her. So she had hidden her past, and she had hidden her talent. All because of her fear.

She glanced at the brochure again. "Land of Eternal Spring." The back panel reminded her that temperatures in January ranged from sixty to seventy-six. The chair whirred as she swiveled to face the grayness and the snow and the ice outside the window. Maybe January would be a good time to go back to Guatemala.

Chapter Twenty-Three

When their plane left behind the Gulf and crossed the Yucatán Peninsula, Ellen's stomach began to churn. She unbuckled her seatbelt, grabbed the paper bag from the seat pocket, and made her way to the tiny lavatory reserved for first-class passengers. Locking herself inside, she held the airsickness bag close to her face and took several deep breaths.

The closer she got to Guatemala, the more she regretted her impulsive decision to make this trip to the country that held so many awful memories.

She tried to swallow the sour taste in her mouth so she wouldn't heave. This trip, things would be different than when she had lived there. The poor orphan who possessed nothing more than a shoe box had been replaced. She didn't even have to go back to the garbage dump. But in spite of her anxiety, the need to revisit the setting of her early childhood had not evaporated since it first arose two weeks earlier.

The tinny voice of the pilot announcing their descent into Guatemala City came over the speaker. She gulped. Time to return to her seat. Almost time to confront her past. She sat down and nudged Erik, who leaned with his head against his seatback. Even asleep, he clutched the thick manila folder he had been studying before he dozed off. "We should be landing soon."

He lifted his head and sat up straighter, glanced out the window, and nodded. He pulled his briefcase from under the seat in front of him, stashed the folder inside it, and returned the case to its resting place.

"Have a good nap, Rip?" Ellen grinned at him. But she

felt like the one waking from a twenty-year sleep.

"It's a good thing my meetings aren't until tomorrow. These early flights get to me."

"Does that mean we can go sightseeing together this afternoon?"

Erik stretched his arms over his head and let one fall around her shoulders. "I think I could manage it. After I make a few calls, okay? You figure out where you want to go."

The place she most wanted to see would not be found in the tourist guidebooks. And she needed to go there without Erik. Maybe the two of them could start with the Museum of Modern Art. As a little girl, she had wanted to visit the museum, but they'd had no money for such luxuries.

They cleared customs, collected their luggage, exchanged some currency, and then met up with the rest of the Neilson travelers. As they spilled onto the sidewalk in front of the terminal, bright sunshine and shirt-sleeve temperatures greeted them while a warm breeze lifted their spirits.

Rosemary raised one arm to the sun and danced a jig. "Now, this is what I need in January. Why did I have to grow up in Minnesota?"

At the curb in front of the terminal, Alan Monroe leaned against a black Mitsubishi Montero. He had been in the country for a week preparing for the others' arrival. He gestured toward an ancient version of a typical American yellow cab parked behind the SUV. "I figured we'd need two cars to handle all the luggage. He's the only driver who would wait."

Rosemary waited by the SUV. "How do we know the cabbie won't steal one of my bags?" She didn't seem to care whether the driver understood her. Manuel offered to go in the cab with the luggage so the others could ride together.

Ellen hugged Alan. "Did Ria come?" From Ria's occasional visits to the U.S., Ellen knew her to be charming and down-to-earth, and she looked forward to seeing her again.

Alan took Ellen's carry-on from her and placed it in the backseat of the cab. "She had a long drive today, so she's at the hotel resting. She'll join us for dinner." Because he travelled so much, the couple lived in Mexico near her parents.

Once they had settled in the cars and Alan pulled away from the terminal, Rosemary leaned forward and tapped him on the shoulder. "Alan, darling, do you need an international driver's license here?"

Alan glanced over his shoulder and smiled at her. "All you really need to drive here are an accelerator, a horn, and strong nerves."

They soon found out what he meant. As he sped through the crowded streets, Alan's horn joined the cantata. Other drivers seemed to have no idea why cars had brakes. The only place no one hurried was behind the hotel registration desk.

By the time they reached their room, Ellen's stomach grumbled about missing lunch. Erik ordered from room service and then called his office.

Exploring the two-room suite, she opened the drapes in the bedroom and stared down at the bustling street. The tall, modern buildings and tidy streets sparred with the images she had locked behind the secret doors of her memory. When she had allowed herself to remember her birth country, her mind brought up images of cardboard shanties and squalor. Now she felt as though she had landed on Mars, not the country where she spent the first ten years of her life.

She turned away from the window and began to empty the suitcases. She arranged Erik's suits on the left of the closet and her dresses on the right, just like at home. She followed the same pattern with things that went in the dresser. She set out their toiletries on top of the dresser, placing each item on the appropriate side.

Erik had not finished his phone call when room service arrived, so she answered the door. She stepped aside to let the short, dark man enter with his cart, pointing him toward a table by the window. She retrieved her purse from the sofa and dug out several bills, which she handed the waiter.

"*Gracias*." She closed the door behind him.

She moved back to the table and peeked under the two metal domes to see what Erik had ordered. Enchiladas, rice, and corn.

She sniffed, and the pungent smells caused her stomach to rumble again. She caught Erik's eye. She mouthed the words so she wouldn't disturb his phone call. "Almost ready?"

He shook his head, covered the mouthpiece of the old-fashioned black phone, and whispered, "Go ahead. Don't wait for me." He returned to his conversation.

She sat down and uncovered her plate. She tasted the enchilada, relishing the peppery food. A moment later, Erik hung up the phone and settled into the chair across from her. "What do you want to do this afternoon?"

An hour later, they walked from the hotel to the museum district. Ellen turned her head this way and that, entranced by how different the city looked. The bright colors of the clothing people wore and the flags flying above the street contrasted with her dreary recollections. The dum-da-da-dum beat of *reggaeton* from street musicians echoed the thumping of her heart.

They found the *Museo de Arte Moderno* all but deserted, and they meandered alone through the quiet rooms, admiring the sculptures and colorful paintings. As they entered the largest gallery, Ellen stared at the four-foot-tall landscape painting across the room. Erik examined the canvases on the nearest wall. When he turned and followed her gaze, he put his arm around her.

"Beautiful scene, isn't it? I wonder if it's here in Guatemala."

"Only someone who knows and loves the place could have painted that," she whispered. "It reminds me of a place where we used to go for picnics."

"In Kentucky?" He chuckled. "I thought all you had were picturesque horse farms and coal mines, not mountain gorges like that."

For Such a Moment

Chapter Twenty-Four

Ellen slapped Erik teasingly on the chest with her rolled-up map of the museum's exhibits. "The things you don't know about Kentucky could fill this building. Come on. Let's see what the placard says about the painting."

She had let her guard down. She had to be more careful, or Erik might suspect that she had kept secrets from him.

They crossed the terrazzo floor, and Ellen read the identifying card aloud. "*La Belleza del la Cerra*, Carlos Elias Rivas, 1965." She remembered the mountain well.

He smiled and translated for her. "'*The Beauty of La Cerra*.' I think *La Cerra* is a mountain near here. Maybe we'll have time to drive up there before we leave."

"I'd like that." More than he knew, and for reasons that had little to do with the scenery. "I hope it's as beautiful as the painting."

He studied the placard. "The artist's name is Rivas. I wonder if there's any connection to Manuel."

"Rivas is a common name here, isn't it?"

He moved toward the door. "He said he doesn't have any living family, but if the artist is dead, he could be a relative. We'll have to ask him." He reached the door and turned. "Ready to go."

The missing question mark revealed he had seen enough artwork for today. She hurried to him and grasped his arm as they walked out.

As soon as Ellen and Erik joined the group for a late dinner, Rosemary declared she had already grown bored with the city. "I say we ladies rent a car and drive to the beach tomorrow. What do you think, Ellen?"

Ellen didn't want to seem unsociable, but she needed an opportunity to go off on her own. "Actually, I thought I'd do a little sightseeing around town tomorrow. I want to check out the handcrafts at the market. Why don't you and Ria go without me? I'll join you the day after." She hoped they would have little interest in seeing the handcrafts.

"You do not need to rent a car," Ria spoke up. "We can take my car. It looks as ugly as me in a bathing suit, but it will get us there. And back."

Rosemary narrowed her eyes and leaned back in her chair. "As long as we get to the beach. Are you sure you won't come, Ellen?"

Once she convinced Rosemary that she would be fine staying behind in the city, Ellen relaxed. No one but Manuel would understand her desire to visit the slums around the garbage dump. She welcomed the distraction when the waiter came to take their orders.

Alan and Ria provided recommendations on which dishes to try, and after extensive discussion, the waiter left. Manuel turned to Rosemary. "This is your first trip here, is it not? What do you think of our country?"

She leaned forward. "The trees and flowers are a great improvement over the icebox we left this morning." Behind her left ear she had pinned a large, freshly cut red flower that matched her colorful print dress. "Anything's better than white. I get so tired of gray and white."

Warren ignored her, as usual, and spoke to Erik. "Alan has set up a tour of one of the plantations tomorrow. Morales has invited us for dinner. Perhaps we can reach an agreement then."

The waiter arrived, and Erik waited until the food had been served. "Like I told you before we came, I need to see what we're buying. All the plantations and how the operations run. Then we can negotiate."

"Of course. But I don't think we should drag it out long. It's a good deal, and if we don't take it, someone else will." Warren picked up his fork and started to take a bite.

Manuel cleared his throat. "Before we eat, I propose that we ask God's blessing for the food and for the negotiations. Erik, would you mind if I pray?"

Erik shifted in his chair but nodded and tipped his head forward. Warren put down his fork and made a show of folding his hands. Rosemary sat frozen, her mouth open in surprise. Alan and Ria closed their eyes. Ellen bowed her head but kept her eyes open.

"Father God, we are thankful that we have all arrived here safely. We ask that You bless this food, that it will nourish our bodies. Please protect and watch over the ladies tomorrow. We also pray that Your will be done regarding the business that has brought us here. Open our eyes to any problems that we are not aware of. In Jesus' holy name we pray. Amen."

No one spoke as they began eating. After a few minutes, Erik broke the silence. "Manuel, Ellen and I went to the art museum this afternoon. We saw a painting by someone named Rivas. We wondered if he was any relation to you." Erik took a drink. "Carlos Elias Rivas. But I'm sure Rivas is a common name."

Manuel dabbed his face with his napkin. "In fact, he was my grandfather."

Ellen dropped her fork, and it clattered to the floor. She bent over to pick it up, hoping she could hide her shock. Could he mean their mutual grandfather? Manuel's mother and hers had been sisters, but her *mamá* had refused to talk about her parents, so she didn't even know their names.

He continued speaking mostly to Erik and the rest of the group. "I was an only child, and my parents died when I was young. I knew nothing of my heritage. After I got out of college, I did some research." He glanced at Ellen and immediately looked back at Erik. "I learned that my grandfather had been a very talented and famous artist. I regret that I never knew him, but at least I have been able to acquire a few of his paintings."

"What a delightful story," Rosemary chirped. "I would never have guessed you came from an artistic family." Tactless as always. She leaned forward and peered at Manuel with raised eyebrows. "Do you really believe that stuff you prayed? You think God will reveal any problems with this plantation deal?"

Warren's lips twisted. "Don't worry about it, darling. We've already identified all the problems. We're not going into this with our eyes closed. We'll be ready to close the deal in a couple of days. Right, Erik?"

With his usual reserve, Erik shrugged. "That depends on what we see, Warren. We'll need to spend the night in the village since it's too dangerous to drive those roads at night. Ladies, you will be careful and stay near the hotel tomorrow evening, won't you?"

Ria turned the conversation to what they could do the next evening, but Ellen had stopped listening. Perhaps she had inherited some talent from the artistic grandfather she had never known.

Chapter Twenty-Five

Amid the early morning shadows, Manuel and the other three men settled into the rented SUV for the four-hour drive to Indiana Plantation.

As soon as Alan pulled the car into the heavy traffic, Warren zipped open his leather attaché case. "I went over the numbers again last night, Erik. I think I found some ways we can make these plantations even more profitable."

He handed a typed sheet to Erik and pointed to a number on the paper. "See here? Look how high their percentage is for wages. I've been looking at the pay scales, and I think these people are overpaid. They'll work for far less."

As Alan wove through the streets, Manuel braced one hand on the dash and half turned to look at the men in the backseat. "Excuse me, *señor*. Is there not a union on this plantation?"

"No, seen-yore." Warren wrinkled his nose. "A few workers tried to organize one several years ago, but it failed. A union isn't really necessary down here."

Erik handed the paper back to Warren as Alan turned the car onto a broad thoroughfare. "Your numbers do strengthen the case. Let's talk about it again after we've seen the operations."

Manuel settled back into his seat and gazed out the window. They passed the Government Palace where, even at this early hour, uniformed schoolboys in short pants played football on the plaza, passing the dirty white ball with their quick feet. He had played on a team a handful of times. Would any of these boys have the opportunity to become executives, like him? Or in ten or fifteen years, would they be raising corn and potatoes on some hillside, grateful to earn a dollar a day?

He prayed silently that God would show him what he could do to bring hope to his country.

Ellen stood on the street corner by the hotel studying a small map she had picked up in the lobby. Traffic fumes filled the air, burning her nostrils and throat. Around her, a small group waited for the next bus.

She had visited the shopping mall connected to the hotel as soon as it opened. Now she wore a red top embroidered with yellow, blue, and white swirls that she had found in a store selling native clothing. A full black skirt carried the same swirls above the hemline. A pretty red and white apron completed the look that she hoped would help her avoid being pegged as a tourist.

"Excuse me." She tapped the arm of a squat woman standing at the curb and spoke to her in Spanish. On her back the woman carried a small boy, held in place with a gaily striped cloth wrapped around her waist and bosom. "Will the next bus take me to—here?" Ellen pointed to an area in *Zona Six*, near the location of the garbage dump.

The woman peered at the map, shook her head and looked up at Ellen. "You don't want to go there. Not safe there."

Ellen remembered enough of the language to understand the woman. "Yes, yes, I do. Will the bus go there?"

The woman put her pudgy brown finger on the map a few blocks from the spot Ellen pointed out. "The bus will go this far. No more. Walk from there. Be careful."

Ellen nodded. "I will. Thank you."

The little boy started to fuss, and the woman jiggled her

body to bounce him up and down. Ellen smiled and made an airplane motion with her hand. The child stopped crying and followed her hand with his large dark eyes. Ellen "landed" her plane on the mother's shoulder, then reached up suddenly and tickled his chin. He giggled. She tapped his soft nose, and he giggled again. She started the "plane" motion once more.

As she played her game with the child, more of the language came back to her. "How many children do you have?"

"Five. The others are in school."

"It must be hard to pay for school for so many."

"Yes. My husband works for the government, but I work, too. I clean that building." The woman nodded toward the office building across the street. "To pay for uniforms and books. The children must finish school to get good jobs like my husband's."

Ellen guessed the child to be about three. "You take him to work with you?"

"Of course. He mostly sleeps while I work."

Ellen imagined the bending and stooping required to clean offices and restrooms. It would be a physical job under any circumstances, but the added weight of a child on her back must make it grueling. Yet this mother seemed to accept it as normal. A bright blue bus with a broad orange stripe across its side appeared down the street. Voices of people around them rose above the honking of traffic and cut off all chance of asking any more questions.

The waiting group pushed closer to the curb, and the bus screeched to a stop at the corner. Ellen peered at the pile of luggage and crates on top, wondering if they would tumble off. She remembered that the "chicken buses" took their nickname from the practice of carrying cages of chickens and small animals inside the bus and on top, along with other baggage.

A small man hopped out the back door and scrambled up the ladder on the back of the bus. He reached down to grab the parcels that people were holding up. As those with no luggage lined up at the front door of the bus, Ellen maneuvered behind the woman she'd been talking to. Furtively, she took two paper bills out of her cloth bag. Making a quick calculation, she estimated their worth at about fifty U.S. dollars—more than a month's earnings for the woman's family, she guessed. After folding it several times, she palmed it and reached up to pat the baby's back.

"Good boy." She slipped the folded money underneath the cloth that held him in place. "You'll make your *mamá* proud, yes?"

Chapter Twenty-Six

As soon as the last passenger climbed onto the recycled school bus, the driver stepped on the accelerator. Ellen grabbed onto the back of a nearby seat but couldn't help being jolted into a man standing next to her. "Excuse me."

The man ignored her. More people found seats, and the little man who had collected the luggage swung from the top of the bus through the back window.

She felt a tug on her arm. "Sit here." The woman she had been talking with patted a tiny patch of bench seat. She held her son on her lap, and another woman and two children squeezed in the space next to the window. Five or six people to a seat seemed the rule, not the exception. She didn't want to offend the woman, so she smiled and perched on the corner offered to her.

"Why do you want to go to the garbage dump?" the woman asked.

"I used to live there." Ellen grasped the back of the seat in front of her to keep from falling to the floor as the bus took a corner. "I—I have to see it again."

They rode without speaking for a few minutes while passengers chattered and children cried. Black soot from vehicles drifted in the open windows and swirled around them. A man in the seat in front of them puffed on a cigar, and the smoke floated back to where they sat, stinging Ellen's lungs.

"You come home with me. My brother is there. He will take you, keep you safe."

Ellen did not hesitate. "Thank you. That is very generous." When she breathed a sigh of relief, she realized how much anxiety had built inside her. "I don't even know your name. Mine is, um, Elena."

"My name is Dolores." The woman patted her son's head. "This is Salvador. He is named for his uncle—my brother I just mentioned. Our parents named my brother after the artist, Salvador Posadas. They were fond of his work."

"I am interested in art myself. Is that a Guatemalan artist?"

Dolores's eyes gleamed. "I thought you must be a visitor. From the United States?"

Ellen nodded. "I was born here. After my mother died, I went to live with my American father. He was an engineer, working on a project here when … when he met my mother." Her face warmed.

Dolores reached a hand up and touched her shoulder. "A common story. It was difficult as a child, no?"

"Yes. Not Guatemalan, but not American either. Other children made fun of me. When I left, I resolved never to return."

The bus stopped. Several passengers got off and others crowded on. Dolores eyed her. "Yet here you are. And you want to go back to the shanties. What changed your mind?"

Ellen adjusted her position, trying to get comfortable on the sliver of seat. "Recently I decided I needed to come back. To see the only home I knew before going to the States."

"It will be different." Dolores tipped her head toward the window. "Perhaps better, perhaps worse than you remember. But it will not be the same."

"Yes, of course. But I must see for myself. I don't feel that I ever said good-bye to *Mamá*. This is my way of doing so."

Dolores nodded. "Perhaps it will help. My brother will go with you."

They rode in silence amid the chattering of the other

riders. After a half-hour, Dolores called out to get the bus driver's attention. "Here. Stop, please." The vehicle swerved to the curb and lurched to a stop.

Ellen stood up, crowding into the narrow aisle. She maneuvered her way through the standing passengers and stepped onto the sidewalk. She stretched her cramped legs and turned to take little Salvador.

"Thank you. We have a little walk. Put him on my back," Dolores said. Ellen followed her instructions and fit the child into the cloth harness again. Obviously used to the routine, the boy cooed and giggled as Ellen held him high and worked first one leg then the other into position. When she settled him in place, he snuggled his head against the back of his mother's neck.

Dolores turned to walk uphill. "This way. It is just fourteen blocks."

Ellen remembered her childhood days of walking and running around town. She could still manage the distance, thanks to her running routine. This area looked more like the city she remembered. Single-story adobe houses crowded up to the uneven sidewalk. Wooden shutters, not glass, covered most window openings. As they passed a house with open shutters, she heard animated voices inside.

In the next block, three women sat on straw mats under the covered entry area of a house. They chattered happily as they sewed beads and colorful yarns onto garments, but their conversation stopped when Ellen and Dolores drew near. The two had to step into the street to go around the little group.

"*Hola, Benita. ¿Cómo están, Selena, Lupe?*" Dolores greeted them. The women smiled and seemed to relax, calling out questions to her. Dolores nodded but kept on walking. A few minutes later, she stopped in front of a bright orange building. "Here it is. My home is your home."

Unlike most of the neighborhood houses, the exterior appeared to have been painted recently. A wide white border highlighted the arched entrance. As soon as they entered, Dolores called out, "Salvador, cover your paints and come meet our new friend from the United States."

Chapter Twenty-Seven

Surrounded by banana trees in every direction, the plantation's main office hunkered under the late morning sun as if it wanted to burrow into the earth. The low concrete-block building had a clay tile roof and a large window opening on each side of the front door.

Manuel stepped out of the SUV and stretched. Slow vehicles and road construction had caused the drive east to take an extra hour, and his legs were stiff. He wished he could run about five miles to get the kinks out. The others joined him beside the vehicle.

A man with sandy-colored hair and bronzed skin, looking like a bored lifeguard, emerged from the building's doorway. He buttoned up his white linen jacket that appeared to have been pulled from the bottom of a laundry basket. "Reckon you're the new owners."

Erik stretched out his right hand and stepped toward the man.

"I'm Erik Neilson, president of Neilson Enterprises. You must be the manager, Mr.—"

"They call me Tex." He reached out and shook Erik's hand then wiped his hand on his pants.

"Nice to meet you, Tex. I believe you've met Alan and Manuel. And this is Warren." Erik paused as each man stepped forward to greet Tex. After each handshake, Tex repeated the ritual of wiping off his hand.

"Guess you're here to find out our dirty little secrets. Whatcha wanna see?" He grinned and spit on the ground.

Warren bounced on the balls of his feet. "It's been a long

drive from the city. Would you happen to have something for a parched throat before we begin the, uh, tour?"

Tex looked Warren up and down. "Might could find some beers inside." He turned abruptly and disappeared into the building.

Erik motioned the others to follow Tex. Warren led the way. Erik whispered to Alan, "I thought they were expecting us. Isn't Morales meeting us here?"

"Maybe he forgot to tell Tex."

Manuel stopped in the doorway. The north-facing openings didn't allow sunrays to pierce directly into the room. As his eyes adjusted to the semi-dark interior, he saw the owner, Ricardo Morales, sitting behind a desk that dwarfed him.

The wooden swivel chair squealed as the man rotated it and tilted the seat. Placing a hand on each arm of the chair, he pushed himself forward until his feet touched the floor and he rose to a standing position. He spread his arms wide. "Welcome to Indiana Plantation. I've been expecting you." He stayed in front of the chair, which sat on a raised wooden platform.

Erik stepped forward to shake his hand across the desk. "*Señor* Morales, I am pleased to meet you at last. I am Erik Neilson. These are my colleagues. Warren Stubbs, senior vice president."

Warren had positioned himself with his back to the wall by the door. Now he shook his whole body as if to wake up. He extended his hand stiffly to Morales. "Happy to meet you, Mr. Morales." He bellowed the words as he might to a deaf man.

Since Manuel and Alan had met Morales on previous trips, they shook hands without needing an introduction.

Tex entered from a back room carrying a tray with six opened bottles of local beer. He set the tray on the desk, swooshed his arm in invitation, and picked up one of the bottles. He grabbed the back of a wooden chair next to the desk, twirled it around, and straddled it facing the back. He gulped some beer, wiped his mouth with the back of his hand, and draped his arms over the top rung of the chair, one hand holding the beer bottle loosely. Everyone else remained standing.

Morales planted himself back in the swivel chair. He put his elbows on the desk and tented his fingers. "Gentlemen, as you know, I am in a financial predicament. My family has owned these plantations for three generations. They have been extremely productive, extremely lucrative."

The chair whined as he rotated it back and forth. "Unfortunately, I made some unwise—shall we say— investments in other areas, and I find myself in the position of owing far more money than I am able to repay. If I do not sell the plantations, the loans will be called and I lose everything. I intend to sell all three plantations—Indiana, Florida, and Missouri—as one unit."

He tilted his head in Tex's direction. "I believe you will find Tex to be a most productive manager, so perhaps you will consider keeping him on despite his, um, less-than-warm personality."

"*Señor* Morales, we may be interested in helping you out of your predicament." Erik set his bottle on the desk. "We already own banana plantations in Honduras and Costa Rica, and we believe Guatemala offers similar opportunities. However ..." He turned to look out the window and stood with his back to the room, hands clasped behind him. When the pause became awkward, he swiveled, stepped up to the desk, placed both hands on its edge, and leaned forward to look Morales in the eyes. "We are not ready to make an offer until we thoroughly examine your operations. We will not be rushed into making a bad decision."

Morales held Erik's gaze for a long minute. "Of course, *señor*. I would expect nothing else from a man with your experience." He spread his arms to include the entire room. "Shall we begin our tour? Tex, bring the car around."

Tex drained his beer and banged the bottle down on the tray. With a grunt, he pushed on the back of the chair to lift himself up. He grabbed a set of keys from a pegboard and headed into the back room.

Chapter Twenty-Eight

Ellen settled onto a floor cushion in Dolores's living room in Guatemala City. She bounced little Sal on her knees and tried not to listen to the low voices in the other room.

Soon, a short man, younger and thinner than Dolores, but with the same round face and expressive eyes, emerged. He spoke in Spanish. "*Hola.* You are the American visitor my sister brought home. I am her brother Salvador. I see my nephew likes you." He grinned.

The boy immediately lost interest in Ellen's game and stretched his arms up. His uncle lifted him and tossed him in the air. The boy's giggles made Ellen laugh. He squealed as Salvador tossed him and caught him again and again.

Dolores entered with a tray of glasses. "Salvador, that's enough. You spoil him."

Salvador caught the child and held him in one arm. "He is already spoiled. But it is good for him." He looked at Ellen. "How do you know my sister?"

"Salvador gets right to the point," Dolores said. "We met at the bus stop this morning. I told her you would take her to visit the shanties at the garbage dump."

"Why would a lady like you want to visit there?" He jostled Sal to quiet him and then put him down on the floor.

Dolores handed Ellen a glass of lukewarm lemonade and gave one to her brother. "She lived there when she was little, and she wants to go back. It was the only home she knew before she moved to America."

Ellen sipped the tart drink and watched the pair.

Salvador eyed her with a curious expression tinged with

humor. "Does she talk?"

She laughed. "Yes, I speak. My Spanish is not as good as it once was, but so far it has served me."

Salvador nodded. He switched to heavily accented English. "Would you prefer we speak English?"

"No, no." She continued in Spanish, "I want to practice."

He settled onto a cushion near little Sal. "Very well. You want to go to the garbage dump. How long since you lived there?"

"About twenty years."

"It is not a safe place."

"It wasn't then either." She brushed aside the memories. "I must see it again."

"In twenty years, the dump has grown and changed. After the big fire a few years ago, they fenced it off. Everyone living there had to move."

At this, she stiffened. "Where did they go?"

"Mostly just outside the fence. Closer together. The whole zone is more crowded than before. More disheartening."

"I don't care. I want to see it." She set her glass down, rose to her knees, and stood. "Thank you for your hospitality, Dolores, but if I'm going to visit the dump, I must be going." She looked at Salvador. "By myself if you won't go with me." She bent to kiss little Sal on top of his head and moved toward the door.

"Why do you think I won't go?" Salvador rose to his feet. "I would not let a friend of my sister's go there alone even if you did just meet. Please wait while I put on shoes."

Minutes later she matched strides with him as they headed up the hill. He walked fast for a man whose legs were shorter than hers.

"How far is it?"

"Fifteen minutes, maybe twenty." He looked at her. "Am I

going too fast for you?"

"No, I'm fine. I'm used to running several times a week."

As they walked, the houses became smaller and more rundown. Soon the sidewalks disappeared, and they walked in the middle of the cobblestone street. After a few more blocks, the stones gave way to rutted dirt. In the alleys, faded laundry dried on clotheslines stretched next to the buildings. An occasional breeze sent wisps of acrid smoke their way.

Salvador broke the silence. "You are American."

"I'm only half-American. My mother was half-Mayan, as I told Dolores—"

"No, you have grown to be American. Headstrong. Independent. Foolish."

She had never thought of herself as any of those things. "I'm really not. At least, not usually. It's just that I am determined to see my childhood home. It has been so long since my mother died and I left. I need to know if conditions were as bad as I remember."

Salvador looked at her sideways. "It's probably worse. Children get used to the poverty, the garbage, and the smells. We're the ones who have difficulty with it, because we know there is something better."

"I knew there was something better." She spat the words. "When my cousin and I begged near the hotels, we saw tourists wearing fancy clothing, driving good cars. Even as young as I was, I wanted that. I understood that if I had money, I would never be unhappy again."

Why was she telling him all this? She had known him less than an hour.

He let her statement hang in mid-air. He lifted his nose into the breeze. "We're almost there."

The sour odor of rotting food reached her nose. She swallowed hard and determined not to gag.

They stopped at the top of a hill where they could look down on the garbage-filled valley. Ellen felt as though she were standing on a derelict beach, staring at an endless ocean of rotting garbage. Vultures circled overhead, competing with men and women for tidbits of food scraps and animal carcasses amid the mountains of rubbish.

A convoy of trucks pulled through a barbed-wire fence, and men and women swarmed around the trucks like rats. She remembered the routine. Everyone knew which trucks came from restaurants and were more likely to contain food scraps. The people scratched out a meager subsistence by going through the garbage looking for usable goods they could sell or exchange for food. As the trucks pulled in, each person fought to place a flat palm on the side of a truck to mark his or her scavenging spot among the waves of refuse as the truck pulled away.

She had rarely gone near the trucks. Even grown men who got careless could get run over by a truck and killed. Instead, the children scavenged among other piles looking for items that could be used in their houses or recycled for a little money. She tried to hide her best finds in a bag before the bigger children could take them away from her. When one discovered valuable material, like aluminum or glass, all the children scurried to the spot to hunt for more. That's when they pushed her away. "Go away, *yanqui*," they yelled at her. "This is for Guatemalans, not for mongrels."

But now, no children were in sight. She looked at Salvador. "We children used to search through the trash, too. Why are there none here?"

He shook his head. "Since they fenced it, the government will not allow children inside."

"Who watches them, then?"

"Most wander the streets looking for work or begging."

She remembered how she and Manuel had done just that after her *mamá* died.

"Sometimes, older children look after their younger siblings. A few go to school when their parents can pay. Some women have started to make and sell jewelry instead of scrambling for garbage so that they can keep their children with them."

He pointed down the other side of the hill, where makeshift houses clutched the steep incline at the margins of the dump. "Do you want to see where they live?"

She nodded and followed him downhill to the haphazard collection of shanties. Remnants of corrugated tin, scraps of wood, and other recycled items formed sheds and lean-tos that clung together as if searching for any trace of protection from the world.

The nearest one had no door, and mattresses were piled on the floor in the dark interior. A few yards away, five children stopped their game of tag to stare at Ellen and Salvador. A lanky boy broke away and ran toward them. He straightened his back to appear taller. "Luis Fernando Barrios," he said in Spanish. "If you need to find someone, I can help you. I'm the fastest." He wore a faded green shirt, tail out, covering worn dungarees. The pants legs were rolled up but still drooped over dirty gray, once white, running shoes. His uncombed, longish black hair stuck out in places, but his dark eyes sparkled in his brown face.

Salvador fished a coin out of his pocket. He extended a hand with the coin lying in the palm. "All right, Luis Fernando Barrios. Show us around, please."

Luis reached out and picked up the coin with two fingers. He quickly slipped it into a pocket in his pants. "Missionary?" He tilted his head at Ellen.

"No. Just looking." Salvador hesitated. "The lady is from

America and wants to see what it is like here."

Ellen smiled. To show the boy that she understood, she also spoke in Spanish. "That's right, Luis. Will you show me where you live?"

Luis looked at Salvador and then at her. Suspicion crept into his eyes, but after a moment, he shrugged his shoulders. "If you wish, I will take you there."

He turned and made his way past the other children who had gathered in a semicircle around them. Ellen and Salvador followed, watching their steps as they made their way across the uneven stones that passed for a street.

After a few minutes, Luis stopped at a cardboard refrigerator-sized box turned on its side and surrounded by large bags that appeared to hold recyclable aluminum cans. He lifted a flap on the end of the box and pointed to a pile of blankets inside. "That is where I sleep. During the day, I live— everywhere." He spread his arms wide, grinning.

Ellen shook her head. "You have no family?"

"No." Luis tipped his head to one side. "Not since I was ten. My papa was run over by a truck—in there." He gestured toward the garbage pit. "*Mamá* died a few months later. Broken heart, everyone said." He placed a hand over his chest.

Ellen blinked back the tears forming at the corners of her eyes. "How old are you now?"

"Fifteen."

Luis reminded her of Manuel. When she left Guatemala, he had been fourteen and sleeping wherever he could. Would someone help this boy the same way her cousin had been helped?

Salvador spoke softly in English. "Be careful, *señora*. The needs are greater than you can imagine, but not all are as they seem."

Wondering if he could read her thoughts, Ellen raised her

eyebrows and looked at him.

"Make no promises, give no gifts," he said, "until you know who is the receiver."

"But you gave him money," she whispered.

"I paid him. He will earn what I paid, and when we leave, I will pay him a little more. He knows this. But you are American. He may take advantage of your soft heart."

Luis stood by the cardboard box, looking from one to the other, waiting for them to finish their English conversation. His face showed no signs of understanding, only open friendliness. Ellen did not think there could be any guile in him. But she chose to listen to Salvador's advice.

Salvador spoke again in his native language. "Luis, the lady would like to see the inside of a shanty. Do you know a family who would show us their home?"

Luis widened his eyes and nodded. "Yes, I have a friend who lives with his mother. Just the two of them. They have a grand home. It is not far." He took off with long strides between the rows of shacks overflowing with bags of scrap metal.

Ellen had to cover her nose and mouth with her hand as they passed two of the sturdiest looking structures. Built out of packing crate boards with no roof, the swollen plywood doors that hung from ropes had crude drawings of stick figures—a man on one and a woman on the other. She held her breath until the desire to throw up passed. She did not remember that sensation from her childhood days.

Luis ran ahead of them to a shanty made of metal and scrap wood. Indeed, a side expansion made it wider than the other huts by half. He knocked on the door, which actually had rusty hinges holding it in place.

A woman cracked the door open and peeked out. Her weather-worn face made her look sixtyish, but Ellen guessed she was much younger. Her hair, which was still dark, parted in the middle and pulled back, was fastened neatly at the back of her neck.

"Luis, Gustav is not home. I am surprised he is not with you."

"Mrs. Vasquez, I want to talk to you, not Gustav. These are friends," he gestured to Ellen and Salvador. "I told them how nice your house is, and they want to see inside."

"Is this a tour?" She sounded suspicious, as though gawkers were common.

Ellen spoke up. "No, Mrs. Vasquez. I am visiting from America, but I lived around here when I was small. It's been a long time, and I don't remember much. I hope you don't mind."

The woman nodded and stepped aside. Ellen ducked her head to step into the dark interior. Surprisingly, the room held two wooden chairs and colorful, though faded, embroidered panels on two walls. Beads and a half-finished necklace lay on one chair. On the floor, a basket made of rough wooden slats of different lengths, brimmed with more beaded items. A small braided rug, frayed at the edges, had been placed carefully between the two chairs.

On the left side of the tiny room, a curtain of various fabrics patchworked together hung by small nails at each corner. Mrs. Vasquez pulled the curtain back to reveal a crude opening into a second room. She gestured for Ellen to go through.

On the floor at each side of the opening lay a pallet neatly made of tattered wool blankets, with a small walkway between. The room looked much as she remembered the tiny room she had shared with her mother. She felt a chill in her spine and backed through the doorway into the first room.

Chapter Twenty-Nine

As Tex drove the battered ten-year-old Jeep, Morales identified the buildings of Indiana Plantation. Manuel hung onto a rumble seat facing backward while Erik, Warren, and Alan were squeezed together in the middle seat of the open vehicle.

Morales pointed to a compound of one-story concrete block buildings. "Housing for the workers there. We added four buildings about three years ago, making two hundred forty total units."

Sets of four buildings, each about a hundred feet long, surrounded large courtyards. "Each family has their own compartment." Morales huffed. "It is wrong they do not show more gratitude."

Manuel's stomach clenched. Open doorways and single window openings repeated every few feet—long, short, long, short, long, short—dark lines one after the other in rhythm. Colorful cloth covered some doors and windows, providing bright contrast to the dull gray cinder blocks. Between the buildings, children played in the dirt.

Manuel turned toward the front. He yelled so he would be heard over the vehicle's motor. "How many people live on this plantation, *Señor* Morales?"

Morales had focused on the other side of the road. Now he looked at Manuel and frowned. "How should I know? We have four hundred workers. Who knows how many *niños* not big enough to work?"

He called Erik's attention to the processing facility as they passed it. "During harvest, the plant operates sixteen hours a day, seven days a week. We ship the bananas out within twenty-four hours after they are picked. That gets them to the consumer with plenty of time before they spoil. We will go through the processing plant when we come back from the fields."

"You run two shifts at the plant?" Erik asked.

"No. We could do that if we had enough workers. But the processing is done mostly by women, and we can't find enough of them that want to work at night. They worry about their children." Morales sneered the last word.

Manuel had visited the plantations Neilson Enterprises owned in Honduras. The company ran two ten-hour shifts during harvest, rather than the single twelve-hour days some plantations required. Apparently Morales expected even more of his employees.

After a few minutes, the last of the buildings gave way to fields on both sides of the road—row after row of banana trees laden with green fruit.

"Let's show them the fruit up close, Tex," Morales said.

Tex rolled the vehicle to a stop in the middle of the dirt road, strolled around to open the door for Morales, and helped him out of the car. He showed no concern for the visitors, so Alan found the handle and pushed open the door.

"You know bananas, do you not?" Morales asked. "You see that these are at just the right stage for picking. Here, down this row, they are harvesting." He trotted toward a cluster of Indian men. Because of Morales's short legs, Manuel and the others had to move as slow as tortoises to keep from going ahead of him.

The workers wore colored handkerchiefs over their faces, making them look like bandits. A short, muscular man perched on a ladder used a long-handled machete to chop through the stem of a banana bunch. He shifted the heavy bananas onto a long pole, and two men below him hefted the pole to their shoulders. Balancing the large bunch between them, they ran soundlessly toward a wagon at the end of the row.

The thick, sweet scent from the fruit took Manuel back to the season when he worked in another company's processing plant. He tasted again the brutality of the supervisors, felt the bone-deep fatigue brought on by twelve-hour workdays.

While the others talked with Morales, he slipped between the plants to the next row being harvested. Two men returning from the wagon came toward him. When he greeted them in their native language, they stopped. They looked over their shoulders before the taller one answered. "You speak our language. Are you Mayan?"

"My grandmother was Mayan, and I have many friends who are also." Above their bandana masks, the men's eyes reminded him of dogs that had been beaten by their owners. "It is warm today. Why do you cover your faces?"

The two men glanced at each other. The silent one shrugged. The other man answered again. "The chemicals. They make us sick."

"Do you not have protective equipment?"

"It is too hot to wear."

The other man tugged at his friend's shirt and pointed. Manuel turned and saw two men starting toward the wagon with a load of bananas. The men he had been talking to ran together in that direction. They passed the men carrying the fruit and headed toward a cutter moving his ladder. Given how fast the men moved, he guessed that dawdling brought severe penalties.

Guatemalan banana plantations had quit using the most toxic chemicals a decade ago. Newer pesticides and fungicides were less effective but safer for the workers. What chemicals was Morales using that would make his employees sick?

For Such a Moment

Chapter Thirty

The small bedroom of *Señora* Vasquez's shanty brought back the memory that invaded Ellen's nightmares. One she wanted to bury.

A man had come home with her *mamá* a few days before Christmas. Not unusual in the years before her *mamá* found Jesus. But this man stayed the night. The next morning, her *mamá* took the money he paid her and went to buy food. Elena's stomach had growled. It had been two days since she had eaten anything more than moldy scraps.

The man smirked at her from where he lay on the lumpy mattress. "Come here, little girl. I'll take away your hunger."

Maybe he had something for her to eat. She'd risen from her pallet and moved toward him. One step, another. He motioned to her. "You're not afraid to be alone with me, are you? Your *mamá* asked me to be nice to you."

Elena wondered why he said "nice" that way. He must have a special treat. She moved closer. He reached out and picked her up, pulling her onto the mattress with him. She struggled a little, but he stroked her hair and her back until she relaxed. He smelled of sweat and soot, and she imagined he was her *papa.* She rested her head on his chest.

Before she knew what had happened, he had removed her thin garment. She tensed, not understanding. He forced himself on top of her, and she began to cry.

When her *mamá* returned, she yelled at him. She grabbed the broken broom and hit the man over and over while he yanked his clothes on and laughed at her. When he had left, *Mamá* took Elena in her lap and hugged her. "I should not have left you with him, little one. I am so sorry. So sorry." *Mamá* cried as much as Elena. They sat like that all morning, *Mamá* saying, "I'm so sorry. It's all my fault."

But Elena knew the truth. She had done something very, very wrong.

Ellen realized that *Señora* Vasquez was watching her with a puzzled expression. "You have made a good home for your son."

The woman folded her arms. "I try. Not easy without a husband."

Ellen touched her chest. "My mother also—" Her throat clenched, and she couldn't finish.

Salvador rescued her. "We must be going, Mrs. Vasquez. Thank you for showing us your home." He opened the makeshift door and waited for Ellen to leave. Her eyes watered when she stepped back into the bright sunlight.

"Are you all right? You seemed alarmed."

"Yes. Yes, I'm fine. It's just … I felt like a time traveler, like I was back in the shack we lived in when I was little. Things I had forgotten. Or tried to."

Salvador's eyes consoled her. "Do you want to see more?"

She rubbed the moisture from her eyes. "Show me."

Luis waited for them. "Come. We go. I will take you to the clubhouse."

They followed him, and after a few moments, Salvador took her hand to lead her across some metal that blocked their way. "Is this not what you wanted? To visit your old home?"

"Yes. But I was not expecting—I don't know what I expected."

As they walked, boys and girls all younger than Luis, began to follow them. She felt like the Pied Piper, and she realized the children knew Salvador. By the time Luis stopped, a dozen children chattered and skipped around them, along with two scrawny dogs.

The "clubhouse" reminded her of tree houses in her Minneapolis neighborhood, except without a tree. Salvador stood at the door of the rickety structure. "Children, we are not painting today, but we are going to show my new friend what you've been working on."

Startled, she jerked her face toward him. He knew these children, and they knew him. Had he been teaching them to paint? "You did not tell me ..."

He grinned at her but spoke again to the boys and girls. "This is Mrs. Neilson. She is visiting from the United States, and she enjoys art. As you go in, pick out your best painting, and wait by your station. She will come around to visit with each one of you."

He stepped aside and the children ran eagerly into the room. She followed them in, surprised to see daylight filling the space. The walls on two sides stopped short of the corrugated metal roof. At the edge of the roof, a second short "wall" hung down about a foot, providing a barrier from wind and rain without cutting off the daylight.

She looked around the room. Each child stood by a square wooden crate that came to about Ellen's knees. They held their paintings, and their voices echoed through the small space.

"See mine?"

"Here!"

"Look at this."

The crates had been turned sideways to create tables. Every crate contained odd pieces of boards and cardboard, a few jars of tempera or watercolor paints, and brushes. At the first one, she stooped to look closer. Three brushes, the cheap kind sold in discount stores in the U.S., stood in an old tin can. The frayed bristles felt stiff, but they were clean. She shook a yellow tempera jar with paint caked on the outside. Nearly empty.

She squatted to eye level with the boy who stood beside the crate.

Dressed in a faded t-shirt and short black pants, he looked no older than five. His bangs had been cut unevenly and hung over his eyes. On the right side, a clump of hair stuck out at an odd angle. He held a two foot piece of chipboard close to his chest and stared at the dirt floor. The lack of expression on his face made her heart lurch. "*Hola. ¿Cómo te llamas?*"

"This is Donato," Salvador answered for him. "He doesn't speak, but he understands what you say."

"I see. I am glad to meet you, Donato," she said in Spanish. "Will you show me your painting?"

Slowly, with his eyes still focused on his feet, he turned the board so she could see the imaginative scene of mountains and birds. The largest and highest bird had a figure on its back that looked like a boy.

"Is this you, Donato?"

A barely perceptible nod.

"Would you like to fly over the mountains?"

He jerked his head up and looked at her with brown kewpie-doll eyes. He jerked his chin up and down, twice, and resumed studying his bare brown feet.

She swallowed hard. "Someday you will. I'm sure of it. It's a beautiful picture." Her arms ached to wrap around him and hold him tight. But she stood and merely patted the top of his head. She would ask Salvador later why the boy had built such a shell around himself.

She moved on to a little girl at the next crate. By the time she spoke with each child and inspected the paintings, Salvador urged her to hurry. "You have a long way back to your hotel before dark."

"Thank you, children." They had waited patiently by their tables as she made the rounds. What could she say that would make a difference for them? "I can tell you have all worked very hard on your pictures. Keep painting. Someday you may be great artists."

The girls giggled, and the boys smiled—except Donato. With the same serious look on his face, he looked up at her. His eyes met hers for an instant. She saw a flicker there. Something that looked like determination.

Salvador clapped his hands. "Would you like to sing our song for *Señora* Neilson before she leaves?"

The children shouted, and Salvador held up his hand. He made a cross in the air with his hand as he counted to four. On the next beat, their voices rang out in English, "Jesus loves me, this I know …"

Ellen couldn't tear her gaze from Donato. He kept his head down and didn't open his mouth.

As the children drew out the last phrase, "The Bi-ble tells me sooooo …" Ellen applauded, holding her tears out of sight.

Chapter Thirty-One

Manuel and the rest of the Neilson group headed for the nearby village, Río Limpio. Maybe they would be able to unwind before joining Morales for dinner.

As they crossed a wooden plank bridge with no railings, Manuel looked out the window at the river. The water rushing over the rocks looked like vegetable soup, murky brown with bits of vegetation and unidentifiable matter collecting against an outcropping of the bank. On both sides of the river, banana trees spread for miles in every direction.

"Great possibilities, don't you think, Erik?" Warren's excitement spilled out. "If Morales's other two plantations are just as promising, we'll be showing a profit in six months. I'm sure of it."

In the back seat next to Warren, Erik didn't answer.

Warren took out his iPad and began making notes as he talked. "The first thing we'll do is bring in more workers. We'll find single men. Each family can take in another man, and that way we won't be adding any more kids. More workers, lower wages, and we'll increase production—"

"Warren," Erik said.

Manuel understood Erik's soft tone of voice demanded attention, and apparently so did Warren.

"I appreciate your enthusiasm," Erik continued. "Now I want to hear from the others. Alan?"

Alan seemed to be concentrating on avoiding potholes in the road. Finally he coughed. "Warren is right. We can improve the profits if we lower wages and hire more workers. We'll need to plant more trees, but all the plantations have enough acreage to double or triple the cultivated area. Morales has some large gambling debts, so he's desperate. I think it's a win, Erik."

"Um-hmm." Erik turned his head. "Manuel, is it unanimous?"

Manuel rotated in the front passenger's seat so he could meet Erik's eyes. "I do agree that we can make Morales's plantations profitable. However ..."

"That sounds like a 'Yes, but' to me. Go ahead. What's the 'but'?"

"I think it may take longer than six months. And I'm not sure crowding more workers into that housing and paying lower wages is the best method. Before we make major changes, we should study the operation, learn where the weaknesses are and what the strengths are."

"That sounds like business school logic, Manuel."

Did Erik mean that as a challenge or an encouragement? Manuel met his intense gaze and held it.

"Is there something else?"

Warren shifted in his seat. "Really, Erik. Manuel doesn't know the company yet. He doesn't understand how we—"

"You had your say, Warren. I want to hear what Manuel thinks—*all* of it."

Manuel tried to ignore Warren's glare. "Did you notice the men were all wearing bandanas over their faces?"

Erik nodded.

"I think Morales may be using hazardous chemicals. By harvest there should be no residues with today's pesticides, yet the harvesters were concerned."

"Hazardous chemicals? Nonsense," Warren interrupted. "Morales took us out there, and we had no problems. Besides, the workers—"

"Warren. Let him finish." Erik hardened his voice and kept his eyes on Manuel. "You think we may have some cleanup to do?"

"That depends on what he's using. As you know, some pesticides are only dangerous at the time of application. But if there are residues in the soil or water, we could inherit some liability. But we can find out by testing."

Erik closed his eyes and leaned back again. "Okay. We have more homework to do."

Chapter Thirty-Two

As the threesome hiked away from the shanties, Luis walked backward to face Ellen. He asked questions about America, her family, when she would be back. His curiosity reminded her of a much younger child. He asked a new question before she had finished answering the previous one, and she laughed.

Finally Salvador stopped him.

"Enough, Luis. Our visitor is not an encyclopedia. It is time for you to go now." He handed the youth several coins. "This completes our bargain."

Luis took the money and tucked it in a pocket, bowed low, and skipped off down the hill, reminding her again of Manuel when they were children. He disappeared behind a row of shanties. "Tell me about Donato."

"Ah, Donato. He is a mystery. No one knows where he came from. He showed up one day at the dump entrance and began helping. When the women came out at the end of the day, he carried things for them and never put out a hand to ask for anything in return."

Ellen remained silent as she matched Salvador's strides. They reached the top of the hill before he spoke again. "After a few days, an old woman called *Tante* Maria noticed that he slept in a different place each night. She told him she needed someone to help her all the time and asked him to move in with her. She looks after him and treats him like a grandson."

"Does he talk to her?"

"No. As far as I know, he has not spoken a word to anyone." He laughed. "It works just fine for *Tante* Maria. She can't hear a thing, so the silence doesn't bother her."

"And there are no clues ... nothing to tell what happened to his family?"

He looked back the way they had come as if longing to find the answer. "He had nothing but the clothes he wore. We don't even know his name. He was wearing an old American football jersey with the name 'Donato' on the back. So that's what we call him. Do you not remember how things are here?"

She could still see Donato's sad, brown eyes. Did his parents abandon him, or had he witnessed something horrible that happened to them? Whatever the case, it seemed to have stolen his will to speak. She wanted to help all these children but especially Donato. "I remember. But seeing it all again—I realize that in my mind, I had changed things."

The buildings improved as they got farther from the dump. They passed a school where children played with a soccer ball in the yard. "I'm glad you are teaching the children to paint. They can learn to put color in their lives no matter where they live. And it is a wonderful way for them to express their feelings. I teach art to inner-city children in Minneapolis, and I see them come alive when they realize they can enjoy drawing and painting."

"Yes! I try to give them something they can carry in here ..." He pointed to his head then to his heart. "And here, all their lives. Some people say I am wasting my time. That what they really need is food, clothing, real homes. And they are right. These children, their families, do need those things. But I can give only a little food to last a few days. I can provide clothes for only a handful. They need more. They need love. And this I can give them. They need beauty. That I can show them, and I can teach them how to find it for themselves, how to create it."

He pulled off his hat and wiped sweat from his forehead.

"Forgive me, *señora*. I am passionate about these children, and I get excited."

"I can tell how much you care. I never thought of it quite that way before." They reached the street where he lived and turned onto it. "I want to help. I want to buy supplies for your art school—real canvases, new paints and brushes." She hadn't imagined she would ever say this. "I'll be your patron of the arts."

"You are an answer to prayer, *señora*."

She turned to him. "How do you mean?"

"I have been discouraged. It is difficult to find even used paints, old brushes. I had tired of the struggle. I asked God to give me a sign if He wanted me to continue. And here you are." He stopped and hugged her like a brother might.

She wrinkled her brow. "So you believe in God? You believe that song you taught the children—*Jesus Loves Me*?"

"With all my heart and soul. It is Jesus' love that I give the children. Do you know the song?"

"Yes, I know the song. My *mamá* taught it to me, after she … changed. But I am not sure I want to believe in a God who allows so many bad things to happen. These people, the children, living as they do. As I once did. I can't be your answer to prayer."

Erik felt like he had fallen into Wonderland when they arrived at Morales's home that evening.

Morales had built his whole world to fit his small size, a deception apparently designed to make him feel normal. He played a cordial dinner host, if somewhat strange. The dining table sat some six inches lower than normal, and the chairs were shortened to match. Erik and the others had to bend their legs at an odd angle to keep from hitting their knees on the bottom of the table.

Only Morales had a normal size chair, which allowed him to sit taller than his guests. The rest of the furniture, like the china cabinet, had either been specially made smaller than normal size or had the legs cut off. Expensive paintings hung at eye level for their host. A low ceiling kept the room in proportion.

Morales's wife served a traditional Mayan turkey soup, followed by *chiles rellenos*, chile peppers stuffed with rice, meat, and vegetables. The concentrated aromas of pepper tickled Erik's nose, and the spices prickled his tongue.

After Morales's wife poured coffee and disappeared into the kitchen, their host placed his palms on the table and leaned back in his chair. "Well, *señores*." He mixed Spanish words with his accented English. "The plantation is good, no? Can we reach agreement?"

Warren answered at once. "Indeed, it is. I am sure we can agree to terms—"

Erik shot a warning look at Warren. "We will see. After we visit your two other locations tomorrow. The deal is for all three as a package, correct?"

"*Sí, sí*. But you understand I know of more buyers who may be interested. I do not wish to delay the sale for much time."

Erik dropped his napkin on the table and rose from his chair. "Very well, then. Contact your other buyers. We will return to Guatemala City in the morning."

Warren shifted, looking from Erik to Morales. "No, no, *señor*." Morales held up both hands. "I did not mean to imply—Of course, you should see the other two plantations tomorrow. Do your—what do you call it?—due diligence?"

Erik sat back down. Warren leaned forward. "Erik,

perhaps we could agree to terms on condition we like what we see tomorrow. Nothing that we can't back out of if things are not up to par."

"We will not discuss it now." Erik directed his cold tone toward Warren. The man should have known by now that Erik wouldn't want to reveal their cards too early. "After we visit the plantations tomorrow, you and I will discuss terms, *Señor* Morales."

Manuel turned down the rough multi-colored blanket covering the antique iron bed, took off his shoes, and stretched out. They had checked into the only hotel in the village of Rio Limpio, a three-story building from the country's colonial era. Before retreating to their rooms for the night, they agreed to meet at seven for breakfast.

The early start, the long car ride, hours in the heat touring the fields, capped by too much food at dinner had exhausted him. He closed his eyes and took several deep breaths.

Lord, open our eyes to any problems ... As he prayed, his body quickly gave way to sleep.

Hours later, his eyes fluttered open. Low voices in the next room sounded intense. At first he couldn't understand the words, despite the paper-thin wall between him and those who spoke.

Gray light filtered in through the flimsy curtains. He glanced at his watch. Five thirty.

As the conversation became more heated, the words came through clearly. In English.

"There's no problem." One man spoke in a loud stage whisper. "We'll get a report showing no pollution, and that will be that. Erik is always convinced by a report."

The other voice hissed, "Yes, but what if one of the workers says something to Manuel?"

"You worry too much."

Manuel now recognized the first voice as Warren's. "Tex has them under control. If they get out of line, replacement workers are always available."

Manuel lay quietly, listening. After more muffled discussion, a door opened and closed. Manuel waited. Only when several minutes passed without further sounds from the other side of the wall did he risk getting up from the squeaky bed. He yawned and stretched then swung his feet to the floor and sat up.

He could not identify the second voice. Perhaps it had been Alan; who else would Warren know in this area? If the conversation referred to pollution of the Morales plantations, Neilson Enterprises might be inheriting an enormous liability. But he needed to learn more before he raised an alarm to Erik, who still seemed to doubt his credibility at times.

After touring the two remaining plantations, the group returned to the village cantina for a late lunch. Warren continued to press for the purchase of all three plantations.

Erik spoke in a low, even tone that Manuel had begun to recognize as a sign of his irritation. "I want to be sure we have all the facts before we sign anything. Why are you so insistent on wrapping up the deal this week, Warren?"

Warren leaned forward. "You know it's a good price. Someone else will buy the plantations if we don't, and we'll be hard-pressed to find any others in this country at an affordable price."

"We have wanted to grow bananas here, but that doesn't mean we should proceed without doing our homework," Erik said.

Manuel suspected the reason Warren pushed so hard, but

he couldn't prove it. "May I suggest …?"

Erik glanced his way. "You have a suggestion? I'm listening."

Warren glared at him, but Manuel ignored him. "The agreement might allow for, perhaps, a ninety-day period before we take possession. During that time, we would have full access to the facilities and to the financial and legal records. The purchase would conclude only if all is acceptable."

Erik nodded. "Yes, I would be comfortable with that if Morales agrees." He leaned back and studied the three men. "Manuel, I think you would be a good choice to do that, um, review and analysis. What do you two think?"

Warren and Alan exchanged a brief look, but both nodded. "Of course, Erik," Warren said. "If you think Manuel has enough experience."

Manuel did not understand what he had done to earn Warren's disdain. He didn't seem to care for Manuel, and the feeling was becoming mutual.

Erik pushed his chair away from the table. "I think Manuel can bring fresh eyes to it. And the fact that he knows the culture and the language will be an asset. He may see something that someone else could miss."

Manuel prayed he could discover Warren's intentions before Neilson Enterprises took ownership in three months. He didn't want to let Erik down.

Chapter Thirty-Three

Ellen didn't mention Cerro La Cerra when Erik suggested the group take a day trip on their last full day in Guatemala. No doubt he had forgotten about the painting, and she decided not to remind him.

Besides, most of them wanted to see a live volcano. Ellen went along with the plan and suggested they end the day browsing the shops and open air market in Antigua.

Golden ribbons of sunlight peeked over the surrounding mountains, but the heat had not yet chased away the blue haze that had settled around the two vehicles. At the base of Volcan Pacaya, they parked and met up with the English-speaking guide Erik had hired.

As the guide distributed bottled water, Rosemary asked, "The volcano won't erupt on us, will it?"

The guide smiled. "No, *señora*. Pacaya is active but has not erupted for many years. But you will be able to see the hot lava inside it."

The trail climbed gradually through farmland until they reached the mesa just below the cone. When they came to the steep final grade covered in hardened lava runoff, Rosemary wheezed, already out of breath. She sucked on her water bottle. "I'm not used to this much walking. My feet hurt." She stooped to adjust the straps on her platform sandals.

Warren pointed behind them. "If you want to go back to the car, go ahead. We'll be back in about three hours." He turned and began to climb.

She looked back at the narrow cinder trail. "Alone?" Her voice trembled. She hurried to follow her husband. "I don't think so."

"You should have worn sensible shoes. Drink some more water, and keep quiet. No one wants to hear your complaining."

Rosemary huffed and crossed her arms, slowing down to hike beside Ellen. "My dear husband." She stuck out her bottom lip, a sharp contrast to her usual attempts at sophistication. As the terrain grew rougher, she uncrossed her arms and began pumping them, but she didn't complain again.

By the time they reached the summit, Manuel and Ellen were the only ones other than the guide who weren't panting. But excitement took over as the others approached the edge of the crater. Rosemary, her face crimson and her hair mussed, stopped several feet away. She waved her hand at the sulfuric smoke billowing from the opening. "Eeewww. It stinks."

Warren went back and grabbed her arm. "Come on, Rosemary. You've come this far. You should look down into the crater."

She allowed him to pull her but kept behind him. "It doesn't look safe to get so close."

Ellen gazed into the chasm, awed as much as anyone. *Mamá* had never taken her to see a volcano. In truth, she and the other children had more fear of their destructive power than curiosity. The smoke burned her eyes, and she tried to breathe through her mouth to avoid smelling the sulfur.

The wind blew the smoke momentarily away from them. Erik moved to her side and pointed to a lava cone glowing bright orange. "I wonder what the temperature of that lava is."

He dropped to the hard, black ground to rest with most of the other tourists, but Ellen wandered along the plateau. Across the valley, clouds kissed the tops of surrounding peaks.

"Beautiful, isn't it?" Manuel stood next to her, gazing with her at the vista. "Do you remember?"

"I remember. The view reminds me of La Cerra."

In spite of the steaming cavity behind her, the serenity of the setting spread over her, bringing peace to the hidden corners of her heart. Her *mamá* had loved the mountains. La Cerra had been close to the city, and she had taken Ellen and Manuel there several times before she got sick. Visiting that mountain had given Ellen hope that she could rise above life in the garbage dump. And she had done it. She had returned to this country with her dreams of wealth and security fulfilled. Only two of her desires remained—becoming a successful artist and being a mother. She lacked the courage to try the first, and God had taken her ability to achieve the latter.

The rest of their group had scattered to various spots, and no one was nearby. Still, she kept her voice soft. "Grandfather loved our mountain, too. The painting that Erik and I saw in the museum was called *The Beauty of La Cerra*. It captures the feeling that I always had there, and that I have now."

"I know what you mean. Perhaps it is a family trait to find something special in high places that one cannot find elsewhere."

They said little. Ellen became lost in thoughts of long ago days. A thousand feet below, pine trees and scraggly bushes marched in ragged lines toward a clear blue lake.

Ellen adopted a little-boy voice. "What do you want to be when you grow up?"

Manuel caught on right away. He mimicked her child's voice, reversing their roles. "A famous artist."

She bowed, with a sweeping flourish of her arm. "And I— I shall sell your paintings all over the world."

They laughed, and she turned to hug him, but she spotted Erik striding toward them and she stopped. "Oops," she said under her breath and stopped smiling. "Erik, come see this view. Isn't it beautiful?"

He looked at her, and then at Manuel. "You seem to be having a good time." She had never given him reason, but she detected the seeds of jealousy nevertheless. She searched her brain for a logical explanation to give him.

Manuel rescued her. "I was just telling *Señora* Neilson about my childhood. She found some of my stories humorous."

"I see." Erik sounded skeptical. "Perhaps you can entertain the rest of us later. The guide says it's time to go." Ellen took the hand that he offered her, and he led her where the others waited.

Manuel hoped to beat Ellen to the corner north of the hotel where they had agreed to meet. But no, there she was, pushing against the building with one leg outstretched. "Again, you wait for me. I thought I would be here first this morning."

Her musical laugh ran up the scale and down. "You should know better by now." She turned and began jogging toward the zoo four blocks away. Manuel matched her pace. The early morning traffic was light, so they crossed the smaller streets without stopping.

While shopping in Antigua the day before, he'd told her they needed to talk, and she had agreed to run with him this morning. That afternoon, she and Erik would fly home while Manuel would return to Rio Limpio to begin his review of the plantations. He would not have another opportunity to tell her of his suspicions.

They crossed a pedestrian bridge over the multi-laned Liberation Boulevard. At the end of the bridge, Ellen asked Manuel which way, and he pointed left. As they followed the walk around the outside of the park, she lengthened her stride, and Manuel increased his speed to keep up.

Muffled sounds of big cats calling for their breakfast drifted over the high zoo walls. "What is it, Manuel? What is this information you want to give me? Not another conspiracy to get rid of Erik, I hope."

"No, cousin, not to get rid of him. But another conspiracy, yes. I believe so."

Ellen frowned. "I was joking."

"I am not."

She took a deep breath and let it out. "All right, tell me."

"I fear this—conspiracy, if you will, puts more at risk than your husband's position. It has possibly already caused the poisoning of hundreds of Maya."

He detailed his conversation with the workers. When they had covered the two-mile circuit twice, Ellen stopped and sat on a low cement wall.

"But if the chemicals are so dangerous, won't Neilson Enterprises stop using them? The workers will be better off if the company buys the plantations and cleans up the soil and water."

He perched beside her on the wall. "Yes, one would think so. But in the hotel, I overheard Warren talking with someone. It sounded as though they intend to continue using the dangerous chemicals and to keep it a secret."

"Not again. How do you always happen to be where you hear these things?"

"Perhaps God is arranging for me to hear so that he can use you and me to prevent tragedy."

Ellen stood and paced. "Why do you keep bringing me into this, Manuel? Erik doesn't want me involved in his business. He made it clear after the last time that I was not to interfere again, even though your story was true, and he fired Therese. He will not talk to me about business, and I don't dare bring it up."

"Yes, yes, I understand. But if you don't tell him, who will?"

"You. Aren't you supposed to do a review of the plantations? Put this in a memo."

"I fear it will never reach him. All memos have to go through my own vice president—Alan—to Warren, who decides if it should go to the president's office. Alan would probably disregard it, and if he didn't, Warren would shred it. Then I could do nothing." If Ellen wouldn't help, what could he do on his own? He prayed silently for a way to convince her.

She stood with her back to him. "Mail the report to him anonymously."

"Why would he take an anonymous report seriously? He would think it was a prank. He would ask Warren to check it out and—dead end. Don't you see? You must tell him. It is—" His mouth felt dry and his heart roared in his ears. "It is your duty, Elena. These are your people, too."

His voice cracked, and she turned to face him, her head tipped to one side. He cleared his throat. He had to tell her everything. "Your—our grandmother came from that village. When I researched my family, I learned that our Mayan grandmother grew up in Río Limpio. That's the village near Indiana Plantation. She left there to come to Guatemala City. In those days, the Indians were treated even worse than when we were children. It seems she married our grandfather, who was not Mayan, in hopes of hiding her ethnicity. She was ashamed of her background—just as you are. Needlessly." He fell silent, his head drooping. He refused to look at her. He hoped this information would dissolve her resistance.

She paced. Then she stopped and threw her hands in the air. "It makes no difference. There is nothing I can do. You must find another way. I'm going back to the hotel."

Ellen walked away briskly, but Manuel caught up with her before she got across the bridge. Neither spoke. He should have allowed her to go ahead of him, so they would not be seen together. But it was too late. As they rounded the corner of the hotel, they nearly bumped into Erik.

Erik looked from Ellen to Manuel. "I was getting worried about you, Ellen. We need to get packed. Where have you been?"

Her face warmed, but she hesitated only a moment. "I told you I was going for a run. I—I ran into Manuel. You know he's a runner, too." She pecked Erik on the cheek and edged around him, leaving Manuel standing there with him, watching as she headed into the hotel.

After showering and getting dressed, she wrapped a towel around her wet hair and walked into the hotel suite living room. Erik was not on the phone or reviewing files. He was just sitting on the sofa.

Puzzled, she sat next to him. "Are you all right?"

His eyes searched her face. "Are you?" He stood and gazed down at her. "And Manuel? Have you been enjoying yourself?"

"Yes, I'm glad I came with you." She lowered the towel from her head and draped it around her shoulders. "Are you glad I came?"

He paced across the room and pivoted. "What's with you and Manuel?"

Her heart thudded. He knew. No, he couldn't. "What do you mean? We were just running."

His eyes pierced hers. "You've been together a lot this trip. And you seem to be enjoying his company."

"What are you saying? You honestly think I would be unfaithful to you?" The tropical heat outside invaded the room. She jumped to her feet as if she'd sat on scalding lava. "That is insane. I can't believe you don't trust me more than that."

She stamped into the bedroom and slammed the door.

Leaning against it, she put both hands to her flushed face. He was right not to trust her, after all the lies she had told him. But it was ironic that he would think she might be unfaithful—something she would never do.

The twelve-hour trip home would be worse than if she had walked on the hot coals of Pacaya unless Ellen could convince Erik she and Manuel were not having an affair.

Erik had not spoken to her since the argument. When they landed in Houston where they had a three-hour layover, she could stand the silence no longer. "Can we have dinner without the others?" she asked him. "I'd like to talk."

"Good idea."

They found a seafood restaurant in the terminal. When they had ordered, Erik eyed her. "Well? What did you want to tell me?"

She held his gaze and reached across the table to touch his hands, which he had clasped in front of him. He didn't move. "I would never be unfaithful to you. Manuel and I are just friends."

He shifted in his chair. "I don't understand. How is it that you know him so well?"

"Before Christmas, when he told me about that meeting at the restaurant, he mentioned that he liked to run." She shrugged. "I thought since he was new in town, I would invite him to join me during my morning workouts. So he did, a few times."

Erik just sat there gripping his hands together. "Why didn't you mention it?"

She looked down at the table. "I don't know. I was afraid you wouldn't understand." She took a deep breath and looked up. "We are just friends, Erik. That is all. It hurts that you would suspect anything else."

His frozen face began to thaw. His eyes searched her face. At last, he unclasped his hands and folded them over her hand. "I want to believe you. I was just surprised to see you together this morning. And yesterday, at the volcano. I don't know. You seemed to be having such a good time with him."

She was relieved the waiter brought their drinks just then. She doubted she could explain the shared laughter yesterday. But when the waiter left, Erik said, "I owe you an apology. I shouldn't jump to conclusions like I did this morning. I'm sorry."

"I just want you to know that I love you, Eric. Only you."

He smiled. "I'll try to remember that in the future."

For Such a Moment

Chapter Thirty-Four

When Ellen returned to class on Tuesday, most of the children gathered to hug her all at once. She laughed, just as glad to see them. They shared the same eagerness to create beauty that she had seen among the children in the garbage dump. "All right, we're wasting time. We have a busy day today since I was gone last week. Find your seats."

Only two students had not come to greet her. Stubborn William Henry, who sat in his usual defensive posture with his arms crossed. Could anything crack his shell?

And sweet Tyrone, who watched her with a grin that reached across his face. Seeing him completed her pleasure at returning. She moved to his side and touched his shoulder. "I'm glad you're back, Tyrone."

"Yes, ma'am. Me, too." He pointed to his leg, still in a cast, which he had elevated on an extra chair beside him. "Sorry, but it's hard for me to get up."

She bent down and put an arm around his shoulder. "I understand. You stay right where you are." She looked at Lateesha on the other side of the table. "We'll make sure you have your supplies."

The girl nodded but didn't look at Tyrone. "Yes'm. I know he might need help."

Lateesha had a natural sense of compassion. She could be a nurse—or a doctor. Ellen made a mental note to encourage her after class.

She crossed the room to where William Henry sulked. She put both hands on his shoulders and whispered in his ear, "I'm glad to see you again, William Henry." He didn't look at her, but she thought she detected a softening of the hardened mask of his face.

She asked three children to help her distribute paper, colored pencils, and soft lead pencils. "Miss Carolyn told me you all worked hard while I was gone. Today I would like you to have some fun. Who remembers the instructions on how to use colored pencils?"

Several hands shot up, and she nodded as she listened to the answers. "Very good. Now I want you to create a picture— the best picture you can make—that shows me the most fun activity you did over the holidays."

The students reached for the colored pencils. "Remember, children. You want to sketch your drawing with a black pencil before you color it in."

Groans. But they put down the boxes and picked up the lead pencils. As she walked around to check on their work, she found Donato's face returning to her mind. She had thought of him every day since leaving Guatemala. A small boy with tousled dark hair she'd seen sledding near Lake Harriet had reminded her of him. Her dreams had been punctuated with images of his sad brown eyes, determined but pleading. Had her own eyes shown such desperation after her *mamá* died? She had sent an e-mail to Salvador asking him to keep her posted on the boy. She wanted to know that he was safe and sound.

She stopped to admire Tyrone's drawing. A large bed with a small figure in it. His hospital bed. Was that the most fun thing that had happened? He had been hospitalized for a whole month. But it looked like the boy in the picture had his hands together, as if in prayer. "Tell me about your picture, Tyrone."

The boy turned his face to her, glowing. "It's me in the hospital, Miz Neilson. The best thing that I did was pray. 'Cause God answers prayers. He answered my grandma's, and

He answered mine."

Ellen had prayed for her *mamá*, but she had died. She remembered her stepmother's prayers after being diagnosed with cancer. Mom Anne had only gotten worse. Then, after her death, Ellen's dad had been injured in the car accident. Desperate not to lose him, she had given God one more chance, but those prayers also failed, and she had been left alone.

She could see that Tyrone believed what he said. And the fact that he was here affirmed his belief. For the first time since her father died, she wanted to believe, too.

Chapter Thirty-Five

Pink streaks spread across the pale blue sky early Sunday morning as Manuel pulled off the road into the tall grass. He edged the twenty-year-old car forward, not sure how firm the ground near the river would be. When the grasses had closed behind the car, he stopped and got out. If anyone passing should notice, the car would appear to be an abandoned vehicle.

He grabbed the canteen he'd bought in the market the day before and threw the strap over his shoulder. He looked toward the road, and then toward the river. His plan was to search the riverbank on this side of the road, upriver from the plantation compound.

He had been working at Indiana plantation for four weeks, reviewing the financial books and business records for all three properties. When he wasn't in the office with his head in the ledgers, he had walked the property—a hundred acres so far. He had talked to employees and their families living in the dormitory-style housing.

As he'd suspected, the crowded, unsanitary buildings provided little more than a roof over their heads. He had begun writing a proposal to improve the workers' housing once the company took over. Better housing could mean healthier and happier workers. From what he had seen since coming to work for Neilson Enterprises, Erik believed in decent treatment for all employees, not just those at headquarters.

Neilson Enterprises would assume control in two months, and he had been unable to find evidence of illegal pesticides. Other than the two men he spoke to that first day, no one had revealed anything useful. He could see fear and despair in the workers' eyes, but he could not persuade them to talk about the working conditions.

Yesterday, he had decided to take a break and enjoy a Saturday at the market. He browsed among wagons and stalls loaded with vegetables and handmade items. As he admired the colorful blankets at one stand, a white-haired old man had moved next to him. The booth's owner, bargaining with a woman a few feet away, paid them no attention.

"You look for truth." The quiet words caused Manuel to glance at the man, wondering if he were talking to himself. His back curved like a parenthesis so that his head did not reach to Manuel's armpit. He wore the bright red, blue, and orange sombrero beloved by the Indians of this village. Had he met the man, perhaps at the plantation? Nothing about him seemed familiar.

The man raised his right sleeve. "You look in the wrong place. You must look here." Out of the overlarge opening came a withered stump of an arm. The arm ended just above where the wrist should have been, and the end was calloused and cracked. With the stump, the man hit the pile of blankets on the table. "*Aqui.*" Here.

Manuel inspected the top blanket where the man indicated. The weave made a picture of a river, and the man tapped the riverbank. He did not look at Manuel. "North."

"What? What am I looking for?"

"Truth. Look deep. When you find it, you will know." The man turned and limped away.

Stunned, Manuel opened his mouth to call after him, but he shut it before any sound came out. Perhaps the man had put himself in danger with their conversation. He glanced around to see if anyone had observed them talking, but everyone nearby seemed preoccupied with their own business.

Manuel strolled around the market for the next hour, hoping to spot the old man again, but he never did. He considered the brief exchange. The river north of the main plantation compound would be on the other side of the narrow road leading into the village.

Since he didn't want to be noticed snooping around, he drove an hour to El Estor, the nearest town. There he had found a school teacher who owned the old, brown Ford sedan, as nondescript a vehicle as he could expect.

"Why do you want to borrow my old car? It will break down any day." The teacher had wiggled her eyebrows. "You run from the authorities? You sell drugs? What is it?"

"I cannot explain. I assure you I have done nothing illegal, and I will not." Manuel held out both hands, as if to show that he had nothing to hide from her. "You can use my car, and I will return yours Sunday evening. I will pay you five hundred *quetzals* if you will ask no more questions."

The woman's eyes opened wide and her jaw dropped. She closed her mouth and nodded slowly. He had offered her more than she made in two months. He handed her the keys to his rented SUV.

Now that he was certain the car would not be noticed, he should start looking. He hadn't come here to stand around. But he did not know what to look for. He hoped the old man had not sent him on a pointless search.

He reached the river's edge. "Look deep," the man had said. Did he mean in the water? No, he had pointed to the riverbank. He had to mean underground.

Manuel needed something to use as a probe. Stunted trees clung to life along the edges of the quiet river. A thick branch, about four feet long and mostly straight, had fallen from one of them. He picked it up by the end, which was as thick as his fist, and tested it by pushing it into the undergrowth near his feet.

He began to systematically poke every foot or so along the bank, working his way north.

For the next hour, he explored the riverbank, finding nothing. He proceeded with the speed of a turtle, searching under bushes and down the steep banks descending to the river.

He looked upriver and decided to venture ten more meters before abandoning the search. As he took another step, his right ankle turned. Pain wrenched up his leg and before he knew it, he fell to his knees. His hands plopped in the dirt. He grasped his ankle and began to rub it, groaning. Probably sprained. How would he get back to the car?

"Oh, God, please make it stop hurting," he prayed aloud.

The pain subsided to a dull throb, and he realized he was sitting in loose soil. Someone had dug here recently and covered it with dried leaves and grass. No wonder he had turned his ankle. He looked around for the branch he had been using and stretched his arm out to grasp it.

Using the pole for leverage, he managed to pull himself up. He tested a little weight on his right foot and winced. Balancing on his left leg, Manuel poked the stick into the loose dirt and pushed. The stick struck something hard. He lowered himself back to the ground and started to scoop soil with his hands. In spite of the pain in his leg, he moved enough dirt to uncover part of a large metal container.

He scraped more soil away until he revealed a piece of a label. The words were weathered, but he could make out the letters *PBM*. His brow wrinkled. CPBM was a chemical he had learned about in college, one of the so-called "Dirty Dozen." Dangerous, even deadly, when ingested, and a possible carcinogen. Once popular for many crops, the pesticide had been banned in the United States after studies found it caused sterility in male workers. Not to mention the harmful effects if the chemical seeped into a drinking water supply. A container, even empty, buried this near the river could only mean trouble for the plantation workers downstream who used this water. This must be what the old villager had wanted him to find. Who would have gone to the trouble of burying the container here, and how many more were hidden nearby? And how did the old man know?

"What do I do now, God?" He was alone, hurting, and a long way from the car. He needed a shovel to unearth the barrel so he could find out for sure what it had contained and where it came from.

Adrenaline had helped dull the pain in his leg, but now it returned. He needed to get back to town and find ice for his ankle. As if ice could be found within a hundred miles. Unearthing the drum would have to wait until his leg healed. He positioned the stick so that he could pull himself up. As he stood, a hand grabbed his arm from behind. Manuel's heart somersaulted into his throat.

For Such a Moment

Chapter Thirty-Six

"I had a call from Tex." The worry in Alan's voice got Warren's attention.

Catching up on some work on Sunday afternoon, he had assumed when the phone rang that it would be Rosemary, checking up on him. Alan should know better than to discuss their plans in the office—or on the company telephone. "What's wrong?"

"Tex thinks it's time we bring Manuel home."

Warren had convinced Alan they could make enough money with the Guatemalan scheme that, in a couple of years, he could retire early and stay in Mexico with his family. But he still became nervous over every detail.

Warren leaned back in his chair and locked his eyes on the ceiling stain. "What's he doing?"

"Tex says he's gotten friendly with the workers."

"So? They won't say anything, will they?"

Alan cleared his throat. "Tex doesn't think so, but—"

"Right now, all he can learn is how Morales ran things, not what we're planning, right?"

"Well, yes, I suppose so."

"Tell Tex to make sure there's nothing for him to find. We bring him home too suddenly, and we'll create suspicion. Meanwhile I'll try to find another project for him."

"I'll tell him, but he won't like it."

"I don't care. As long as he does as he's told." Warren hardened his voice. "And don't ever call about this on my office phone."

Manuel turned to see who had found him in the woods so far from the road. He looked into the dark eyes of the old man from the market. "What?"

"God sent me," the man said in his native language. "You are hurt. Come, we go." The man gestured for Manuel to lean on him.

Manuel feared the man would fall under his weight, but he was as tough as he was old. Manuel hobbled beside him, grimacing with each step. "My name is Manuel. And yours?"

"Felipe." A man of few words, Felipe said nothing else until they got to the car.

Manuel looked around. "How did you get here? Don't you have a car?"

"Walk." They were two miles from the village, but Manuel knew the Maya people walked everywhere.

The old man helped Manuel get behind the steering wheel. He would have to use his left foot on both the clutch and brake. It would be a slow trip.

A week later, Warren and Alan met for lunch at Zelo on the Nicollet Mall. Halfway through the meal, Warren asked, "What do you hear from Guatemala?"

"Not much. Manuel hurt his ankle, so he's been stuck in the office all week. He says the financials look good."

Warren swallowed a bite of walleye. "Hmm. That should keep him from snooping around. What does Tex say?"

Alan leaned back in his chair. "He's found a storage place for the chemicals for the next couple of months. Once we close on the property, he'll quietly move the containers back and start spraying the plants again." He picked up his glass and sipped. "I am concerned about all the sick workers."

Warren eyed Alan, wondering if he had developed a conscience. He wiped his mouth with his napkin. "What do you mean?"

"I've been thinking. With the high rates of cancer, the breathing problems ... What if Manuel or Erik get suspicious?"

Warren laughed too loudly. He glanced at the tables near them. Empty, but he lowered his voice anyway. "Are you blind? The nurse in the village is Tex's friend. As long as we keep Tex around, they have no illnesses. The cancer can't be traced to us. Slackers who claim to be sick are sent packing."

Their waitress, an amiable twenty-something with gold hoop earrings and blue streaks in her brown hair, approached their table. She asked if they wanted dessert, but both declined. Warren pulled out his company credit card and handed it to her. She blazed a smile his way. "Thank you, sir. I'll ring this up for you."

His eyes followed her as she pranced away. Then he turned back to Alan. "How about the other arrangements?"

Alan nodded. "Tex has a plan for siphoning off money so no one will notice it missing. That man has more ideas than Minnesota has mosquitoes."

Warren tapped his shoe on the tile floor. "So tell me."

The waitress appeared beside him and held out the black folder. She waited, swiveling her hips to the restaurant's background music. He scribbled his name and added a generous tip and picked up his credit card and receipt. As he handed the folder back to her, he looked in her sultry eyes. Her lips parted, and she winked at him. "Thanks. Come see us again."

He watched her walk away, his mouth dry. It didn't matter

that she was half his age. He intended to follow the advice she
had just offered.

"As long as you can still get the chemicals, we'll keep
using them." Warren kept his voice under control. He felt like
yelling at Tex, but he might be overheard here in his office.
"You let me worry about Manuel. Your job is to grow more
bananas and make sure insects don't ruin them and the trees
don't rot. Can you handle that?"

He slammed the phone receiver down. He couldn't believe
Tex had called him on this line. He'd thought Tex would make
a cool-headed and smart plantation manager, but now he
wondered if the man would become a liability.

Speaking of liabilities, he had to do something about
Manuel.

He pulled his personal cell phone out of his pocket and
walked to the window. He scrolled through his phone book
until he found the name he wanted. The man had kept tabs on
Therese after the debacle with the board in December. Warren
had wanted to make sure she didn't tell Erik about his
involvement. He pressed "send" and waited for an answer.

"Yeah?"

Warren turned his back to the view of the city. "I have a
research project for you."

"What is it?"

"A man from Guatemala. Manuel Rivas. Works for my
company now. I want everything you can find on him—where
he was born, every place he's lived, schools, relatives, friends.
You know the drill."

"I'll have to go there," the man on the other end said.
"You want him followed, too?"

Warren hesitated. Maybe they should be worried about Manuel snooping. "Yes. He's in Guatemala now. I want weekly reports."

He clicked off and stuffed the phone in his pocket. By using CPBM, the plants would produce more bananas than Erik would expect. With Tex's help, he and Alan would be able to siphon profits from the plantations. Enough to make up for his failure to steal the company away from Erik last winter. He only had to make sure Manuel didn't get in his way.

By the time Manuel returned to Minneapolis in early April, he was relieved to find the snow had melted. He had exercised his ankle to help it heal, and he looked forward to running with Elena again.

His first day in the office, he went to see Alan. Although he had no proof, he had become convinced that Tex planned to continue using dangerous chemicals, and he needed to find out whether Alan knew.

After a few minutes chatting about Manuel's trip, Alan picked up a file folder. "I've read the reports you've sent. What's your overall opinion?"

A vise clamped around Manuel's chest. "Well, sir, I believe the plantations are a good buy. I did not find anything in the records to indicate otherwise."

Alan leaned his elbows on the desk and steepled his fingers. "So, you don't have any reservations about moving forward?"

"At this time, I do not. But I have not received the laboratory report yet." He had taken water and soil samples from several locations. If pollution already existed, the cleanup costs would affect the purchase price. But his concern had more to do with what happened after Neilson took over.

Alan smoothed his hair. "It should be here soon, right?"

"Yes, sir. I'm expecting it this week."

"Good, good," Alan answered quickly. Too quickly. "What about the personnel?"

Manuel rubbed his hand over his cheeks. "I am not sure that Tex will be loyal to Neilson Enterprises."

Alan raised his eyebrows and leaned his body to one side of his chair. He looked down at his desk. "What makes you say that? He seems like a good manager."

The tightness in Manuel's chest grew. "He does know how to run a plantation. But his salary and bonuses seem large for this size operation. And ..." He needed to express his reservations without revealing his suspicions, at least until he knew whether Alan was involved in the scheme. He cleared his throat, considering his words. "I do not believe that he understands this company's philosophy. He does not seem to care about the employees like Mr. Neilson does. He seems more interested in, ah, making money."

"Is that all?" Alan waved his hand, flipping away Manuel's comment like an annoying insect. He turned to his computer. "We want to make money, too. I'm sure we can bring Tex around to our way of thinking."

That was that. Whether Alan sanctioned Tex's plan to keep using illegal chemicals, instigated it, or did not even know about it, he wanted to keep the plantation manager. And he left no opening for Manuel to disagree. At least for now.

Manuel received the laboratory reports in an interoffice envelope a week after Neilson Enterprises took ownership of the Morales plantations. Despite his protests, the transfer had occurred a week earlier than planned. Alan told him Erik decided not to wait for the test results on the soil and water samples Manuel had collected.

A note from Alan was attached to the report. "Warren and I looked these over and everything appears fine. Good work. Transfer of ownership is complete."

So his superiors had intercepted his mail and read the results before giving them to him. That seemed unusual.

He reviewed the summary sheet, which indicated that chemical levels in fifteen of the twenty soil and water samples were within acceptable levels. The other five showed slightly elevated levels of CPBM, chloropropanebromide, in the soil. CPBM—the same chemical as on the label of the empty containers Felipe helped him uncover. He had been unable to prove who had buried them or where they had come from.

According to the memo, the chemical took only six months to break down to nontoxic levels in soil. But Manuel knew it had devastating effects while it remained active. That's why it had been banned in so many countries.

He scrutinized the individual printouts. On several forms, the numbers were blurred. Was that a three or an eight? Must be a three, since eight would fall into the "very high" concentration level. When he got to the bottom of the stack, he leaned back. "Lord, something is not right. Show me what I am missing."

He picked up the packet and began to go through the individual sheets again. He sorted them according to the locations where he had collected the samples. Ten soil samples and ten water samples. Wait. A report on one of the water samples was missing. He counted them all. Nineteen, not twenty. He checked the interoffice envelope. Empty. Probably an oversight. He decided to call the lab and ask for the missing report to be faxed to him.

He dialed the number and spoke to the scientist who had signed the report. "Doctor Faulkner, I received your report on the samples from a plantation in Guatemala. But—"

"Yes, I remember those samples, Mr. Rivas. Serious contamination in the water."

Chapter Thirty-Seven

After listening to Dr. Faulkner's brief explanation, Manuel waited at the fax machine to intercept the printed sheets as soon as they arrived.

Based on what the scientist had told him, someone had tampered with the results before forwarding them to Manuel. He knew Alan and Warren had seen the report. But which version? He could not imagine what motive they had to falsify the report before sending it to him. The company had just bought the plantations.

As the pages printed, he grabbed each one and scanned it. The summary had been changed. Every line he read caused the acid in his stomach to increase. "Moderate to extremely high levels … serious contamination of groundwater, with potential to move over large areas … recommend immediate remediation."

He glanced at the sections where the numbers had been hard to decipher on the first version. Sure enough. Eights, not threes. He compared the pages to the version he had received in interoffice mail. Someone had used correction fluid and then made a copy to make it appear like a blurred original. He rocked on his heels while he waited for the machine to spit out the final page, the report on the missing water sample. His hands shook as he read the numbers. The well where the workers and their families retrieved their drinking water showed dangerously high levels of CPBM. The people were being poisoned.

And either Alan or Warren—or both—had tried to hide the facts.

As Ellen and Manuel rounded the south end of Lake
Harriet, her eyes watered, partly from the April sun glinting off
the lake, partly from what he had just told her.

"Elena, don't you see? You must tell Erik. He will listen
to you."

Manuel had spent the first half hour of their run describing
the conditions at the plantations and the altered laboratory
report. The thought of children being poisoned sickened her.
But she still sensed Erik's suspicion over her friendship with
Manuel. And he remained steadfast about not discussing
business with her. He seemed to think his wife should be
insulated from the details of company operations.

Her steps pounded in rhythm with her heart. "I can't. He
won't listen to me."

"How do you know unless you try, cousin? Perhaps he
will listen this time. If he does, you could convince him to stop
using the chemicals. You could save hundreds of lives." He
stopped and grabbed her arm, forcing her to halt and look at
him. "Please, Elena. It really is a matter of life and death.
These are our people—your people."

She studied his face, wrinkling her forehead as she
considered his words. She shook her head sharply and jerked
her arm free of his grasp.

"No, Manuel. I can't do it. I'm trying to make my
marriage with Erik work. Even meeting you for a run is a risk."
She glared at him for a long moment, turned, and jogged away
from him, away from the sorrow in his eyes. But she could not
run away from the pain in her own heart.

Ellen's art class that day left her feeling like a squeezed-out sponge. Most of the Thursday afternoon students cared more about showing off their latest technological gadgets than they did about painting. Still, the fees their parents paid enabled the Walker Foundation to underwrite the classes for less privileged children.

She checked the paint brushes to make sure the students had cleaned them thoroughly. Today she could not get her mind off Manuel's request. Though he had been back in town for three weeks, she had not mentioned to Erik that she had been running with him again. Erik did not understand her friendship with Manuel, and she wanted to avoid more questions.

The cold water ran over her fingers, washing away the remaining bits of color. How she longed to rinse away the secrets, to tell Erik everything. Perhaps then she could convince him to get rid of the poisonous chemicals. But if she told him about her mother and the abuse by the man who haunted her dreams, her entire life would pour down the drain. Her husband would consider her not only dishonest, but tainted.

With the water running, she didn't hear footsteps approaching. The light knock on the open door caused her to jump. She turned to see the Walker Center director crossing the room.

"I didn't mean to startle you, Ellen." Geri Mitchell's clipped accent had not changed since she had moved to Minneapolis three years earlier. Her polished New York bearing and brusque mannerisms had clashed initially with the Midwestern politeness of most of the staff. But her efficiency in running the museum, matched by her genuine kindness, soon won their loyalty.

"How are the children doing?" Geri nodded at the paintings Ellen had tacked on the bulletin board. She smiled without showing her teeth. "Any budding Rembrandts?"

Ellen grabbed a paper towel and dried her hands. "You never know. Two or three are learning very quickly. I'll show you." She took a step toward the wall, but Geri placed a hand on her arm to stop her.

"That's all right. Actually, I want to talk about the summer classes." The Walker's summer program provided a variety of half-day classes. Students could specialize in watercolor painting, sculpture, photography, or other art forms. She laid a purple file folder on the counter and opened it. "Here's the schedule I've worked up so far, but I wondered if you had any ideas for classes that might especially interest boys." She handed Ellen two sheets of paper.

Ellen leaned against the stone counter and scanned the list. "I've been thinking about that, and I thought of something that might work. Could we try a class where they learn to use found objects to create collages and paintings?"

As Ellen outlined the idea, Geri perched on a nearby stool and jotted some notes. "You could take them outside to hunt for things from nature and miscellaneous trash. I can see how boys would enjoy that." She wrinkled her nose. "Just make sure they wear gloves when they collect the items."

She closed the folder and motioned Ellen to take the other stool at the counter. "I wanted to talk to you about something else, too. Please sit. It won't take long."

Ellen sat on the edge of the stool, reminded of being called to the principal's office in high school. But Geri had never spoken a harsh word to her, or to anyone else. She couldn't think of any reason the museum would fire her, and it wasn't as though she needed this job.

Geri tilted her head. Behind shiny designer glasses, her hazel eyes gazed at Ellen with a strength Ellen wished she possessed for herself. "Ellen, dear, you have a gift." She cleared her throat then gave a casual wave around the classroom. "You're wonderful with the children, of course, and I can tell they enjoy your classes."

Ellen's cheeks grew warm. She did not want to be praised for doing something she loved as much as she did teaching.

Geri removed her glasses and dangled them by the frame. "But you should be showing and selling your own paintings."

The familiar pounding began in Ellen's ears. Echoes of laughter and teasing from her childhood. She shook her head. "I can't. I—I paint for myself. Because I enjoy it. They're not good enough for anyone else."

Geri slapped a palm on the counter. "Nonsense. This is what I do, and I'm very good at it. I'm working on the fall schedule of exhibits, and I want to set up a show of your work."

Ellen jumped up from the stool and paced away from her. She covered her mouth with one hand, rubbed her cheek, then reached for the back of her neck and began to massage the knot she felt forming there. "No, Geri. You'll have to leave me out of your schedule." She turned to face her again. "I'm sorry."

The other woman looked at her, unspoken questions apparent in her face. When Ellen said no more, she finally nodded. She set her mouth in a thin, tight line, and rose. "I hope you will change your mind one day. When you do, let me have the first opportunity, won't you?"

For Such a Moment

Chapter Thirty-Eight

Warren had just exited the interstate on his way to work when the pay-as-you-go cell phone rang.

"Got something that might help you," the investigator said.

"It's about time. Talk to me." A month had passed, but so far the weekly reports had provided no useful information.

"Manuel Carlos Rivas, born in Pena Verde, Guatemala, only son of Maria Rivas Cuat and Juan Garcia Ordoñez. Mother's parents were Carlos Elias Rivas Flores, a nationally known artist, and ..." The man fumbled over the next words. "Na Ixchel Balam Cuat, a Mayan woman. Grandparents died before he was born. Mother disappeared when he was still a toddler, I guess. Father died when the son was eight. The boy lived on the streets 'til he was fifteen, when he was taken in by missionaries. Graduated with honors from Universidad de San Carlos in Antigua. Employed by Neilson—"

"That's what you've got?" Warren jerked the steering wheel sharply as he cornered onto Hennepin Avenue. "I need something I can't read in his personnel file, you idiot."

The man said nothing. Warren had angered him, but if the moron didn't give him something good soon, Warren would do more than insult him. He would fire him.

After coughing in Warren's ear, the investigator continued. "Try this. His mother had a sister, who had a child out of wedlock. Lived in Lomas de Santa Faz for a while. That's a slum area in Guatemala City. Her death was reported ten years after her kid was born."

Warren pulled next to the curb a block before the Neilson

Building. The sign proclaimed *No Parking or Standing*, but he might lose reception in the parking garage. The driver behind him honked as he swerved to go around. Warren gestured at him. "Listen, I've got to go. Is all this going somewhere meaningful?"

"I'm getting to it. The kid's birth certificate—her name is listed as Elena Moore Rivas —shows the father as American. Government records indicate that the girl left Guatemala after her mother died. I tracked her to Kentucky."

Warren knew someone from Kentucky, but he couldn't think who. Probably not important, anyway. "Go on." He grew tired of the conversation and didn't see what this had to do with Manuel.

"So the kid was legally adopted by her American father and his wife. Changed her name. Graduated from Trigg County High School and the University of Minnesota. Married—are you ready?"

Warren cursed. "Just get to the point."

The investigator laughed. "This is worth the wait. So Manuel's cousin, the illegitimate daughter of a poor woman who seems to have been a prostitute, married into a very wealthy, three-generation Minnesota family. Want to guess who?"

Warren clenched his teeth. The man must have a secret desire to write suspense. "Just tell me."

"Her husband is Erik Neilson."

Ellen leaned on the railing at the bow as the chartered yacht, the *Princess Elizabeth,* pulled away from the dock on Lake Minnetonka. The string of days with weather in the eighties, unusually warm for the last week of May, provided an ideal prelude to the annual managers' outing.

Abigail and Andrew Andersen joined her in gazing at the water parting to make way for the sixty-foot cruiser. At ages eleven and eight, the two children sported the blond hair and blue eyes that revealed the Scandinavian heritage common in Minnesota.

"Mrs. Neilson, doesn't that water look like it has jewels in it?"

Ellen leaned over to see where Abigail pointed.

"There, the bright blue spots with the white circles around them. It looks like a necklace."

"Yes, I see it," Ellen said. "It's beautiful, isn't it? Look, Andrew."

Andrew wrinkled his nose. "That's dumb. It's just water."

She faced him. "All right. Tell me what you see in the water."

He watched the ripples for several minutes. Finally, he pointed. "There! Now, that's cool! The weeds floating in the waves look like snakes and spiders." He cast a triumphant look at his sister.

Ellen laughed and put her arm around his shoulder. "That's wonderful, Andrew. You can see whatever you want. It's great to use your imagination. Abigail sees what makes her happy, and you do the same."

Abigail broke in. "That's what you always say about art. That we can create whatever we want to."

"That's right, Abigail. We have to use our imaginations and not be afraid to try new things." The words slipped out. She shouldn't talk about fear since it kept her from trying to sell her own artwork.

Andrew stepped up on the lower bar of the railing and hung his upper body over the water. "Are you teaching again this summer?"

"Yes, I am." His position caused knots in her stomach. She put her arm around him and gently pulled him back. "Are you going to take another class this year?"

He looked down at the water and mumbled. "Maybe."

Typical boy. He enjoyed art but wouldn't admit it. "I hope you do. I'm offering a class where we're going to use sticks and leaves and stuff to create paintings and sculptures. It's called Found Art. I think you'd like it."

"Cool. I'll go ask Mom now if I can sign up."

He ran off, and Ellen smiled.

Abigail bounced on the balls of her feet. "What class should I take?"

Ellen studied Abigail and frowned. The girl had an aptitude for art and would do well in the watercolor class. But she also enjoyed being teased. "Hmmm. I don't know. We might have to put you in the Color by Numbers class with the five-year-olds."

"Nuh-uhh. I could teach that one. What else ya got?"

"Well, I suppose we could let you try—that is, if you promise to work really, really hard—"

"I will. You know I will, Ellen." Her head bobbed up and down like the weeds on the water. "What class?"

"All right. How would you like to try watercolors?"

The girl's eyes rounded. "Could I? Do you think I could do it?"

"I'm sure of it." Ellen stooped down and gave her a hug. "Now you'd better go ask—"

A shrill shriek came from the stern of the boat, followed by several voices in a confused uproar. Someone yelled, "Stop the boat!"

Ellen's heart raced. Abigail's mouth gaped open. Ellen grabbed her hand and rushed toward the sounds.

Chapter Thirty-Nine

The engines slowed and the boat stopped just as Ellen and Abigail reached the cluster of guests crowding around the railing on the port side. Ellen couldn't see anything but the backs of heads.

She touched the arm of Jean Gibbs, whose face had turned white as a sheet. "What happened?"

"A child fell off. I think it's the Morgan boy. Manuel went in after him." Jean kept moving her head to see around the crowd.

Ellen's heart pounded in her ears. Manuel? Her cousin had gone in the water?

Abigail whispered, "Taylor Morgan? He's only three."

"Abigail, stay back here with Jean, okay?" Ellen pushed her way through the crushing bodies. "Excuse me. Let me through, please." When she reached the rail, she grasped the warm chrome and held on tight, leaning out over the water as far as she could. She peered into the water, squinting against the glare.

Manuel moved away from the boat, his strokes awkward. She didn't know he could swim. And there—a tiny blond head bobbed away from him. Ellen realized the boy floated face down, and her throat closed. From here, his body looked no larger than the lake trout Erik used to bring home from his Lake Superior fishing trips.

Crew members watched the two bobbing heads in the water as the captain started the engines and turned the boat. The sudden movement caused the passengers to grab each other to avoid falling. The Princess Elizabeth completed the circle and pulled within a few feet of the spot, and a deckhand signaled the captain to stop.

Kelly Morgan stood at the rail, her arms outstretched toward the water, her face contorted. "Please, please, let him be okay. God, please."

Her husband, Bruce, stood silently behind her, his arms clasping her waist as if trying to prevent her from going in the water, too. Ellen edged through the cluster of spectators until she reached the couple. She touched Bruce on the back and put her arm around Kelly's shoulders.

Despite the recent warm days, the lake would remain cold. Manuel reached Taylor and grabbed the boy's arm. He pulled, turning the slender body over. He cradled one arm under Taylor's back. With his other hand, he put a finger in the boy's open mouth. Manuel paused, eyes closed—praying, Ellen guessed. He put his mouth over the boy's and blew gently. The little body jerked and Manuel turned the boy's head to the side. Taylor wheezed and retched, then began to wail and flail his arms.

The onlookers cheered. Kelly turned and collapsed against Bruce.

Taylor wrapped his arms around Manuel's neck and tried to climb higher, pushing Manuel lower in the water. Kelly's body tensed again. Manuel grabbed the boy's tiny arms and pulled him close to his chest, speaking soothing words that Ellen could hear across the water but could not understand. Soon Taylor stopped crying and appeared to go limp in Manuel's arms. Manuel held the boy close to his chest with one arm and looked around the boy's head. Someone threw the life ring near the pair, and Manuel grasped it with one arm. He shifted Taylor to that side and used his free arm to dog paddle toward the boat.

"Come on, Manuel. Bring him here," a man's voice cried.

Two men pulled the rope attached to the life ring until Manuel reached the back of the boat. Another man said, "Way to go. You got him."

Manuel grabbed the ladder with his free arm. Exhaustion showed on his face and his teeth chattered. He tried to pull himself and Taylor up the ladder, but he sank back into the water. Erik called down to him. "Hang on, Manuel. I'll come down and get the boy."

Erik climbed over the railing and backed agilely down the ladder, reminding Ellen of the man she fell in love with—the compassionate man who cared about helping people. Holding onto the ladder with one hand, he leaned down to take the boy with the other arm. Ellen held her breath until he had passed the boy up to Bruce, who tenderly laid his son on the deck. Then Erik returned to Manuel, grasping his hand, and helping him to keep his hold on the ladder.

Kelly knelt next to her son, whose lips were blue. "Taylor! Taylor, dear God. Are you okay?"

His whole body shaking, Taylor lifted his arms to Kelly, who embraced him. The boy nestled his head against his mother's chest and started blubbering, taking quick breaths. He wrapped his arms around his mother's neck in a death grip as if he would never let go.

Someone draped a blanket around Taylor as he clung to Kelly. A blanket and towels were handed to Manuel, who took them and headed below.

The captain started the boat and turned it back toward the marina. Erik pulled out his cell phone and called 9-1-1, asking for an ambulance to meet them at the dock. He hung up and looked at the group who still gathered around.

"Folks, let's give the Morgans some privacy now."

Bruce held his wife and son in an embrace. Taylor had cried himself into a state of frenzy. Bruce stroked the back of his son's head, murmuring low, soothing words.

Taylor's cries settled to low, gulping sobs as he shivered under the blanket. Bruce rubbed his son's arms and legs to warm him. Then he began to rub his back, gradually taking his hand closer and closer to the boy's head as he pressed against Kelly. He worked his hand up to the side of Taylor's face and switched to one finger. That finger inched its way in until he could tickle Taylor's chin. A few more pokes and prods and tickles, and Taylor giggled.

Bruce obviously knew that laughing would help Taylor relax and recover from the traumatic event. Ellen, smiling to hide the pain she felt, headed below deck to find Manuel.

Manuel removed his wet shirt and shoes and socks and laid them out on a bench to dry. He dried his head and back with a towel. Bumps covered his skin, and he couldn't stop his teeth from clicking together. He wrapped the blanket around himself and did a high step on the coarse carpet to get blood flowing to his feet.

He did not remember jumping in the water. Had he really saved that little boy? No, God had saved them both.

A woman's deck shoes appeared on the narrow steps, followed by tanned legs wearing white capri pants. Ellen stepped into the cabin, raised her head, and looked at him.

"Manuel!" She rushed to him and hugged him. "I can't believe what you did. You saved Taylor's life!"

He looked into her eyes. He tried to form a question, but his cold lips didn't cooperate. He sat on the bench and worked his lips until he could speak. "Is he all right? He will live?"

"Oh, my goodness, yes." She sat on the bench next to him and put her hand on his arm. Did she want to comfort him or reassure herself? "Bruce has him giggling already. We're going back to port so they can get him checked out, but he seems fine. He was terrified, though. It may take a while for him to get over the scare."

Still shivering, he pulled the blanket tighter around his shoulders.

"Did you learn lifesaving in college?" Ellen asked.

"No. I can't even swim very well."

She gaped at him. "You looked like a lifeguard out there. How did you know what to do?"

He picked up a dry towel and began to rub his thick hair. "I don't know." He shook his head. "It must have been God helping me. I just tried to do what I've seen them do in movies."

For a few minutes, only the whine of the engines broke the silence. Ellen stared at the opposite wall. "Why, Manuel? Why would you jump in the water if you can't swim?"

"The boy was drowning, Elena. Someone had to save him."

"But why you? I was so frightened … You could have drowned, too." Her eyes filled with tears. "Why did you risk your life?"

He reached over and wiped a big drop of water from her cheek with his finger. "Why not me? Neal and I were watching the waves off the back of the boat. We were the only ones close enough to help, and I couldn't let Neal go in the water at his age."

"Weren't you afraid?"

"When I heard Kelly scream, I just jumped in. All I could think about was that little boy, and I prayed that God would help me save him. And he did. I could not have done that on my own." He took Ellen's hand and turned her face toward him. "Elena, when you were a little girl, you heard that Jesus went to the cross to give us life, right?"

She nodded. The tears streamed down her face, dropping to her lap.

"If He was willing to go through that for me, the least I can do is try to save someone else." He thought again of the families at Morales's three plantations and in the nearby villages. Many of them were sick, perhaps dying, even now. He glanced around the cabin to make sure they were still alone. It seemed like a strange time to approach the subject again, but he couldn't help it.

"Elena ... Ellen. Have you thought any more about my request? About talking to Erik?"

She tensed, pulled her hand free, and wiped her cheeks with both hands. She stood up. "No, Manuel. I won't. I can't. Please don't ask me again."

She whisked away up the stairs before he could stop her.

His hands crunched the rough white towel he held on his lap. He drew in a deep breath and forced the air out through puckered lips. Putting his elbows on his thighs, he dropped his face into his hands. He hated asking her again, upsetting her, but he lay awake nights worrying about the villagers.

He moaned. "God, what do I do now? I have to find a way to stop Warren. Show me how, God. You have to show me how."

Ellen stumbled up the steps to the deck. The boat had slowed; they were nearing the marina. The lights of an ambulance in the parking lot flashed, and two EMTs waited on the *Princess Elizabeth*'s dock with a stretcher and equipment.

The Morgans stood next to the gangplank, arms locked around each other with Taylor in the middle. Other guests talked quietly in small groups around the deck.

Ellen searched for a spot along the railing where she could avoid speaking to anyone. She moved with her head down to a place away from the others. She pretended to watch as the captain maneuvered the boat into place. She couldn't see through her watery eyes, and the activity did not register in her brain.

What could she do about the illegal chemicals? That question had nagged at her for weeks, ever since Manuel had told her about them. Something had to be done, but not by her. Someone else had to stop the killing.

She felt a hand on her back and jumped. She had not heard Erik approach.

"You okay?"

She nodded. She wiped at her wet eyes again and turned to face Erik. She scrambled for an excuse for her smudged face. "I can't believe how close we came to losing Taylor. I hope he's going to be all right."

Erik pulled her close. "The hospital will check him out and make sure there are no lasting effects." He glanced over his shoulder as the boat nudged the dock. "I suppose the fright will take longer to disappear. Maybe he's young enough that he'll forget about it soon."

Leaning against his chest, Ellen brushed her cheek against his shirt. "Can you believe how brave Manuel was? I spoke to him below, and he said he doesn't even swim very well."

She felt Erik bristle. He dropped his arms from around her. "He was just being modest. From what I saw, I'd say he used to be a lifeguard." He didn't wait for a reply. "I'd better see the others off and settle up with the captain. I'll see you back at the car." He whirled and strode away.

Whenever she mentioned Manuel's name, Erik turned into an ice cube. Another reason she couldn't be the one to tell him about Manuel's disclosure.

They couldn't very well arrange another restaurant meeting, but there must be some other way to expose Warren's intentions. But how?

Chapter Forty

Ellen settled cross-legged on the floor of her studio in front of an unfinished piece. Cerro La Cerra, the mountain where she and *Mamá* and Manuel had picnicked when she was little. She started it after the trip to Guatemala in January but had set it aside. She had given up when she couldn't bring her memories to life on the canvas.

A landscape of Lake Harriet on a bright spring day captured her attention. The wind that day had rocked the boats anchored to buoys at the north end of the lake, and the choppy waves crashed up against the retaining wall. She had tried to make the scene realistic. When she finished, she had a rare feeling of satisfaction, that she had finally achieved her goal with a painting. Now she wondered if others who visited the lake regularly might like it. Did she dare make prints of it to try to sell in local gift shops?

She worried that no one would buy them. But what had she told Abigail on the boat? "We should not be afraid to try things." And then Manuel had jumped in the water to save Taylor, without regard for his own safety. Maybe the time had come to act in spite of her fears. Not just with her paintings but with her marriage.

She loved Erik and wished she had not concealed any of her past. Keeping secrets had created a wall between them even though Erik didn't realize it. She longed to tear down that wall. If only she could be sure their marriage would not be crushed against the wall in the process.

The next morning Ellen voiced her thoughts to Manuel while they ran. "I want to tell him the truth, but I'm afraid."

A woman with a spaniel jogged toward them. Manuel waited until she had passed. "Whoever lives by the truth comes into the light."

"What does that mean?"

He shrugged. "Simple. In hiding your past, you have been living in darkness. You cannot see beyond right now. You have no reason to believe in the future." He slowed down, turned, and jogged backward so that he faced her. "It's like me, now. I can't see where I am going. If I am not careful, I will run into a tree or fall down."

She reached out to him, afraid that exact thing would happen.

He turned again. "But if I face the right direction, I have sight. I come into the light, so to speak, and I can see. You have more peace when you can see, yes?"

She glanced at the blue-gray water of the lake surrounded by leafy trees. White sails of a lone yellow-hulled boat glided past, guided by a little girl and a man wearing matching black-and-gold jackets. Had she missed out on the joys of life because of her fear and her secrets? But she had a good life, didn't she?

No. She had been kidding herself. She and Erik spent little time together, and her loneliness involved more than just not having children. "But if I tell him, and he wants a divorce, what will I do?"

Manuel veered around a pothole. "I do not believe he will do that. But if he does, what is the worst that could happen? You have a job. You have your art. You can take care of yourself. But ..."

He seemed reluctant to finish his thought. "What is it?"

she asked.

"You must trust God. He is big enough for you to tell Him that you're hurting, or scared, or angry. Jesus promised that He would never leave or forsake you. He can give you the courage and strength to face whatever happens."

"You truly believe that, don't you?"

"Not only do I believe it, but I experience it every day." He touched her arm as they ran side-by-side. "Do you think it is easy to come here to America knowing no one? To have a position of such responsibility, yet feel like an outsider? I could not do it if I did not have Jesus to show me what to do, how to live."

She hadn't realized that he felt like an outsider, but she could identify. "When I came to America, I didn't know anyone. At least my father and stepmother welcomed me into their home. But God took them away from me. Without Erik, I would have no one now."

"Then you must let God be your father."

A watercolor palette of emotions swirled inside her, the colors of anger, fear, longing, all mixed with a dash of hope, a slim golden ray of sunlight. She wanted to let the light flood in, as Manuel suggested, but too much time had passed.

He must have sensed her turmoil. He stopped by the big oak tree where they typically stretched. "Elena, God is calling to you. Is it not time you answered Him?"

Confusion lodged in her throat. She could do nothing but shake her head.

His face pleaded, and he placed a hand on her shoulder. "Do you mind if I pray for you, at least?"

She didn't answer. He squeezed her shoulder. "Father, I know how much You love Your daughter Elena. She needs to know it, too. I ask You to wrap Your arms around her now. Take away her fear and help her to speak the truth, to reveal the secrets she has buried for so long. As the Psalms say, Lord, let Your love and truth protect my dear cousin."

She blinked away the water in her eyes and mumbled, "I need to get home now, Manuel."

She ran up the hill and crossed the street without checking for traffic.

Erik examined the report from Warren. On paper, the transition after they assumed ownership of the Guatemala plantations had gone smoothly. Why did he have this niggling sense that something wasn't right?

Maybe he could identify the problems if he could keep his mind on the business. But he couldn't stop wondering about Ellen and Manuel.

He had no reason to distrust Manuel. The man had worked hard, and his reports on the plantations before the sale had been detailed and thorough. He had believed Ellen when she told him she and Manuel were just friends. But it bothered him that they ran together twice a week.

Ellen had other running friends, both women and men. Sometimes she ran with one or two, other times with a group. He didn't know why her friendship with Manuel should concern him so much. But they seemed to have a connection that he hadn't felt with Ellen for many months.

He pushed back from the desk and stood, looking around his office. He needed to erase from his mind the pictures of her and Manuel together, laughing, talking. But the images kept returning. They seemed to share many interests, like running and a love of art.

He paced to the window and looked out. Bits of green brightened the cityscape, interspersed with the buildings and roads. He enjoyed this view because he could see the small blue speck that represented Lake Harriet and the slightly larger spot of Lake Calhoun. He wished he could see the house. See what Ellen was doing right now.

Shaking his head, he returned to his desk. He needed to trust her. If he couldn't trust her, they didn't have much of a marriage. He picked up his father's photo.

"What do you think, Dad? Can I trust her?" Silence. He sighed. "Okay, then. What about this plantation business? Maybe you can help me see what I'm missing in these reports."

Manuel's words echoed in Ellen's mind as she ran at full speed back to the mansion. She pushed up the sleeve of her bright blue running jacket and checked her watch.

Good. She had the house to herself. Erik would have already left for work, and Angelica wouldn't come until nine thirty. She wanted to be alone for a while.

Some time back, Manuel had said, "His yoke is easy and His burden is light." She had heard those words before. Perhaps Diane had quoted them, or maybe her father. But today, for the first time, the scripture had seemed to touch something deep in her soul.

Words came to her in her native tongue. Over and over as she ran, creating a melody in her head. *Dios te ama y quiere lo mejor para usted. God loves you and wants the best for you.* She had practiced thinking in English for as long as she had been able to speak the language fluently. Hearing the Spanish words in her head seemed surreal.

She reached the front walkway to her home and bent over to catch her breath. *God loves you, Elena. All He wants is for you to love Him back.*

She stood up and looked around, but the street was empty. She had heard the voice clearly but still not in English.

Mamá. It had to be something her *mamá* used to say. But how could her *mamá* have believed it? Ellen remembered how difficult life had been for them and for the many others who lived around them. People with nowhere else to go moved into the open city garbage dump and built huts around the edge, using whatever scraps they could find. Her *mamá* did whatever she could to earn money for food. Until the day *Mamá* had gone to the small chapel at the mission orphanage. After talking with Papa Thomas for hours, she told Elena that Jesus had changed her. Instead of bringing men to their little one-room shanty, she began scavenging in the garbage dump every day. They had less money, but *Mamá* had been happier. And so had Elena.

But then her *mamá* got sick. Elena sat beside her and cried, begging her to get better. One of the other women who lived in the dump brought soup a few times. But no one they knew had much food to spare. With no money for medicine, Elena had been afraid. When *Mamá* did not improve after a week, Elena began going to the mission chapel every day to pray, but *Mamá* got weaker. Then Elena herself got sick. She recovered, but her *mamá* did not, no matter how hard Elena prayed. After her *mamá* died, Elena begged on the street with Manuel. Even at age ten, she had known that she needed the protection of her older cousin to keep her from a life like *Mamá* had lived before Jesus changed her. In the end, only the letter her *mamá* wrote before she died had saved Elena.

Fighting back tears, Ellen untied the house key from her shoelace and let herself in. The shrill tone of the security system reminded her to shut off the alarm. As she punched in the numbers, her mind protested. *Mamá, Mamá. Why did you have to die?*

She kicked off her shoes, leaving them on the oriental carpet in the middle of the hall, and took the stairs two at a time. By the time she reached the top, she had unzipped her nylon shell. She wrestled out of it and tossed it toward the bedroom door to the right as she continued up to the third floor.

When she reached the closed door of her studio at the end of the hall, she pushed it open. Sunlight had begun to slide across the wood floor. She ignored the half-finished painting of the sunrise that still sat on the easel and the other paintings that leaned against the walls and made her way to the attic access door. She picked up three canvases that leaned against the door and set them off to the side. Her hand on the doorknob, she took a deep breath. She hadn't been in this closet for more than a year.

Chapter Forty-One

Ellen twisted the knob and pulled, but the old door stuck against the jamb. She turned her shoulder to it and bumped hard, hoping to loosen it, and then tugged again on the handle. She kicked the bottom of the door, ignoring the pain that shot through her heel. She pulled again on the knob, and the door jerked free. The caustic odor of mothballs and heat rushed out at her.

Ducking her head to enter the attic, she shivered as cobwebs brushed her face. She pulled the string in front of her and light filled the dusty space. The shelves on three sides housed boxes full of Neilson family treasures—linens, photos, files, collectibles from her in-laws' world travels. She had promised Erik that she would go through them and determine what could be sold or thrown away. But as long as the boxes were stored here, out of the way, she had no need to dig into them.

Where was *her* box? She knelt on all fours on the wooden floor and peered under the grimy shelves. There! In the corner, pushed far out of sight. She lowered her head and shoulders and stretched her arm under the shelf until she could grasp the corner of the shoebox with her fingers.

She maneuvered the box until she could get her hand around the end and pull it out. When she had it exposed, she picked it up reverently, and sitting cross-legged, she cradled it on her lap. The green and red wrapping paper covering the box and lid was torn in places, but she saw the box as it had looked on the day she received it.

Two weeks before Christmas, some men from the United

States had brought hundreds of boxes for children who lived at the garbage dump. Her *mamá,* too sick by then to leave her bed, had given her a letter to take to the Americans.

As she used her fingernail to slice through the brittle, yellowed tape that had held the lid on her box all these years, she could still remember the excitement in the mission church. She and Manuel waited as Papa Thomas and the American men made sure that every child received a shoebox. Elena decided that she must give *Mamá*'s letter to the tall man who appeared to be in charge. Though dressed in black, he looked like no priest Elena had ever seen. His dark hair brushed the collar of his pullover shirt, and his black jeans covered the tops of black cowboy boots.

Through an interpreter, he told the children that boys and girls in America packed the shoeboxes with gifts because they love Jesus. "They want you to know that Jesus loves you, too." Then, speaking Spanish, he called, "*Uno!*" The children joined him, shouting in unison, "*Dos! Tres!*" At that, she pried off the tape and lifted the lid.

There, smiling up at her, lay the most wonderful doll she had ever seen. It had blond hair and blue eyes, and wore a bright red dress and tiny plastic high heels. "Look, Manuel! I'm going to look just like her someday!"

"Good, Elena. I knew you'd get something nice." From his box, he pulled out a shiny aluminum flashlight. He found the switch and turned it on, flinching as the light momentarily blinded him. He pointed it at the ceiling and waved it around the room, following the beam with his eyes as it moved in and out of the sunshine streaming through the windows. A grin spread across his face. "I'll be able to find lots of treasures at night."

Clutching the doll in one hand, she pawed through the other contents of her box. She found a small red rubber ball, red gloves, three pink hair clasps, and a little book with a green cover. She ignored it and reached for the box of colored pencils and a small pad of paper. Setting the doll beside her, she took out a green pencil and turned to the first page. Her very own clean paper to draw on. She began to sketch a tree, bending her head to her work.

Manuel interrupted her. "Elena, didn't your *mamá* give you a letter for the Americans?"

She looked up, worried that she had waited too long. The children chattered and showed their toys to each other. The tall American shook hands with Papa Thomas. Frowning, she looked at her cousin. He nodded. "Hurry. Go wait outside for him."

She put the green pencil back in its box and closed the top. She put the paper and pencils back in the shoebox and laid the doll on top, arranging the delicate red dress. She put the lid in place and, grasping the box of treasures close, she slipped out into the cool day and ran around to the side of the building. The door opened and the visitors came out. She stepped toward them and held out the letter as the tall American strode by.

Mamá had scrawled something on the envelope that she had scavenged from the dump. Taking the letter from her hand, the tall man held it up and studied the writing. He handed it to the short man who had translated for him. They spoke in English while Elena looked from one to the other.

The interpreter spoke to her in Spanish. "You would like the letter delivered to this man?" He pointed to the name on the back of the envelope. "There is no address, just a city and state."

"Yes," she whispered. "Please. For my *mamá*. She is very ill."

"We may not be able to find him. Does your *mamá* know his address?"

She shook her head.

The tall man squatted down and looked her in the eyes. He spoke again, and the short man translated. "He says he will try to find him. He cannot promise, but he will pray and trust God to help him find this man for your *mamá*."

The American gave Elena a warm smile. As he stood up, he reached out to pat her on the head. "*Adios, el niña.*" He said something in English, and his friend repeated it in Spanish. "God bless you."

As they walked away, she whispered, "*Gracias.*" She wondered what *Mamá* had written in the letter.

Chapter Forty-Two

Ellen blew dust off the old box and lifted the tattered lid. She turned it over and saw the long-forgotten writing on the inside of the box top. Several days after they had received the gifts, Manuel had done his best to translate the English words. The message had made her *mamá* smile, but Elena and Manuel had not understood what it meant.

The writing had faded, but she could make out most of the letters. "When you pass through the waters, I will be with you. Isaiah 43:2." The words reminded her of what Diane had told her over the years. How had she put it? "Cast all your cares on Him, for He cares for you." But after her *mamá* died, she had found it impossible to believe that God cared for her. She envied the faith her stepmother and her father possessed, but she never did accept it for herself. When they both died, she had been left alone. The Bible promised that God loved her, so why had she always felt that He had abandoned her?

She set the lid beside her on the floor and stared at the doll with her matted hair and her faded dress. The miniature shoes had been lost a few days after she took the shoebox home. Two buttons on the dress had come off years ago, and her stepmother had replaced them with tiny beads. Gingerly, she lifted the doll and smoothed the wrinkled red skirt then laid the doll on the box lid.

Next she pulled out a small comb and the one remaining pink barrette. The box contained a few other mementos she had collected as she grew. Shells from her first visit to the beach with her dad. A lace handkerchief that had belonged to her stepmother. A torn photo of her *mamá*.

She examined the photo, holding it closer to the bare light bulb in the attic ceiling. As she looked at the black and white photograph, she saw her own narrow face and sharp chin, the same black hair, and dark eyes. She wondered that Manuel hadn't recognized her at once that first day in Erik's office.

"Oh, *Mamá*," she whispered. "I know you believed God loves us. Why can't I believe like you did?"

She rubbed her eyes with the back of her hand, brushing away tears. Even after all these years and miles, she could still remember waking up on her pallet one morning and finding that *Mamá* had stopped breathing. Elena had thrown herself on her *mamá*'s still body and sobbed. Around noon, Manuel had found her motionless, dried tears on her face, with her arms wrapped around her *mamá*. He had gone to the orphanage and brought back Papa Thomas. Manuel had always known what to do.

Placing the photo back in the box, she noticed the little book, the green-covered New Testament. She picked it up and opened it to the first page.

Mamá had loved the book most of all. As Elena had showed her the treasures in the gift box, she had tried to reach for the Bible.

"Here, *Mamá*." Elena placed the green book into her hand on top of the blanket. "This is for you. When I learn to read English, I'll read it to you until you get well enough to read it yourself. Would you like that?"

Mamá smiled, her head inching up and down. *Mamá* had learned to read a little English before Elena was born, and she had begun to teach Elena before she got sick.

"Manuel got one, too. He'll help me learn to read it."

"For God so loved…" *Mamá* took a deep, raspy breath. "You. That He gave His only son…"

"Shhh, *Mamá*. Don't try to talk." Elena set the precious

shoebox on the floor by the bed and pulled out a small booklet with large colorful pictures. "Here. They gave us this, too. It's in Spanish, so I can read it to you. It's about Jesus."

Elena opened the booklet and began reading. A few minutes later, she stopped reading when she saw that *Mamá* slept.

Now, sitting in the attic, tears streaming down her face, Ellen read again in Spanish, "All you have to do is say a prayer like this one."

How many times had she read this booklet to *Mamá* before she died? She and *Mamá* had both memorized it. *Mamá*'s lips would move soundlessly as Elena read.

Mamá had believed. She had known Jesus even before Elena had brought home the booklet and the New Testament. She had trusted God's plan.

"God, why have You always seemed so far away from me? I always blamed You for everything that went wrong. *Mamá* getting sick and dying. I thought it was Your fault that I didn't have a father. Even after I came to America, anytime something didn't go the way I wanted it to, I blamed You."

A tear dripped onto the booklet, and she dabbed at it with the tail of her still-damp running shirt.

Her father and stepmother had insisted that she join them for church. Her father had become a Christian sometime after the year he spent working in Guatemala when he had known her *mamá*.

"God has forgiven me," he told her soon after she came to live with them. "And Anne forgave me for being unfaithful to her. But I regret that I didn't know about you before now. I never had the chance to tell your *mamá* I was sorry for the way I treated her. But I hope you can forgive me."

She did not think *Mamá* had been angry with him, and she hadn't been either. She blamed God, no one else. When she turned sixteen, she begged to stay home on Sunday mornings. "Why should I go to church when I don't believe in God? That just makes me a hypocrite."

Eventually, her father conceded—reluctantly. But he continued to remind her that God loved her and had a plan for her life. She could still hear his voice saying, "I pray that someday, dear Elena, you will learn that for yourself. I will pray this every day for as long as I live."

Neither of them guessed that would be such a short time. The accident that killed him only two years later confirmed for her that God had abandoned her.

Still, the life insurance proceeds were enough to pay for college where she met Erik. Once they married, she had enjoyed luxury and security. Everything she had longed for as a small girl in Guatemala. Maybe her father—and Diane—had been right. Maybe God had taken care of her, even when it didn't seem that way.

She thought of how Manuel had been there to watch out for her after her *mamá* died. "I never realized that You cared, God. I guess You helped the American find my father, didn't You? Just like he said You would." She sucked in her breath and wiped at her nose with the back of her hand. "You sent Diane to be my friend. You gave me a good Dad and stepmom. I had so much more growing up in America than ..."

She knew this to be true, but she didn't want to disrespect her *mamá,* who had struggled to get food and clothing for them and had managed to show Elena she loved her. Life had been difficult, yet she had believed in God. She had found forgiveness and had trusted in Jesus. If *Mamá* had not blamed God for the problems in her life, perhaps Ellen could also stop blaming Him.

"You've been there all along, haven't you, God? Just waiting for me to come to You?" She snuffled and hiccupped.

Now what? She had been wrong about God all these years, but what more did He want from her? Manuel told her God wanted to help her carry her burdens, but what did she have to do?

The prayer. She picked up the booklet and turned to the last page. "OK, God. I want that joy and peace that *Mamá* had, that Diane and Manuel have. I'm tired of trying to do things on my own." She rubbed her eyes and tried to read the blurry words in the booklet. They wouldn't come into focus.

She decided to use her own words. "God, I know I've messed things up. Forgive me for not believing you. Forgive me for all the secrets I've kept and the lies I've told. Come into my life. Jesus, help me to understand and to live the way You want me to." She paused, waiting for something to change. "Amen."

She leaned her head against the wall and sat there, letting the tears cleanse her soul.

"Mrs. Neilson? Mrs. Neilson!" Angelica's distressed voice broke into her consciousness.

"I'm in here, Angelica. In the studio."

"Mrs. Neilson, I've been calling and calling. I was so worried when I saw your clothes all over—" The plump, fifty-ish woman stopped when she saw Ellen sitting on the floor in the attic closet. "You all right?" She knelt beside her.

"Yes, yes, I'm fine. In fact, I think I'm better than I've ever been!" She wiped at her swollen eyes. She knew her face must be streaked red. But an unexplained joy welled up inside her. "I was looking for some of my old things, and I ... I guess I found Jesus. I don't hate God anymore."

"Well, glory be!" Angelica put her arms around Ellen's shoulders and hugged her. "I've been praying for that a long time, no?"

"I didn't know, but I'm not surprised." She began picking up her mementos and putting them back into the box. "I guess I'd better find out what I'm supposed to do now."

Angelica laughed. "You'd better start by taking a shower and getting out of those smelly running clothes!"

Chapter Forty-Three

The skies opened up just before noon, so Erik and Warren jostled through crowds in the skyway on their way to City Center for lunch at Lee Ann Chin.

When they had picked up their food and settled at a table in the little restaurant, Warren surprised Erik by asking about Ellen. "I haven't seen her since the excursion. I thought maybe she'd been hiding."

Erik opened the white cardboard container of rice. "No, she's fine." Actually, he had no idea. Their house seemed more like a library the last few days. She had left to go running this morning before he got up. Last night, business concerns occupied his mind and she had been quiet. Their brief conversation consisted of a polite exchange: "How was your day?"

"Fine. Yours?"

He picked up his chopsticks. He never shared his personal life with Warren, so instead he returned the courtesy. "Rosemary?"

Warren gave a half laugh. "She's being Rosemary. What can I say?"

"Tell me about the plantations in Guatemala."

Warren licked his lips. "What do you want to know? The numbers are all in the last report."

He had read the monthly report. "I want you to tell me what's going on there, Warren. The numbers don't feel right. Expenses are extremely high compared to our other locations."

"It's early still. It's only been a few weeks since we took possession."

"Capital expenses would be higher at the beginning, of course. But not operating expenses. Not that much."

Warren busied himself with chewing a piece of shrimp. He swallowed. "I don't know, Erik. The numbers looked right to me. We had to give Tex a raise to get him to stay, and you wanted to raise the workers' pay, too." He took another bite.

Erik chewed his Kung Pao chicken. He prided himself on knowing the situation at each of the company's facilities. Maybe he had not paid enough attention to the Guatemalan operations.

Warren, who didn't bother with chopsticks, waved his fork at him. "Remember, Morales cleaned out all the materials. Fertilizers, pesticides, even the gasoline for the machinery. It all disappeared right before the closing. We had to replenish everything."

Erik nodded. Morales had been underhanded. He claimed the supplies had been used up in ordinary production. Left just enough that they couldn't prove otherwise. Still, replacing those items would only account for half of the reported expenses. "How is the next harvest shaping up?"

Warren studied his food, attacking the last shrimp with his fork. "Actually, not as good as we had hoped."

"Why not?"

Warren cleared his throat and wiped his mouth with his napkin. "Seems Morales stopped taking care of the plants once we had signed the agreement. Stunted the growth of the fruit. Looks like the crop will be only half as large as it should be." He sipped his water.

"Why didn't we know this before we took over ownership? We could have at least asked for compensation. Where was Tex?"

"Manuel was there. We'll have to ask him." Warren's voice held an unspoken accusation.

"Maybe I should go down to Guatemala with Alan and Manuel to check on operations personally."

Across the table, Warren twisted his napkin. "You know, I haven't trusted Manuel Rivas from the day I met him. Maybe he's taking care of his friends. Why don't I go and check it out first? It may not be necessary for you to get involved just yet."

Erik considered that. Ellen trusted Manuel. Liked him, a little too much. But the man seemed like a straight shooter, and he had saved Taylor Morgan. So why did he have this lingering suspicion about him?

Ellen could hear the joy in Diane's voice when she told her she had prayed to receive Jesus. "I knew God would answer my prayers. I just didn't know how long you would keep running from Him."

Ellen smiled. She had curled up in her favorite chair by the window in the living room. "You make it sound like He was chasing me."

"My pastor likes to say that God chases you until you find Him."

"Hmm. I guess that's what happened." She drew her knees up to her chin, propping her feet on the edge of the chair. "What do I do now that He's caught me?"

Diane's laugh crackled across the phone line. "Now you get to know Him. You read the Bible, find a good Bible-teaching church, spend time alone praying. You talk to God and listen for His voice."

"You make it sound easy. But I don't know where to start." Her mind raced, threatening to drive away the inner glow that had washed over her.

"I won't tell you following Jesus is always easy." Diane

sounded serious now. "But He is always there to help you. Anytime you feel worried or confused, just stop and pray. He'll clear away the confusion and replace it with peace. Hold on a minute."

How did Diane know her thoughts? She heard Diane soothing one of the children. While she waited, she tried following her advice. *Jesus, I don't know how to do this,* she prayed. *I need Your help. Please take away this confusion and help me to follow You.*

Diane returned. "Now, where were we? Oh, I know. Where to start? The Book of John is always a good place to start reading the Bible. And I'll e-mail you some information on finding a church."

"Thanks." Ellen visualized herself, walking alone into a packed Basilica of St. Mary's on Hennepin Avenue with every eye turned on her like at her wedding. She couldn't do that. "Um, Di? How do I tell Erik? You know he's not really keen on religion. What if he can't deal with me becoming a Christian?"

"Who says you have to tell him right away?"

"But I—I can't lie to him about this."

"I'm not suggesting you lie. But nowhere does the Bible say you have to tell everything to everyone. Given Erik's attitude, I think you wait until he notices a difference in how you live. By then, he'll know that it's real, and he'll listen to what you have to say."

"But not saying anything seems, well, dishonest."

"Now you're worried about being dishonest? Jesus really has changed you."

Ellen did not reply.

Diane drew an audible breath. "I'm sorry. That was uncalled for. But listen, in the New Testament, Peter wrote something to wives whose husbands were not believers. Wait, let me find it and read it to you." A minute later she came back on the line. "Here it is. It says, 'they may be won without a word by the conduct of their wives, when they see your respectful and pure conduct.' If Erik asks you why you're different, you don't lie to him. But there's no need to tell him until the time seems right. Pray about it, and God will let you know the right thing to do or say."

Ellen tried another quick, unspoken prayer asking God to take away her negative thoughts, and the peaceful feeling returned.

She spent a few more minutes asking questions but realized that she had kept Diane from teaching the children their lessons. She promised to call again in a few days.

After hanging up the phone, she picked up the New Testament she had laid on the side table. She thumbed through the book until she found the first page of the Gospel of John and started reading.

Chapter Forty-Four

Ellen pulled a brush through her hair as Erik entered the bedroom that evening. He came up behind her and began to rub her upper arms. "I just talked to Bruce Morgan."

Ellen held her breath and waited for him to continue.

"Taylor saw the doctor again today. They poked and prodded and ran a bunch of tests, but they didn't find any damage. They want to see him again in a month just to be sure. Bruce and Kelly are overjoyed."

Ellen let out her breath and smiled. "That's wonderful. Thank God!"

"Do you really think He had something to do with it?" His light tone lacked the sarcasm of his usual comments about religion.

"Yes, I do. I think God had everything to do with saving Taylor." She caught his eyes in the mirror. "What do you think, Erik?"

"I thought you didn't believe in God."

"I do believe in God. I've been mad at Him because it seemed like He took away everything I had that was good." She waited. How much should she tell him? "But I've decided to give Him a chance to prove me wrong."

After a full minute, he removed his arms from her shoulders and started to unbutton his shirt. "I'm not sure you were wrong."

Other than their wedding and his parents' funeral, Erik avoided church. That had suited her just fine, until now. Now she hoped to find a church they could attend together. But that discussion would have to wait.

Erik removed his shirt and tossed it in the hamper. "Well, whether it was God or just luck, we should find a way to thank Manuel for saving Taylor."

She put down her hairbrush and stood up. "You're right. That's a—" She started to say "wonderful," but she didn't want to sound too thrilled when it came to Manuel. "It's a good idea." She went into her closet and began undressing.

"Why don't we throw him a surprise party?" she called out over the sound of water running in the bathroom. "He wouldn't—he doesn't seem like the type who would want a big fuss, but if we surprise him, he can't get out of it."

Erik came out of the bathroom, toothbrush in his mouth. He took the brush out of his mouth and tilted his head back to keep the toothpaste from dripping. "Okay, we could do that. Do you want to have it here?"

Ellen pulled her nightgown over her head. "Sure. I'll talk to Kelly to find a date that suits them and ask Angelica about the food. I wonder what kind of food says, 'Thanks for saving a life.'"

Erik looked up as Marcie opened the door to his office.

"Sorry to disturb you, Mr. Neilson." Her face looked tight. "I know you're busy, but—"

"It's fine, Marcie." He motioned to a chair. "You never interrupt unless it's important. Besides, I can use a break." He leaned back in his chair, stretched, and reached up to rub the back of his neck with his right hand.

Marcie sat on the edge of the guest chair and pulled it closer to the desk. She held a white envelope in her hand but did not extend it to him. Not good. She could not resign. He would never find a suitable replacement.

He put his arms on the desk and assessed her. "Is there a problem?"

She licked her lips, looked down at the envelope, and then looked in his eyes. "No, sir. No problem. But I found something that I think you need to see."

He nodded. She had discovered something that distressed her. Not wanting to upset her further, he tried to gentle his voice. "What is it?"

She adjusted herself in the chair and squared her shoulders. "You remember when your parents—um, after the plane crash, how we had to get this office ready for you quickly?"

Not something he could forget. It had been four years, and he still could not block out the memories of that day. His father and mother were returning from a week's vacation. His dad had loved to fly, so he was piloting the King Air Ninety when they encountered a severe thunderstorm over Iowa. The authorities determined that "adverse weather conditions, including turbulence—and failure of the airplane's primary attitude indicator—led to the pilot's subsequent loss of control." When the officials released the report several months later, those words had blazed themselves into Erik's mind. He preferred to forget them, but like gum on a shoe, they remained glued to some lobe in his brain.

He thought it ironic that the report blamed the attitude indicator, the instrument that showed how level the plane flew. His father always seemed to maintain his balance more than anyone. And without him, Erik felt as though his world had tilted.

He had not wanted to use his father's office, or even to become president, but his father's close friends on the board had insisted. "The company needs to show strength and continuity," one advisor had explained. "Our customers and trade partners will expect you to take over."

Two days after burying both parents, he forced himself to act the role of president. Marcie, his father's secretary of many years, had immediately transferred her loyalty to him. She had cleaned his father's office and moved Erik's things into it while he took a few days off for the funeral.

Her voice cracked. "I packed some of his loose papers in a box and put them in the storeroom down the hall. I'm really sorry, but things were so crazy in the weeks after that I totally forgot about that box."

She tapped the edge of the envelope on the arm of her chair. "I came across the box this morning and decided to go through it to see what needed to be filed and what could be tossed. After all this time ..."

Erik became concerned. Papers on his father's desk could have been vital documents—or notes of no consequence. "You found something important—related to the company?"

She shook her head. "Not related to the company. Just to you." She handed the envelope across the desk. "This has your name on it—in your father's handwriting. It's sealed. The fact that he wrote it himself, instead of dictating it to me, tells me that he considered it important. And private."

He stared at the business-size envelope. His father had not been a letter writer other than official correspondence. He reached out and took the envelope with two fingers, laid it on the desk in front of him, and studied the writing. One word. "Erik."

Marcie cleared her throat. "I apologize for missing it when I packed up his things. And for not finding it until now." He hardly noticed that she stood. "I'll leave you alone to read it."

He did not know how long he sat there, eyes focused on the rectangle in front of him, yet seeing images of his father as if on a movie screen. His dad showing him how to pitch a baseball when Erik was about seven. His fifteenth birthday when the two of them had flown in the King and Dad had let him take the controls for about three minutes. His summer internships with the company, learning the intricacies of growing and marketing fruits and vegetables on a large scale. College graduation, when his father had arrived just as the processional started and slipped out as soon as Erik received his diploma. Always eager to return to the office. His father's warm reception of Ellen when Erik first brought her home for Thanksgiving dinner.

With each memory, good or not so good, his hopes rose or fell. This letter could resolve some of his doubts, or it could leave him devoid of answers once and for all. Maybe there was no letter at all but only a note regarding some business project. But his dad would not have handwritten and sealed that.

He turned the envelope over and reached for the gold-plated letter opener that his mother had given to his father. He unfolded the single sheet of paper and struggled to read the scrawled writing covering both sides.

Son,

As your fifth official anniversary with Neilson Enterprises approaches, I wanted to write a personal note of congratulations.

In a few years, you will take over the company so that I can retire. I have tried not to control your life or tell you what to do, but it pleases me that you have decided to join the business that your great-grandfather founded.

Though we are now an international corporation, I hope that family will continue to be a basic foundation for our operations. I have always considered employees like family, but in the process, I forgot how to treat my own family. I hope you and your mother will forgive me. Perhaps it is too late for this old dog to change, but I intend to try. That is why I am taking your mother on this trip—our first real vacation in a long time. I will be asking you to do more so that I can spend time with her as we near our "golden years," but I do not want you to repeat my mistakes.

You have chosen a lovely wife in Ellen. She is intelligent and talented, and she loves you. Do not let your work consume you, as I did. Treasure her.

I don't believe I have ever told you how proud I am of you. You have always worked hard and applied yourself to every task, whether school or sports, or now, your duties in the company. You have become a fine man. I give your mother the credit for that, since I was rarely around to show you the way. I spent too much time building the business, trying to provide for my family, when I should have been spending time with my wife and son.

Take time to nurture your marriage and to love your children (I do expect you to give me grandchildren some day).

I love you, son. I am, and have always been, proud of you.

Dad

Erik closed his eyes and used one finger to push back the single tear that threatened to escape. He missed his father more than ever.

"I am proud of you," the letter said. All these years, Erik had assumed his father did not love him or that he felt ashamed of him. To earn his respect, he had tried to act like his father, made decisions based on what he thought his father would do.

He stood and crossed to the bookcase, where he picked up the baseball he kept there. He would need time to comprehend this different side of his father. Four years after his death, Dad had finally given him advice. Advice he had longed for his entire life but never received.

He rolled the ball in his hands, stroked the red stitching on the white leather surface. Habits had become ingrained in the last four years. He had woven a tight pattern to his life, mostly wrapping it with work as yarn wrapped the cork center of the ball. Once, playing on the high school team, he had picked up a baseball that had split and fallen apart, creating a tangled mess. He could not allow his well-ordered life to unravel that way. His father's advice may have come too late.

He carefully placed the ball back on its holder and returned to the desk. He picked up the letter, glanced over it again, then folded the paper, inserted it back into the envelope, and stuck the envelope into his top desk drawer.

Chapter Forty-Five

Warren reported to Erik's office for their weekly meeting.

"Your trip to Guatemala is in two weeks, right?" Erik asked.

Warren looked forward to this trip. He would be able to check on Tex and make sure the man had been following instructions. He'd been pleased to see cash flowing into his secret new offshore bank account. Already more than fifty thousand. But that didn't mean Tex wouldn't try to cheat him. "Right. I'll find out what Manuel was up to while he was there."

Erik frowned. "If anything. We don't know that he was up to anything."

"Of course not. But if he was, I'll find out."

"Look, I know you don't trust him. But I don't want you going with a preconceived idea. It's too easy to see something that's not there. I've done that myself recently."

Warren nodded, even though he didn't know what Erik meant. "I understand. Anything else?"

Erik handed him a folder. "Yes, I want to know how you think the company should honor someone who has shown outstanding service."

Warren kept his face impassive but his chest expanded. About time Erik recognized all he had done for this company. The sacrifices he'd made, staying here instead of going over to Target or somewhere else. He sat up straighter, adjusted his tie.

"Sure. Let's see. A substantial bonus, of course. Maybe a plaque." A company car came to mind, but he didn't want to seem too greedy. "How about a preferred parking space with his name on it?"

Erik jotted notes on a legal pad. "Good. Ellen and I thought we could host a dinner in his honor, too."

Warren remembered the holiday party when all the managers and spouses were gathered around the table. He imagined himself as the center of attention, standing and making a speech. Everyone smiling and applauding. "I like it. I should have thought of that."

"Does this Saturday work for you and Rosemary?"

When he nodded, Erik made another note on his list. "We'll do everything you suggested."

Warren stood and stretched.

"On your way out, talk to Marcie about the details, would you?"

He smiled. Odd to be preparing his own recognition, but he didn't really mind. He moved to the door and reached for the handle.

"Warren, let's make it a surprise. We'll make him think it's a small dinner party, just the five of us."

The blood left his face. He turned to face Erik. "A surprise? Who are we surprising?"

"Manuel. We're rewarding him for saving Taylor's life. Who else would it be?"

Warren didn't stop to talk with Marcie. He would have to give her instructions about the ridiculous "awards" for Manuel. But it could wait a few hours.

He stopped the elevator one floor down and stormed into his office. He grabbed his briefcase and slammed his office door shut. His secretary jumped out of her chair. "Sir?"

"I'm going out for a while," he said. "I need to go visit my mother. Should be back mid-afternoon." She didn't need to know an exact time. And he didn't want to commit to a particular time.

"Yes, sir. If something comes up, should I call you?"

"It'll wait 'til I get back." He punched the elevator button again. He just got off it. Where had it gone? He had to get away.

Thirty minutes later he sat with his mother in the lounge area at the convalescent center. The huge-screen television on the other side of the room blared some soap opera. Why couldn't they turn the blasted thing off when no one was watching? He wanted to storm over and turn it off himself.

His mother patted his hand. "It's such a pleasant surprise to see you in the middle of the day, dear."

"I had to come see you, Mom. I have news."

Her sunken cheeks dimpled and looked almost normal when she smiled. Her eyes lit up with pride. Like when he graduated with honors from the U of M. "That's wonderful, dear. Did you find a job?"

He swallowed hard. "No, Mom. I have a job. At Neilson Enterprises, remember?"

"Oh, that's right." She shook her head. "I get mixed up sometimes. You run the company. I don't know how I could forget that."

He did run the company, practically. Just didn't have the title. He didn't correct her.

"Mom, I'm getting an award from the company. It will mean a bonus and a big presentation dinner." She would never know the difference. He would make up a phony certificate and frame it. To make her proud. "I'll bring in the certificate afterwards and show you."

She reached over and pinched his cheek with her bony fingers. "Why, aren't you good? You're always so thoughtful to include me in these things. You must be excited."

Excitement did not describe what he felt. Irritated perhaps. Cheated. Deceived. Manuel would get the rewards he should have. But his mother did not know. Would never know. "Yes, Mom. And I wanted you to know right away. I haven't even told Rosemary yet."

"How is she?" Her voice lost its warmth. The two women had never liked each other. "Is she coming to visit me?" Rosemary hated to visit here and had been only once in the past year—at Christmas. But Mom loved company. Any company.

"Of course, she will, Mom. She'll be coming soon."

His mother nodded. "Good, good." She sat, holding his hand and rocking in her chair for several minutes. Her eyes closed and her head drooped toward her chest. She jerked it upright and blinked. "Is it time for breakfast yet?"

Chapter Forty-Six

Ellen tried to focus on the page in front of her. She had been thinking about Taylor, Tyrone, and Donato all afternoon. She began to read Psalm 113:

Who is like the Lord our God, who is seated on high, who looks far down on the heavens and the earth?

She rejoiced with the writer over God's goodness, and continued reading.

He raises the poor from the dust and lifts the needy from the ash heap, to make them sit with princes, with the princes of his people.

She thought of how God had delivered her from poverty, literally from the burning garbage dump. She read the next words:

He gives the barren woman a home, making her the joyous mother of children. Praise the Lord!

She gasped and slammed the book shut. She stood and paced around the bedroom. The word wounded her. Barren. She was barren and would never be "a joyous mother of children."

How could she praise God when she wanted children so much, yet couldn't have any? Everywhere she went, she saw wonderful children. Tyrone. Lateesha. Little Salvador. Donato.

Her heart twisted. Why couldn't she have just one?

She stopped next to the bed and fell to her knees, tears streaming down her cheeks.

"Why, God? Erik and I would make good parents, wouldn't we?"

She remembered her stepmother telling her about an infertile woman in the Bible. How God healed her and gave her a child. That's what she would pray for.

"All right, God. I'm asking You for a miracle." That would persuade Erik that God is real. "I'm asking You to give me a child, to heal me so I can get pregnant. Please, God?"

The last words came out as a moan, and she sat there, resting her head on her arms on the bed as her body shook. The tears began to subside as her heaves gradually took on a soothing rhythm. Finally her sore eyes closed, she settled into a sitting position, and she dozed with one wet cheek against the bedspread.

"Mr. Neilson, is something wrong?" Marcie perched in the chair in front of Erik's desk waiting for instructions. He had called her in to talk about the headquarters employee picnic in the fall. But he had not spoken for several minutes. His mind had wandered back to Warren's comments about not trusting Manuel.

"Yes, Marcie, something is wrong. I just don't know what."

"Would you like to talk about it?" Marcie listened when he wanted to talk, but she didn't pry. And she was always discreet.

He ran a hand through his short-cropped hair. "I feel like I'm losing control."

She waited. No judgment showed on her face.

"Ellen and I have scarcely talked since the boat trip." Where did that come from? He thought the Guatemala financial statement was his biggest concern.

"Did you have an argument?"

He leaned back in his chair. "That's just it. Things were rough for a while after our trip to Guatemala, but lately things seemed to be improving. But since the E-team boat trip, she's just not talking to me much. I—I wonder if she's seeing somebody."

Marcie uncrossed her legs and leaned forward, peering at his face. "Mr. Neilson, can I be perfectly honest?"

"Of course."

She cleared her throat. "When was the last time you dated her?"

Dated her? They hadn't dated since before they married. "What do you mean?"

"Well, Mr. Neilson." She never used his first name, and it made him feel old. She sat up straight and smiled. "Women like to be courted. Even after we're married. We like romance. We like our man to pay attention to us. I think you ..." She stopped.

He motioned to her. "Go on. Tell me what you think."

She shifted in her chair and grimaced. "I think you're acting too much like your father: working long hours, not spending enough time with Ellen. And when you're together, do you listen to her—really listen?"

His heart beat faster. He exploded from his chair and walked to the window. She was his secretary. She had no right to talk to him like this.

Yes, she did. He had asked for her opinion. And she had nailed it.

He had taken Ellen for granted. Treated her like a prized

poodle. Someone to pet and pamper, to show off, but to ignore when he had no time for her. He certainly hadn't treasured her as his father's letter had urged. No wonder she would have an affair.

He turned back to Marcie. "How do I fix it?"

"Well, sir. You plan a romantic evening. Wine and dine her, so to speak. And you start by asking her forgiveness."

He moved to the bookshelf and picked up his baseball. Could he really ask Ellen to forgive him? What could he do to earn her forgiveness?

"Thank you, Marcie." He dismissed her with a wave of his hand. "Make the arrangements for the picnic. I'll think about your suggestions."

Chapter Forty-Seven

Ellen inhaled the fragrance of the lilacs blooming behind the bench where she waited for Manuel Thursday morning. The morning smelled fresh and new. She couldn't wait to tell him that she had made up with God.

He strode toward her, but he was not jogging like he usually did. And he wore dress pants and a shirt instead of his running clothes.

He carried a large manila envelope and her heart caught in her throat. He would want her to give it to Erik. "You're not running today?"

"Not until I show you what I have. I believe there is enough to convince Erik that Tex, Alan, and Warren are all involved in using illegal pesticides. And I hope to convince you to tell him about it."

Her arm felt like a fifty-pound weight as she reached for the envelope. How could she explain that Jesus had changed her, yet had changed nothing between her and Erik? "I'll look at it, but it's too soon to talk to Erik. I need more time. Our relationship is improving, but if I tell him now—"

"Look at the pictures, please. Every day we delay means more suffering for our people."

Her fingers quivered as she opened the metal clasp and slid the contents from the envelope. She glanced at the printed report. Manuel jittered as she shuffled the papers until she got to the enlarged photos.

The first photo showed pesticide containers, with a small Mayan crouched beside them. Manuel pointed. "That's Felipe, the man who helped me after I sprained my ankle. He lost part of his arm because of cancer on his hand that did not get treated."

She flipped to the next picture, two men about Manuel's age standing in front of a tiny stucco building. "Julio and Diego," he said. "They are so sick they can no longer work."

She nodded and turned to the next image. A small girl sat on bare ground, her eyes reflecting her smile, her thin legs stuck out in front of her. Ellen sank to the seat of the park bench.

Manuel sat beside her. "Isabella. She's five years old, but she can't walk. Her mother worked in the processing plant while she was pregnant, and Isabella's bones did not develop properly." With one hand on her belly, Ellen stared at the child for several minutes. This girl looked so much like she had at that age, they could be cousins. Rage rose in her throat, and she feared she would retch.

Manuel reached over and pulled the next photo from the stack, placing it on top. Three women, younger than her. "These women cannot have babies, Elena. Like you."

She massaged her stomach. "Because of the pesticides?"

"*Si*, I believe so. They worked in the processing plant, cleaning the fruit and packing it for shipment. I could find no other explanation."

As if she were moving through water, she stacked the papers and photos and stuffed them back into the envelope. She handed the package back to him, saying nothing.

He rose and paced a few steps, turned and stood in front of her, his free hand out in supplication. "Elena, please. Don't you see? We must tell Erik as soon as possible."

"I'll do it." How could she stay silent and allow these people to go on suffering?

"You'll do what?"

"I'll tell Erik you're my cousin. I'll tell him about being

part Mayan, about living on the streets, about my mother. I'll tell him about the chemicals and that my family came from this village—everything."

He bent to embrace her. "Praise God. Praise God." He pulled back, his face searching hers. "You are no longer afraid of losing your husband and your safety net?"

"I'm terrified. But ..." Her voice cracked. "Those people in Guatemala—our people—how can I sit in my beautiful house, wear designer clothes, enjoying this life I have, this life that God has given me, while they're being poisoned? When I can do something about it."

He perched next to her again. "What did you say?"

She cast a sideways glance at him, and smiled. "I said that God has given me this wonderful life. I am no longer angry at Him."

He began to laugh. He hugged her again, squeezing her until she also began laughing. "Tell me what has happened," he said.

"My friend Diane says that God chased me until I found Him. I have become a follower of Jesus."

"But how? When?"

"First, you saved Taylor. You overcame your fear and did what needed to be done. And God was faithful. He has always been faithful. I know that now."

For the next few minutes, she explained how their last conversation had affected her. She told him about the shoebox where she had hidden her most prized possessions, the objects that had helped her to realize how God had always cared for her. Even when she had wanted nothing to do with Him.

They both stood and began walking. A woman ran by leading a furry Samoyed puppy that barked at them.

"You once told me about Queen Esther. What was it she said? 'If I perish, I perish.'" She stopped, and so did he. "If I don't do this, Manuel, I might as well perish. I would be no better than Warren if I know about this situation and do nothing."

She stopped to pick up a discarded plastic cup lying in the grass by the path. "Erik will be shocked and hurt that I haven't been truthful with him. If he chooses to divorce me, I can't blame him. But God is God. Even if I lose everything, I will still have Him."

"I'm proud of you. Your decision will make God smile." They walked in silence for a few minutes. "Do you want to take the package with you?"

They reached the corner of the lake, where the trail turned east. She dropped the cup in a trash barrel as they passed. "No, I think you should bring it—oh, dear. I haven't told you yet. We're giving you a surprise party."

"What?" He stopped. "Me? Why would you do that?"

She turned to him. "To thank you for saving Taylor's life. It's this Saturday night. You think you're just coming to dinner, but the whole group will be there."

"No, I don't want a party. I don't need any thanks. Just knowing he's alive is—"

"I thought you'd say that. But don't you see? It's the perfect opportunity. Somehow, by the time the evening is over, we will find a way to give this information to Erik. I pray he will believe us—and do something."

She smiled at him, and she knew the smile radiated from her heart. "So you'll come. And you'd better act surprised."

Chapter Forty-Eight

The afternoon of the party, Ellen retreated to her studio with her Bible. She didn't know what passage to read, but she knew she needed the comfort that God would offer her through these pages.

"Oh, Jesus," she prayed. "I don't know what's going to happen tonight. I need your strength to go through with this."

Once she told Erik her story, she would be at his mercy. If he chose to divorce her, she wouldn't contest it. After all, she had misled him. But she couldn't continue the deception. Her life had been a sham, and the time had come to reveal the truth.

Still, the uncertainty frightened her. She had few resources if she had to move out. Her friends were mostly Erik's friends, too. Would any of them help her?

Diane would. But she couldn't impose on her and Mike. She took a deep breath. She would use the tools God had given her. Geri wanted to hold an exhibit of her paintings at the Walker. Maybe she could sell enough to start over—

But she had jumped ahead of herself. First, she had to find an opportunity this evening to tell Erik the truth.

She flipped open her Bible. She had been reading through the Psalms and had found that they dealt with the same problems she faced. She turned to the 102nd chapter:

"A Prayer of one afflicted, when he is faint and pours out his complaint before the Lord. Hear my prayer, O Lord; let my cry come to You! Do not hide Your face from me in the day of my distress! Incline Your ear to me; answer me speedily in the day when I call! For my days pass away like smoke, and my bones burn like a furnace."

The words expressed her feelings today with precision. Her troubles threatened to overwhelm her. After tonight, the life she had known with Erik could be gone forever. He might not forgive her for deceiving him. But no matter what happened, she had no choice. The lives of the plantation workers and the villagers of Río Limpio might depend on the outcome of this evening.

She slipped to her knees and turned to put her hands on the chair. "Dear God, my life is about to disintegrate like smoke. I know that You love me and that You've always been with me, even when I didn't know You were there. I'm asking You to hear me now, like the scripture says. Give me the right words to speak to Erik. And show him the truth of what Manuel has to tell him. Help Erik to make the right decision with the information we give him."

Chapter Forty-Nine

Warren punched the doorbell of the Neilsons' home with one finger. Their house might be historic and have a great view of Lake Harriet, but he preferred his mansion with two hundred feet of lakefront in a prestigious area of Long Lake. Erik didn't understand the importance of demonstrating his prestige and power.

Rosemary leaned her head against his shoulder. She had started drinking an hour earlier. "It was so thoughtful of them to plan this party for Manuel, don't you think?"

He turned his face away from the stench of her breath. The door opened. "Straighten up, Rosemary. Don't embarrass me."

Ellen showed them into the living room where the others had already gathered.

Rosemary teetered on her stiletto heels toward the sideboard and poured herself a glass of vodka.

Warren went to stand next to Alan near the wall. "What a dog and pony show," he muttered. He could feel the envelope with Manuel's check in his jacket pocket, searing through to his skin. He did not want to make the presentation, but Erik had insisted. Maybe he could salvage part of the evening, if he could get a few minutes alone with Ellen. With what he now knew about her background, he could make sure that she and Manuel kept their noses out of his business.

The doorbell rang. "Shhh!" Rosemary flapped both hands to make her point. She had already downed her drink. "Here he comes. We're going to surprise him now. We have to be quiet." She giggled and lowered her voice to a stage whisper. "We have to be quiet."

Ellen headed for the front door, sliding the paneled door closed behind her. Erik turned off the light.

After a few minutes, muted voices filtered in from the foyer. The door opened as Ellen said, "Erik's in here."

Erik hit the light switch, and the others—even Alan—called out, "Surprise!"

Manuel stepped back, confusion on his face. "No, no. It's not my birthday. Why would you do this for me?"

Rosemary moved to him and threw one arm around him. "You're a hero, Manny, don't you know that?"

Most of the group gathered around, patted Manuel on the back, and murmured congratulations. From his position leaning against the wall, Warren said, "Sure, we're so proud of you."

After dinner, Erik stood and held up his wine glass. "Manuel, I know I speak for Bruce and Kelly when I say there is nothing that can adequately repay you for your courage and selflessness in saving their son."

The Morgans both nodded. Warren thought he would vomit. To hide his discomfort, he picked up his own glass.

"Your actions represent the selflessness and courage that my father admired," Erik said. "He built Neilson Enterprises on such character values, and I want to make sure that our company continues to honor employees who embody these qualities. So here's to you, Manuel Rivas." Erik raised his glass, and the others followed. Warren touched his glass to his lips but set it down without tasting the wine. Next to him, Rosemary gulped hers.

Manuel looked at his plate, color rising in his face. He pushed back from the table and started to stand. "Thank you, but—"

Erik lifted a hand and smiled. "You can make a speech in a moment, Manuel." Manuel slid back into his seat. "First, we have a little presentation for you. Warren, go ahead."

He felt strangled. This party should have been for him. He had to make this presentation, but he didn't have to enjoy it. He rose and pulled the envelope from his inner pocket. Unsmiling, he looked around the table and cleared his throat. Manuel did not look at him, but everyone else watched, no doubt anticipating a great speech.

"Erik asked me several days ago what I thought the company should do for someone who deserved recognition for going above and beyond." He looked down at the table. Rosemary reached out and patted his arm. She knew how upset he had been about this honor for Manuel instead of him. He didn't want her pity, so he shifted away from her touch. She dropped her hand, picked up her glass, and drained the last drop of wine from it.

"I told Erik that such an employee should be given a special parking place, a plaque, and a sizable bonus. The sign was installed this afternoon so you can park in your special space beginning next week." He reached down and picked up a bag from the floor by his chair. He pulled out the wooden plaque and held it so everyone could see the brass plate as he read the inscription. "In recognition of your remarkable service to Neilson Enterprises."

He paused. "Manuel." He added extra emphasis to the name and handed the plaque and the envelope across the table. "I guess it's true that a good deed never goes unpunished. I'm sure this won't be the last time that you go above and beyond the call of duty."

He dropped into his chair. He had stunned the gathering. But he didn't care what they thought.

Kelly and Bruce began to clap. One by one, the others joined in. Manuel stood, shaking his head, and the applause grew in enthusiasm. Warren glared down the table at Alan, who dropped his hands.

Manuel raised a hand. "Thank you." He paused until the clapping stopped. "Thank you. I am humbled by your generosity. I do not deserve any of this. I only did what I could. God gave me the courage and He saved the little boy. I am just His instrument. The Lord deserves all the glory." He sat down.

As the applause started again, Warren leaned over to Rosemary and whispered, "I suppose he'll give all the money to God." Rosemary tittered, but she kept clapping and smiling at Manuel. Warren put his hands together precisely three times.

Chapter Fifty

As Ellen and Erik said good-bye to their guests, her stomach tightened. Her ears flushed with warmth, and her tongue seemed to grow fur. She had promised Manuel—and herself—to tell Erik everything before the evening ended.

Erik would hate her when he found out she had lied to him. That she had pretended to be someone else. Why hadn't she told him the truth from the beginning?

She felt as she had twenty years ago, the day she boarded the airplane to leave Guatemala. She couldn't wait to leave the place where she had felt so hopeless, but she had no idea what lay ahead for her. What her father would be like. Whether his wife would accept her. How long it would take her to learn English. She never again wanted to be poor. Or alone.

Now she faced similar uncertainty. How would she support herself? She would be alone again.

No. She wouldn't be alone. She had reconnected with Manuel. And she had Jesus. But that didn't take away the twisting inside her. She wanted to run away. Yet she had promised. No more secrets. The time had come. She imagined stepping once again onto the airplane that would begin her new life, whatever it might be.

As Manuel prepared to leave, he asked Erik, "Are you pleased with the way things are going at the plantations in Guatemala?"

Standing next to Erik, she felt her heart beat faster. They had arranged this as her cue to give Erik the report. But she couldn't do it with Warren still here. Manuel looked at her, and her face heated up. She looked away.

Before Erik could speak, Warren answered. "It's too soon to show a profit. We have to give it time."

He had an answer for everything. His plans might be working, but that would change. She should speak up. She moved toward the hall tree where she had stashed the envelope containing Manuel's report.

No. She needed to wait until Warren left. He would bluster, try to convince Erik to ignore the situation.

Children were dying. She had to make sure Erik understood that.

She stepped back to the group to say good-bye to Manuel. She met his eyes and, without speaking, tried to convey to him that she would follow through.

Erik let Manuel out and closed the door. "Warren, I have some papers in my office I want you to look over. Can you wait a few minutes while I get them?"

Warren agreed, and Rosemary said, "I need to use the little girls' room." She stumbled down the hall behind Erik. Ellen could not stay in the hall with Warren, so she went into the living room and began to pick up glasses from the tables.

She heard the soft sound of the sliding door closing and whirled around. Warren had followed her. He stood there watching her with an odd expression. "What's wrong, Ellen? You're not afraid to be alone with me, are you?" He walked toward her.

Alarm bells rang in her head. She had heard that tone before. Only this time the words were in English. She stepped backward and bumped into the coffee table. He reached her in time to grasp her arm and put a hand on her back to help her recover her balance.

He kept his hands on her and smirked. "There, you see. You can trust me. I'll make sure no harm comes to you." Something about his manner implied an unspoken condition.

"What do you mean?" Her voice croaked. "Why would I be worried?"

"You tell me, *Elena*." He licked his lips.

Her body went cold. He knew her birth name. She tried to move away from him, but his grip on her arm tightened. One hand stroked her back as if she were a cat.

"That's right. I know all about you. You and Manuel are cousins. You lived in the slums of Guatemala. Erik doesn't know any of it, does he?"

She couldn't let him smell her fear, couldn't let him see the truth in her eyes. She turned her face away.

"You know he wouldn't keep you around if he found out, don't you? And you're afraid of losing this Cinderella life you've found." His voice softened, but it insinuated something other than reassurance. "It will be our little secret. All you have to do is cooperate."

She whipped her head around. "Cooperate? With what?"

His hand on her back pulled her close. He released her arm and reached up to caress her cheek. "I think you know what I want. I'll call you. You're not so different from your mother, after all."

Her stomach turned and her face flushed. She struggled against his embrace. He leaned his face close to kiss her, but she managed to get one hand to his cheek. She scratched, and Warren stepped back, howling.

The door slid open with a bang. Erik appeared in the doorway, his stance like a restrained bulldog. "What's going on here?"

Behind him, Rosemary looked from Warren to Ellen, her eyes narrowed, her bottom lip stuck between her teeth.

Ellen collapsed onto the couch. She couldn't hold back the tears.

Warren held his hand to his face. "She scratched me. She

tried to kiss me, and when I wouldn't, she scratched me."

She began to shiver and shook her head. She kept her eyes on Erik's face. "I—He—" She couldn't get the words out.

Erik reached her in two long strides and sat beside her. "Ellen." His voice caressed her as he put an arm around her. "Take a deep breath, and tell me what happened."

She followed his instructions and she calmed a little. "He followed me. In here." She gulped in air and leaned into Erik. "He—he grabbed me and threatened me. *He* tried to kiss *me*." She buried her face against his shoulder.

Warren huffed and crossed his arms. "Oh, come on, Erik. Do you really think I'd be stupid enough to make a play for your wife in your own house? She probably only married you for your money. There are things you don't know about her—"

Erik's quiet voice cut him off. "I don't want to hear you or see you right now. Go home. Get out of my house."

"But, but—surely you don't believe—"

Erik kept his arm tight around Ellen's shoulder, but she felt him turn to look at Warren. "I said go home. We'll talk about this in the office. Monday."

"We certainly will. I'll tell you everything. And you'll wish you had listened to me."

Chapter Fifty-One

Erik wrapped his arms around Ellen as she sat on the sofa and sobbed. She had never cried like this before. A torrent of tears and terror seemed to be pouring out, finding escape.

He didn't know what to do for her, but he didn't let go. He pulled out his handkerchief and handed it to her.

"I—I'm so sorry." She hiccupped. "I should have told you."

Should have told him what? Had Warren tried something before tonight? Or ... had there been others, Manuel perhaps? But this tension he felt in her weeping seemed to come from somewhere deeper, from some ancient chasm in her soul.

Her weeping slowed to sniveling. She took several deep breaths and sat up straight. She wiped her eyes and blew her nose.

He squeezed her shoulder and released it. "I'll get you some coffee."

She swallowed hard and shook her head. "Angelica left an hour ago. I'll have to make it."

She started to stand, but he pushed her back down gently. "Stay here and relax. I know how to make a pot of coffee."

In the kitchen, his mind whirled as he poured water into the coffeemaker, found the filter and coffee, and flipped the switch. Warren must be having a mental breakdown. He had acted odd all evening, practically insulting Manuel when he should have been honoring him. But to make a pass at Ellen right under his nose? Surely, he didn't think Erik would tolerate that kind of insult.

But what was Ellen's part? Was she as innocent as she claimed? Warren had said there were things he didn't know. Apparently he was about to find out.

He poured coffee into two cups and carried them through the dining room into the living room. Ellen stepped through the door from the hallway carrying a large manila envelope. His eyes searched her face. "What's that?" He set the cups on the table in front of the couch, and they sat down.

She handed the packet to him. "It is very important that you look at this, that you read every word."

He frowned. "That sounds serious."

She nodded. "It's from Manuel. Before you open it, I have to tell you about him—how I know him."

Erik placed the envelope on the table and stood up. He took a few steps and turned to study her. He put his hands in his pockets to control them, to keep from shaking the truth out of her. "So I was right—about you and Manuel?"

"No, no. Please. I have never been unfaithful to you, and I would not be, ever. But I have kept secrets from you." She picked up her cup, inhaled the steam and seemed to be drawing strength from it. "Manuel is my cousin."

"Your cousin? What—" That explained why they seemed so fond of each other. "But when he first came, you said you didn't know him. I thought ..." He shuddered at the suspicions he'd had, even a few moments ago when she was so upset. "Why didn't you tell me?"

"Because I would have to explain about my childhood. Things I never told you. But I want to tell you now."

He knew all about her childhood. She'd been born in Guatemala but her father brought her to Kentucky as a baby. His lungs contracted, and he couldn't breathe. What more could there be?

For the next hour, he listened as she told him the whole

story, as he tried to understand why she had kept parts of her background a secret. She told how she had felt guilty, ashamed. He paced, he sat beside her, he moved to another chair. He asked questions, but he tried to keep his tone objective, inquisitive, hiding the confusion he felt. Her vulnerability touched him even as he struggled with the hurt that she hadn't trusted him before this.

Only once did he show anger, when she told him about the man who forced himself on her. And that anger was not directed at her, but at the unknown man who had molested her.

When she finished, he sat motionless. Only his chest moved in and out.

"I am sorry I lied to you all these years, Erik. I love you so much, and I didn't want to lose you. I know it was wrong not to trust you. But right now, there are people in real danger.

"I told you all this so you would know why I trust Manuel completely. I need you to read what's in the envelope. Put aside how you feel about me right now, and study these documents and photos. People are dying, and the evidence is here." She touched his hand. "Please. You can stop it. You must stop it."

More? He couldn't comprehend what he had already heard, and she wanted him to read the information in this packet? But her eyes pleaded with him, and he couldn't deny her. He reached out and picked up the envelope. "I'll read it in my office. Then we'll talk again."

Chapter Fifty-Two

An hour later, when Erik came out of his office, Ellen sat curled up on the sofa where she had spent the time praying. She couldn't remember ever seeing his face so pale.

He sat down hard in a wingback chair. He had put the documents into a file folder, which he laid on the coffee table. "I need to talk to Manuel. Do you mind if I ask him to come back?"

"Of course not. I doubt he's asleep yet. He knew I'd be telling you all this." She paused. "Do you want me to call him?"

He nodded, and she rose to make the call.

As she expected, Manuel had waited to hear from her, and he arrived in fifteen minutes. She let him in and led him into the living room.

Erik had been alternately reviewing the folder and watching Ellen. While they waited, he had not spoken. He stood and extended a hand. "Manuel, thanks for coming back at such a late hour. Let's go into my office." He picked up the folder and looked at Ellen. She saw a change in his expression, one she didn't recognize. "On second thought, let's just stay here. Ellen—or *Elena*—you may as well stay."

Except for the odd emphasis on her birth name, his voice gave no hint of his emotions. She gratefully accepted the chance to listen to their conversation. "Shall I bring coffee?"

Both men nodded, and she hurried to the kitchen. A few minutes later, she returned with a tray and three cups. She joined Manuel on the sofa. He described how he had found the empty chemical containers buried next to the riverbank. "I was fortunate the old man came to help me. I could not have managed alone after hurting my ankle. He told me he was afraid to come at first, but that God had spoken to him. And he decided there was little they could do to hurt him any more than he'd already been hurt."

Erik flipped through pages in the folder spread on the coffee table. "Tell me about this report on the soil and water samples."

Manuel explained how he had collected the samples and sent them for testing. He went on to tell Erik about Isabella and other children who could not walk because of birth defects, of young married men who were unable to father children, of men and women who died before the age of fifty. Tears rolled down Ellen's face by the time he finished.

"But why didn't you bring me this information before we closed on the property?" Erik's voice cracked. She had only heard him lose his composure once—immediately after his parents died in the plane crash.

"I only received the report a week ago, *Señor* Neilson. Without the report, I could not prove what was causing the illnesses." He shifted his position. "I was told that you chose to go ahead with the purchase and not wait for the test results."

Erik tapped a drumbeat with his pen on the legal pad resting on his lap. "Who told you that?"

"Alan. He is also the one who sent me the report." He reached for the folder Erik had laid on the coffee table. He sifted through the pages until he found the one he wanted. He handed a sheet of notepaper to Erik. "This is the note that was attached to the falsified report when I received it."

Erik nodded. "I saw it." He stared at the handwritten note for several minutes. Manuel shifted his position and looked at Ellen. She shared the anguish that she saw in his eyes, but neither spoke.

Without looking up, Erik spoke in a low, flat voice. "Warren told me three weeks ago that the reports had arrived and showed nothing of concern. Both he and Alan said you concurred that we should proceed with the purchase." He shook his head as if waking from a bad dream. He picked up his coffee cup, and holding it below his chin, he pressed his lips together in a flat grimace. "I guess they didn't expect that you would ever talk to me."

Manuel nodded. "They do not know that I spoke with Dr. Faulkner or that I obtained the actual report."

Erik leaned back, took a deep breath, and seemed to release tension as if from a spring. "All right." He drank the last of his coffee, and Ellen rose to get refills. "Let's talk about what we're going to do."

Marcie showed Manuel into the president's office. Erik stood by the window holding a baseball in one hand. Warren, sitting in front of the desk, appeared ready to strangle someone—probably him. Alan, in the other chair, looked squeamish. Marcie had said Erik wanted to see him but he hesitated, unsure whether to interrupt.

Erik waved him in. "Join us, Manuel. We were just discussing the tests on the soil and water samples from Indiana Plantation. I believe you've seen a copy of that report."

Manuel couldn't sense Erik's mood. He took one step into the room and stopped.

Erik strode to his desk and dropped into the executive chair. "Warren says he had no idea about the chemicals. He's blaming Tex and says we should fire him. What do you think?" He motioned to Manuel again. "Come on. Come on. Pull up another chair."

Manuel picked up an armchair from the arrangement by the sofa and moved it near the desk. He still did not understand. This was not part of the plan they had decided on Saturday night.

"Well?" Erik tilted his chair back. "Speak up. I want to know what you think."

He looked at Warren and Alan, then back at Erik. "I do agree that Tex should be released. But I do not think he acted alone. There were others directing his actions. Tex is not—shall we say—sophisticated enough to develop such a complicated scheme on his own."

Erik brought his chair level and hit the desk with his palm. "Exactly. That's what I was just saying. What I didn't tell them yet"—he shuffled through the papers in the file folder lying open in front of him and picked up two pages—"What I didn't tell them is how you learned that the test results had been falsified."

He laid the papers on the stack and closed the file, folding his hands on top. He peered at Warren then at Alan. "I asked Manuel to join us so there would be a witness, in case you gentlemen would like to confess to what you've done."

Alan leaned forward and buried his face in his hands. Warren shot Manuel an evil look and sputtered a few words of denial.

Erik interrupted the incoherent sounds. "Cut the bull, Warren. It's over. I trusted you, and you repay me by covering up this pollution and letting children die. I don't know—or care—whose idea it was, but you condoned it."

He turned to Alan. "And you, Alan. Your biggest crime is probably being too weak to speak up, to go against Warren. Although, I think I know now why the financials don't add up." He stood up and walked behind Manuel's chair.

"Now I know that the evidence against the two of you is

too weak to press criminal charges. But I'm sure if we were to dig deep enough, we could find that evidence. However, it won't do the company's reputation any good, and I don't think my father would have gone that route."

He stepped back to the desk and pulled two envelopes out of the top drawer. He flipped them against one palm. "So here's the deal. You are both, of course, fired. And so is Tex. Effective immediately. You go quietly and Neilson Enterprises never hears from you again. Then that's the end of it. You don't, and I will hire investigators, get the evidence I need, and press charges. We'd start by looking for embezzlement and go from there, and I'll report you to the Guatemalan authorities for using illegal chemicals." He held out an envelope to each man. "You don't deserve it, but here's a severance check—a month's salary. If you're as smart as I think you are, you've got plenty in savings to get by on after that's gone. Any questions?"

Alan accepted the envelope. Without looking at him, he whispered, "I'm sorry, Erik."

Warren snatched his envelope and stuffed it in his jacket pocket. "You'll never be able to run this company without me, Neilson. I know more about this business than ten of you." He stood and stalked to the door, and Alan followed him.

Without softening his stern expression, Erik tipped his head in Manuel's direction. "Oh, didn't I introduce you to your replacement? Meet Manuel Rivas, my new senior vice president. I believe he's quite capable. That is, if he will accept the job."

For Such a Moment

Chapter Fifty-Three

Erik ordered a pizza delivered to his office, and worked late into the night, reviewing the files from Indiana Plantation. He could identify some areas where Warren and Tex had overstated expenses and funneled money into their own pockets. No wonder things had felt wrong. But it would take a team of auditors to trace all the rabbit trails. They had been clever. Very clever. The company would recover only a small portion of the funds. Going after all of it would consume too many resources. At least, thanks to Manuel, he had stopped the bleeding before it proved disastrous. Though he still had an environmental problem to clean up.

Tex's bouncer image had been a good façade for a crafty mind. But he considered Tex's scam minor compared to Warren's. Twenty years, Warren Stubbs had been with the company. His dad trusted him, thought of him as his best friend. While Erik hadn't considered him a friend, he had respected his knowledge of the business. And his experience.

Warren had risen to the second highest position in the company and had been well paid. What made a man betray the company—and people—who had contributed to his success?

Betrayal perplexed him. His parents had taught him the importance of trust, of keeping your word, honoring your promises, even insignificant ones. The first time he used his dad's car for a date, he had been ten minutes late getting home. Dad had been out of town, but his mother grounded him for a week.

"Life is not just about you, son." She peered up at him from her reading chair. Her tone held compassion but allowed no argument. "If you're late getting your date home, you cause unnecessary worry for the girl's parents as well as for your father and me. How can you be trusted with major decisions in the future if you don't keep your commitments now?"

His mother had known how to speak to his heart in a way that he understood. After that, he had always been home at least five minutes early.

He rose and took a blanket and pillow from the storage unit in the corner. He'd packed an overnight bag Sunday morning before he left the house and hadn't been out of the office since then. Tomorrow morning he would go out for breakfast.

As he lay on the improvised bed he'd made up on the sofa, he tried to find a comfortable position. He thought he knew Ellen, but she'd kept secrets from him. From the beginning. He didn't care about her background, or that she couldn't have children. But he'd taken care of her, and she had made him look foolish.

His heart seemed to be shrinking in his chest. Did she even love him? Maybe she had only married him for his money as Warren suggested the other night.

No, he didn't believe that. His mother had an ability to look inside a person, and she had liked Ellen. "She loves you, Erik," she told him. "She's reserved, but she'll be a fine wife. You need to ask yourself if you love her."

Diffused moonlight seeped through the vast window, creating a shadowy presence in the room. In the dim light, he could imagine his father sitting at the desk, studying him, tossing him the baseball. Would he catch it and hold onto it, or would he throw it back?

Chapter Fifty-Four

"I am still in shock." Manuel told Ellen of his promotion as he ran beside her Tuesday morning. "To go from managing director to senior vice president overnight is too much. I do not know the company enough."

Misty rain watered the grass and dripped from her nylon running jacket. Their shoes splattered droplets as they splashed through tiny puddles. She had heard nothing from Erik for two days.

She tried to keep her voice cheerful, upbeat. "You'll do a wonderful job. Erik needs someone trustworthy and reliable who will give him good advice." They passed several weeping willow trees, their branches drooping toward the ground. "You want what's best for the company, but you also care about people. Like he does."

Erik had not looked at her Sunday morning while he threw socks and underwear into a small suitcase. "I need time to think" had been his last words to her. The lack of sleep evident in his face only emphasized the betrayal and hurt she saw there. She did not blame him for wanting to leave. She had always known the truth would drive him away.

She focused on Manuel. "You know, Erik's father and grandfather ran the company with a concern for people. Warren obviously didn't have that."

He glanced sideways at her. "Was not Warren also his father's advisor?"

She nodded. "But I think his father was …" She did not want to criticize her husband. Not now, not to his new SVP. Not when she already worried their marriage would not survive. "Erik's father had more time to learn from his own father, to see how to balance profit and ethics. His strength kept Warren from wielding too much control."

A tall man in red running shirt and shorts, cropped gray hair above glistening black skin, neared them. He flashed a smile. "Good morning, Ellen."

"Good morning, Judge." She no longer needed to fear being seen with Manuel. A mass seemed to lift from her back, replaced seconds later by a tightness in her chest as she considered the possibility of a future without Erik.

Manuel's voice interrupted her thoughts. "You believe Warren saw Erik as weak and took advantage of his lack of experience."

"Yes. I think Warren viewed lack of confidence as ineptitude. Erik allowed him freedom to manage things without interference because he thought his father had trusted him."

"And Warren took advantage of that trust."

"Yes. But Erik's not weak, and he's not stupid. He proved that by promoting you." She grinned at him, the first smile she had managed since Sunday.

Hours later, she sat in the kitchen, eating lunch only because Angelica insisted. She had not been able to face the large, empty dining table since Erik left.

Outside, the skies had released a torrential rain, casting a gloom over the normally sunny room. After forcing down half a chicken salad sandwich, she pushed the plate away. She leaned her head on her folded arms on the table.

"What am I going to do, Angelica?"

She had not told anyone, not even Manuel, that Erik had left. But she couldn't hide that fact from the woman who cleaned and cooked for them. Besides, Angelica had been helping her learn about the Bible and teaching her about prayer, and Ellen considered her a good friend. She treated her like her *mamá* would have, if she had lived.

Angelica reached over and patted her back. "God will take care of you, *señora*. He will show you what to do. Just keep talking to Him, no?"

She hadn't talked to God much this week. She had finally been honest with Erik, and now she faced life alone. Erik wouldn't be back unless he returned to tell her to move out.

"I can't," she mumbled into her arm. "God doesn't hear me."

Angelica sighed, rose, and came to stand by her chair. She wrapped her arms around Ellen. "Now, *señora*, you know this is not true. Remember how He take care of you since your *mamá* died? How He brought you here? He will not leave you now."

Her tears flowed then, as thunder shook the windows.

Chapter Fifty-Five

Friday was a day of endings. The end of an exhausting week. And the end of Marcie's silence.

Erik noticed her curious looks every morning at finding him in the office when she arrived. Every evening before she left, she made a point to say, "It's time to go home, Mr. Neilson."

Each time, he ignored the comment. "Good night, Marcie."

Apparently by Friday morning she'd had enough. She marched into his office like a boxer ready to tangle. She stood just inside the door, hands on her hips. "Mr. Neilson, we need to talk."

He had just finished shaving. He unplugged the razor, stored it in the cabinet, rubbed his face, and examined it in the mirror. He knew what she meant but didn't want to admit it to anyone. "What about, Marcie?"

"You know what about. Why you're sleeping here in the office. Why you haven't been home all week." She moved toward him. "I know I'm your secretary, but your mother's gone, and I think you need a mother right now. To help you think straight. And I have known you since you were knee high to a grasshopper." She wagged a finger at him. "So talk to me."

He had to chuckle. He raised his hands in mock surrender and crossed to the sofa. He had not yet folded the blanket and stored it, so he pushed it aside and sat. He leaned over, placed his arms on his knees, and rested his forehead in his hands. "It's complicated. Ellen's been lying to me."

Marcie moved to sit beside him and placed a hand on his

back. She rubbed lightly in a circle. "I'm sorry to hear that. But knowing her, she must have had a good reason."

He talked to her as he used to talk with his mother, and he felt the tension leave his muscles. Marcie already knew about the chemicals, of course, and his dismissal of Warren and Alan. The other details poured out of him. Saturday night. The episode with Warren. Ellen's revelation about her life. About her real name. *Elena.* "I don't know why she didn't think she could tell me."

Marcie stopped rubbing and patted his back. "I can see why you've been upset. None of us guessed she was hiding such things."

She leaned back and closed her eyes. He expected her to agree that he had a right to be angry, to leave. The next step would be to file for divorce and ask Ellen to move out of the Neilson family home.

Marcie opened her eyes and lifted her head. "Have you thought about it from her side?"

He stood and paced away from her. "What? Her side?"

"That's right. She must have had a terrible background if she thought she needed to hide it from you. Imagine, a little girl—you said she was ten? She lived in horrible conditions, just her and her mother. She lost the only home she knew."

Marcie pursed her lips and shook her head. "She came to a strange country to live with a father she had never met. She didn't speak the language. And she lost everything again when cancer took her stepmother and that drunk driver killed her father. I just can't imagine a woman her age dealing with so much tragedy in her life."

Erik stared out the window. "That didn't give her the right to deceive me."

"No, it didn't. But it does explain it, don't you think? You were the best thing that had come into her life in a long time.

She was probably afraid of losing you, too. It must have taken a lot of courage to tell you now, after all this time."

The pendulum of his heart swung one way and then the other. Was Ellen someone he didn't even know who had deceived him, or was she the woman he loved, the woman of courage that Marcie described?

An hour later as he and Manuel concluded their daily briefing, Manuel closed his notebook. "May I say something?"

Erik tensed, wondering what bad news Manuel would give him. He stood and walked to the credenza. He motioned to Manuel's coffee cup on the table in front of the sofa where they had been sitting. "Want some more?"

Manuel shook his head. "No, thank you. I have enough."

Erik poured coffee and added a packet of sugar. "What did you want to talk about?"

"Elena. I know this is personal, but I would not be fulfilling my responsibilities to you if I do not speak up."

Erik opened his mouth to snap at him. But as he turned, he saw the set of the other man's shoulders and curbed his tongue. "Go ahead."

"I know that what Elena did—excuse me, what Ellen did—was wrong. She should not have hidden from you her past. But she was very brave to tell you everything now."

Again he was being told about his wife's courage. Why couldn't she have been brave—and truthful—when they first met? He sat in his desk chair and placed his cup on a coaster. He looked at Manuel and waited.

"I do not know what is happening between you this week, but I know that she is broken. My heart hurts to see her like this. She loves you. And I pray you can find it in your heart to forgive her, to love her as she deserves." He rose. "I have said enough. I will go now."

Erik lowered his chin to his chest and did not look up as Manuel left the office and closed the door without a sound.

Chapter Fifty-Six

Erik's mind wandered more than his feet did as he reviewed the European field reports. He couldn't stay in his chair, so he roamed his office, document in hand. But his thoughts kept going back to Ellen. Both Marcie and Manuel had told him he should forgive her. They asked too much of him. She had lied. Their whole relationship was built on lies. How could he forgive that?

After two hours, he gave up and dropped into his chair. He pulled out the letter from his father and read it again. *Nurture your marriage*, his dad had written. His dad hadn't known the truth about Ellen. But Erik did—now. "What would you do in my situation, Dad?"

Knowing he would get no answer, he raked his hair with his fingers. He knew no one he could trust, who would understand his quandary. Maybe he needed to get out of the office, go someplace open, where he could think with no walls to barricade his mind. The mile-long walk to Loring Park would do him good.

Marcie had not returned from lunch yet, so he jotted a quick note to her. He paced as he waited for the elevator, which of course took longer than usual. Must be the lunch traffic. The building felt stuffy. He punched the button again, and finally the chime sounded.

The car stopped on the twentieth floor. When the door opened, he saw a young woman with her back turned, talking on a cell phone. She glanced over her shoulder and tossed her shoulder length black hair. She reminded him of Ellen: tall, slender, fair skinned. She snapped the phone shut as she clumped onto the elevator.

He remembered her face, probably from new employee orientation, but couldn't recall a name or department. She grimaced, drawing her eyebrows together in a scowl that made her appear older, but he guessed her age at just over twenty. Without looking at him, she turned immediately to the control panel and stabbed the already-lit button for the lobby. She tapped one platform shoe. Once the elevator started moving, she put her back to the wall and glanced at Erik. Her expression switched instantly to surprise. "Mr. Neilson, I—I didn't see you." She sounded alarmed, as if she had been caught stealing.

"That's all right. You seem upset. Is everything okay?"

She tilted her head to one side, her mouth twisting into a half smile. "Just having an argument with my boyfriend. He's being unreasonable and..." Her hand went to her mouth. "I'm sorry. You don't want to hear about—I mean, it's nothing."

"Relax. I don't bite." He held up his hand, wanting to put her at ease. He glanced at her ID badge and read her name. "Stacy. I can't remember which department you work in."

She focused on the floor and then back at him, then shifted her eyes to the wall behind him. "Accounts Payable." The words came out small and squeaky, and she seemed relieved when the elevator stopped. "Bye, Mr. Neilson." She hustled into the lobby as she opened her phone and began to punch the keys.

Once outside, Erik stopped on the sidewalk and breathed deeply, relishing the hot, sunny day. A trio, two women and a man in suits, split to go around him, waking him from his musing. He swiveled left and headed toward Hennepin Avenue. At the corner, he turned left again, following the major thoroughfare southwest toward Interstate 94. He began to perspire, so he pulled off his suit jacket and slung it over one arm.

After he passed Tenth Street, the pedestrian traffic thinned out, and he could lengthen his stride. He passed several empty storefronts and a parking lot. Traffic zoomed past, cars and trucks slowing only when forced to by a red light. A bus pulling away from the curb spewed exhaust fumes that made him cough. He would be glad when he reached the park, a green refuge where the air would be clearer, and he hoped his thoughts would be, too. He needed to sort out his feelings for Ellen, to decide what to do about his marriage.

On one hand, why would she have confessed everything about her childhood when they first met? He hadn't really asked; he had made some assumptions. Everyone knew what happened when you assumed. Had he proven to be a fool for not realizing she had kept secrets? But she had never taken advantage of his money, although she enjoyed the luxuries they had. She always thought of others first, she loved children, and she was pretty and talented. He enjoyed spending time with her, although she could not have known that from the last few years. But she was not who he thought she was.

In the middle of the block ahead of him, he spotted Stacy, the young woman from the elevator, walking fast in the same direction. She used one arm to make frenetic gestures while she held her cell to her ear with the other hand. She must still be arguing with her boyfriend. She zigzagged around the trees that had been planted along the sidewalk every few feet. From the way she wobbled, he guessed the built-up shoes made it difficult to walk.

He checked for traffic as he crossed Eleventh Street. When he looked ahead again, he saw Stacy jerk the phone away from her head, hold it in front of her face as she continued to walk, shove it back to her ear. She collided with a young man heading toward her. And then she twisted to the right. Her heavy shoe turned off the edge of the sidewalk and she lost her balance. Her momentum carried her into the street—right into the path of a large, white delivery truck.

Chapter Fifty-Seven

Ellen took her cell phone and went for a walk. She punched the speed dial number for Diane. She couldn't put off the call any longer.

"Hey, I've been wondering where you disappeared to." Her friend's voice always carried a smile across the miles, and Ellen couldn't help but feel better when she heard it.

"It's been a hard week, Di."

"Tell me all about it. The kids are out with Mike feeding the animals, so I've got time."

Ellen watched a rider pass on the cycling path that paralleled the walking path. The bike wheels spun away from her just like her secure life. "Erik knows everything. And he's left, just like I knew he would."

A long pause on the other end. "What happened?"

Ellen related the events of the party. How Warren had tried to kiss her, and Erik had walked in. How she had gained the strength to tell him her secret so that she could convince him to believe Manuel's report about the Guatemalan plantations. About the danger to the employees and the villagers.

"He believed it all." She stopped and plopped on a bench overlooking the lake. "But he walked out Sunday morning. I haven't heard from him since. And—" Her voice broke. She swallowed the toxin that had risen in her throat. "And I think God's abandoned me, too. Again."

"Oh, Laynie. I know it feels like that. But He hasn't. He promised never to leave you or forsake you. He has brought you through so much. And it seems as though He allowed this situation for a reason—so you could tell Erik about those chemicals. And stop people from being poisoned. All of your life, He's been preparing you for this moment."

"But what will I do now?" She hated sounding so helpless, so desperate.

"First of all, you don't know that Erik's not coming back. He said he needed time to think, right? But even if he doesn't come back, Laynie, you will survive. With God's help, Elena Ellen Rivas Neilson, you survived the slums of Guatemala, the teasing of kids at school, the tragic deaths of your father and stepmother. You have a degree from the U of M, and you are a gifted artist."

"I'm not."

"Look, God has given you talent, and it's time you stop denying it."

"But—"

Diane didn't give her a chance to argue. "You will keep praying and listening for God's voice. You will take one step at a time, following His guidance, until one day, you wake up and find that you have built a new life. With or without Erik, you will find joy again. Because God is faithful."

On the way back to the house, she decided to take Diane's advice and make a plan. If Erik decided to divorce her, she would have to support herself. She needed to find out whether other people liked her artwork, and if she could earn any money from it.

She left a phone message with Geri, director of the Walker, asking if her offer to arrange an exhibition still stood. Ellen knew the main exhibit hall schedule had been set for the next several months, but perhaps Geri could arrange for a small showing in one of the other rooms.

She prayed for God's direction as she pondered which paintings might interest buyers. Maybe none of them were good enough, but she had to try. She started the CD player, then she picked up a painting and placed it with the ones she had decided to show or sell.

A year ago, she had worried about losing Erik, losing the security of their marriage. She had hoped having a baby would solve their problems but even that had proven to be impossible. The last few months, their relationship seemed to be improving, and they had even talked about adopting an infant. But having children no longer seemed important.

She knew now that she could be happy without children or money, as long as she and Erik could stay together. But it might be too late. She would never forget how he had stopped at the door before leaving Sunday morning. As he turned and stared at her without speaking, his blue eyes had revealed a mixture of rage and anguish. She had wanted to protest, to beg him not to go, but she could not conjure up one good reason that would convince him to stay.

Not that she blamed him for leaving. Now that he knew her secret and realized that she had not been honest with him all these years, he probably wanted nothing more to do with her. Perhaps he had already decided that he could no longer trust her.

He'd be wrong, of course. Never again would she mislead him. No matter what he thought of her. If only he would give her a chance to prove her new commitment, to show how Christ had changed her.

The aftermath of Saturday's party had shattered Erik's world. In addition to her confession, he had learned about Warren's betrayal. Warren, who had been a trusted advisor to Erik's father for years. Warren, who had counseled Erik since his father's death. Yet Warren and Alan had concocted a deceitful plan, lining their own pockets while violating company principles. Erik had been quick and decisive in firing them both. He may decide to discard her the same way, and she deserved it as much as they had.

The air in the studio seemed to press down on her, and she moved in slow motion. Every painting she picked up seemed to be heavier than the last. Even the music dragged. She shook her head. She recognized the familiar fear, and she refused to give in to it. Even if Erik couldn't forgive her, she knew that God already had. Would He give her the strength she needed to handle whatever lay ahead?

Chapter Fifty-Eight

Erik's heart thudded and his stomach flipped. He ran toward the middle of the block where the young woman from Accounts Payable lay motionless on the pavement. The activity around him continued as if the world had gone into slow motion. The white delivery truck swerved into the next lane, brakes squealing through the intersection, then pulled to the curb and stopped. The young man that Stacy had bumped into swiveled, dropped the backpack he had been carrying, and froze.

Erik reached Stacy and knelt on the hot blacktop next to her. He tried to recall his first aid training from Boy Scouts. He put his fingers on her neck, checked for a pulse. "Call 9-1-1," he yelled at no one in particular. He looked up.

The man—no, only a kid, probably a college student— with the backpack had not moved. Erik stared directly at him. "You! Call 9-1-1! Now!" The student jerked from his stupor, pulled out a cell phone, and tapped the keys.

A pudgy man appeared from the street and sank to his knees next to Stacy. His sweat-stained white shirt bore a company logo on the pocket. The truck driver. "Oh, God, no," he screamed. "She just jumped—or fell—" He put his face in his hands, his entire body heaving. "I don't know where she came from. Oh, God, please!"

Several people, phones held to their ears, poured out of nearby buildings and the pizza shop down the block. The first student hovered nearby, mumbling into his phone.

Erik could not feel a pulse in her neck. He picked up her slender arm and touched the cool wrist. Still no pulse. He needed to try CPR. Taking her shoulders gently, he rolled her onto her back. "Come on, Stacy. Don't die. Not now, not like this. You're too young." She was not breathing. He pinched her nose and blew into her mouth. Once. Twice. He listened for a response. Nothing. He shouted at the student with the phone. "Is help coming?"

The student nodded. "Yeah, they're on their way." His voice broke. "They want to know if she's breathing." When Erik shook his head, he spoke into the phone. "She's not breathing. Some guy's using CPR."

Erik put his hands on her chest and pumped. One, two, three, he counted silently. Fourteen, fifteen. Back to her mouth. *Breathe, Stacy, breathe.*

He heard a siren. Finally. A police car halted down the block. Vaguely, he knew that an officer jumped out and began to direct traffic around the scene.

Stacy's black hair splayed out onto the street, reminding him again of Ellen. *Don't die.* He couldn't lose her. He returned to pumping her chest.

With one corner of his mind, he tried to save his employee, a young woman he hardly knew. He had talked to her in the elevator just minutes ago.

In a separate place in his thoughts, he visualized Ellen lying on the street, unable to talk or move. Unable to hear him say he loved her. That he could forgive her. That he understood what courage it had taken for her to relive those early years of her life in order to tell him her story. That he wanted to know the real woman he had married. Elena.

"No, Ellen. Don't leave me. I love you." The sirens were close now.

He heard a voice at his side. "Sir? Is she breathing? Any bleeding?" He continued to count the chest compressions as he answered the questions. "All right, sir, let us take it from here."

When he didn't stop, the EMS responder grew more insistent. "Please, sir. I need you to move out of the way." Strong hands grasped his arms, pulling him away from her unresponsive body.

One man helped him to his feet while the other took over CPR. Holding his arm, the uniformed EMT led him over to a police officer. "Okay. I've got him." The officer helped him down the block to a waiting cruiser with its lights flashing. He opened the front passenger door. "We'll want to talk to you about what happened, but sit here for now. You've done all you can for her."

Erik's bones chilled his insides despite the heat of the summer day. He had failed. She had been killed right in front of him, and he had not been able to save her.

The fog in his brain cleared, and he made his decision. The past made no difference. He wanted a future with Ellen. He needed to go home to her, to tell her. He got out of the car, but the officer waiting nearby stepped in front of him. "Sir, I have to ask you to stay here. We need to get your information."

Erik nodded but remained standing. Beyond the police officer, he could see the medics lifting Stacy onto a stretcher. They covered her body with a blue blanket and rolled the stretcher to the ambulance. The two paramedics closed the doors and got in the front. The lights on top went off, and the vehicle moved, without hurrying, around the abandoned delivery truck and up Hennepin Avenue toward the hospital. Stacy's platform shoes remained, one turned sideways in the middle of the street where it had landed, the other sitting on the sidewalk as if she had just stepped out of it.

Chapter Fifty-Nine

Erik thought of himself as Ellen's protector, but he couldn't even protect Stacy. Not that he knew her, but as her employer, didn't he have some responsibility?

After he told the police what had happened, the officer gave him a ride. In the front passenger seat of the cruiser, he closed his eyes. All he could see was the white delivery truck and the way Stacy's body had been flung onto the hot pavement, landing with a *thud*. He should have grabbed her, pulled her away. Protected her.

The police officer's gentle voice interrupted his thoughts. "You couldn't have saved her, you know."

Erik opened his eyes. The officer pulled to a stop in front of the Neilson Building and turned a penetrating gaze at him. "I've seen it before. A bystander feels responsible because he couldn't save the victim. But it's called an accident for a reason. It happened too fast, and she probably died on impact. Don't blame yourself. You did everything possible."

Erik nodded. The man spoke the truth. But that didn't make it easy to forget what happened, to squelch the voice in his head telling him he had failed the young woman. He thanked the officer and assured him in a hollow tone that he would be all right. As he forced his body to get out of the car, his limbs felt as if they wore fifty-pound handcuffs and leg irons.

He entered the lobby and trudged to the security desk. Ed put down his newspaper. He pushed his glasses up on his nose and peered at Erik. "You okay, sir? You look like you got run over by a bus."

Erik looked down at his clothes. He carried his suit jacket carelessly over his arm, and his gray shirt, loose and wrinkled, showed several smudges. His pants had dust and dirt from the street stuck to the knees. The guard had no idea how close his comment came to the truth. He sighed. "I'm not hurt, Ed. No need to be concerned about me."

Alone on the elevator, he tucked his shirt in and put the jacket on, buttoning it up to hide the smudges from Marcie. She noticed everything, and he did not want to alarm her. He bent and brushed off his pants then straightened his tie.

Marcie stood up when he got off the elevator. "Mr. Neilson, I was beginning to think you had left for the day in spite of what your note said." She observed him as he approached. He hadn't fooled her. She stepped out from behind her desk and moved to his side. "What's happened, Erik?"

He continued into his office, and she followed him. "Marcie, I'll tell you all about it, but not right now. I need time to think."

He closed the office double doors, leaving her standing there with a puzzled expression.

It seemed like days since he had left, not hours. His eyes fixed on the baseball, and he crossed to the bookcase and touched it. With three fingers, he rotated the ball on its holder, and he noticed each rough spot. Scuffs from being hit by a bat, bouncing in dirt, tossed from father to son.

When had he decided to quit using it, to save this particular ball? A few weeks after receiving it for his eighth birthday. One day, he sat on the back steps tossing the ball and catching it as he waited for his father to come home from work. He knew they would play catch like they did several times a week. Finally Mother came out and told him that something had happened, that Dad would be late. He and Mother ate dinner alone.

Dad didn't arrive home until after dark. Erik stood in the living room door watching as his father hugged Mother for a long time without speaking. Finally, Dad let go, touched Erik on the shoulder as he passed, and went upstairs to bed. The grandfather clock in the hall chimed, breaking the silence of the big house.

Mother crossed to Erik and squatted to look at him. Tears spilled from her eyes. "Erik, son, there's no easy way to tell you this. Your Grandpa Neilson has, um, passed." Her voice sounded weak.

"Passed what?" His small voice came out as a squeak.

"Passed … away. He had a heart attack today, and he died."

Erik knew Grandpa Neilson was old, but he couldn't imagine that the sturdy, active man was gone. He had never been an affectionate man, but Erik liked the way he always gave him a strong handshake and treated him like a grownup.

After the funeral, Dad began working late just about every night and started traveling more. When fall came and his father had not played catch with him again, Erik accepted that life had changed permanently. Though he didn't give up baseball, he took the special ball—the one he and Dad had played with together—and hid it in his bottom dresser drawer.

After his parents died in the plane crash, he found the ball again and ordered a special holder for it. Since then, the ball had sat in a prominent place on his office bookshelf—not within his vision all the time, but he often picked it up when he had a decision to make. Holding the ball gave him a sense of connection with his father, as though it would tell him what Dad would do.

Today, he knew without picking it up what his father would want him to do. It might not be what Dad had done every time, but it was what he talked about in the letter.

He should pay his condolences to Stacy's family. But they would probably need time to grieve and plan the funeral, before a stranger—even the head of the company she'd worked for—intruded. So that would wait until Monday. He would meet with all the headquarters employees first thing and then go to Stacy's house.

Right now, the uncertainty of life made him want to hold Ellen again. And to urge his employees to tend to their own relationships. Only a couple hours remained of the workday, but every moment counted.

The accident would make the news that evening and would be all over Twitter in no time. He wanted his employees to spend time with their families. He would make that a basic value for the company, just as his dad had wanted.

Lifting his hand from the baseball, he turned and strode to the office door. When he threw open both doors, Marcie turned in her chair. She looked startled.

"Marcie, I want you to call the department heads. No e-mail. Call each one yourself. Tell them all employees have the rest of the day off. With pay. I don't want anyone—" He looked at her. "Make it clear. No one is to remain in the office. Not a single person, including you once the calls are made. Everyone is to go home and spend time with their families."

Marcie's mouth gaped open, but she closed it quickly. "Yes, sir." She hesitated. "Does that include you?"

He pressed his lips together. "Yes, Marcie. I'm going home to Ellen."

She smiled and nodded approval. "Anything else, Mr. Neilson?"

He looked down and then back at her. "One more thing. I'd like you to ask personnel for the folder for a young woman in Accounts Payable. Stacy. I don't know her last name. I'll need it Monday morning."

"I'll find it, sir." She reached for the telephone, though her face showed unasked questions.

He moved to his desk and grabbed his key ring out of his briefcase. For a moment, he jangled the keys and considered the framed photo of his father. He knew Dad would be proud of the decisions he had just made. He dropped the keys on the desk and took two long strides to the bookcase.

With both hands, he lifted the ball and the polished wooden holder. Carrying them both to his desk, he placed them next to his father's picture.

Chapter Sixty

"Looks like you're packing up."

The sound startled Ellen, and she turned to see Erik leaning against the doorframe. She had been so absorbed in sorting and wrapping paintings that she had not heard him enter the house.

His clothes looked as though he had slept in them all week. She wanted to rush into his arms but waited for him to make the first move. She needed to know whether their relationship had a chance or if he wanted her to move out.

She shrugged. "I've decided to try a show of my work. Geri's going to add it to the Walker schedule this season. She's been after me to exhibit my work. I—I hope you don't mind."

He nodded. "Sure. I've told you before you should display your paintings." His tone lacked the enthusiasm she had hoped for. He walked around the room, glancing at various pieces. He stopped in front of her easel, which held the unfinished painting of the mountain. "Is that—" He turned and looked at her, his eyes shadowed.

She reached out and brushed her hand across the top of the canvas. "This is Guatemala, and it's a beautiful spot, but it's only a small piece of my country. Where I lived, the part I remember most, was just the opposite. *Mamá* and I lived in ugliness, in the garbage dump."

She put both hands up and brushed her hair away from her face, closing her eyes and leaning her head back. Every cell of her body felt drained. She had given him the facts on Saturday night but hadn't shared her feelings. "You really can't imagine what it was like unless you've been there."

She recalled the small shanty, her mother lying on the bare mattress, shivering from fever. She saw a younger Manuel running and laughing, and suddenly Donato's sad face replaced Manuel's smiling one. She opened her eyes and realized that Erik waited for her to continue.

Unable to face him, she wandered to the window and rested her head against the glass. "Besides being destitute, I was mixed race. Guatemalan-Mayan mother, American father. Even among the garbage dump kids, I was an outcast. After *Mamá* died, my father sent for me. When I came to America to live with him, I wanted to put all that behind me. So I pretended."

She heard Erik pacing across the room. "And you couldn't tell even me?"

Her shoulders rose and fell, but she didn't move. "I was afraid. None of my college friends knew except Diane, because we grew up together. When I met you, you seemed so— refined, so perfect. Then I met your parents and realized the importance of the Neilson heritage and how different our backgrounds were. It became easier to not mention it."

"I never cared about your background. Neither did my parents."

She turned to face him. "Are you sure about that? This house, all the antiques … it's status. And status is everything in business. And in your social circle."

He put his hands in his pockets. "Even if it had mattered to them—and I'm sure it wouldn't have—I am not the same as my parents."

"Aren't you?" She took two steps toward him and halted. "Since they died, haven't you become just like your father? You work all the time. You won't talk to me about the business—just like your father treated your mother." She breathed heavily. She had never spoken to him this way. She wiped moisture from her forehead.

He stopped pacing and eyed her. His body seemed to wilt in front of her, and her stomach clenched. She wanted to repair their relationship not make it worse. She softened her tone. "I'm sorry. I shouldn't have—"

"Don't." He held out a hand to stop her. His voice filled with years' worth of regret. "You're right. I have become too engrossed in work. I've been trying to make my father proud, to make sure I didn't ruin the family business."

He crossed to her in two strides, and his eyes caressed her. He cupped her shoulders with his hands. "I'm sorry for shutting you out and ignoring you. You are smart, capable, and talented, and I can't imagine my future without you. Can you forgive me?"

She tilted her head up and blinked. Tears filled her eyes. "Forgive you? Does this mean—you aren't angry that I wasn't honest with you?"

He wrapped his arms around her and held her in a bear hug. "Oh, Ellen. I've struggled with this all week. I thought you had made a fool of me. At first, I didn't want to admit it, but I think it bothered me that I had married the daughter of a prostitute. I did worry what that would do to the Neilson image."

He took her face in his hands and thumbed the tears from her cheeks. "Mother would be disappointed in me for even thinking that. She taught me better than that. It's not like you had a choice."

Deep in his eyes, she saw pain as intense as her own. Pain that had not been there before today. She kept her tone soft. "What changed your mind?"

"This afternoon, a young woman from Accounts Payable got hit by a truck. I saw it happen, right in front of me. She looked a little like you. And I—"

He pulled her into his cocoon again and leaned his head on top of hers. "I couldn't save her. I tried, but she died immediately." His voice cracked.

As she pressed her head against his chest, Ellen heard his heart thudding, and she felt hers beating in unison. She waited for him to continue.

He stroked her hair. "Her hair was black like yours. About the same length. When I saw her lying there on the pavement … I realized how much you mean to me. I don't want to lose you."

A seed of hope began to grow, watered by her tears and nourished by his touch.

"Ellen, you are still the same woman I married. You've been carrying pain and shame that I didn't know existed. That doesn't mean I love you less; if anything I love you more, and I want to take all that pain away."

He slowly moved his feet in time with the music she had playing, guiding her to follow his lead. "I love you. I've loved you practically from the day we met. Nothing can change that." He stroked her hair and nuzzled his face in it. "We've both made mistakes. What do you say we put the past behind us and build a new future together?"

As if his lengthy speech had not made her feel like she was standing on her mountaintop, his next words sent her soaring over the edge. "In a few months, after we get our marriage back on track, maybe we could figure out a way to have kids. Lots of them."

Epilogue

By the time they returned to Guatemala the following January, Ellen felt they had found the "eternal spring" the travel brochures promised.

With the help of counseling and Erik reducing his hours at work, their relationship had flourished. Erik planned a full two weeks of vacation—his first since his father's death—and he wanted to explore her home country with her. They agreed that the starting point should be the garbage dump and shantytown. She wanted to show him where her painful memories originated.

When she led him to the hilltop above the dump, Erik gaped at the huge pit where trucks were pulling in to deposit their loads of trash. She explained how the people gathered around the trucks to reclaim what they could from the piles of waste in order to survive.

"That's no way to live." His voice sounded choked, whether from emotion or smoke she couldn't tell.

"But it's all they know. The only hope they have is to find a better life for their children."

He put one arm around her. "We must find a way to do more. With the resources we have …" His voice trailed off and she peered at his face. The man she had fallen in love with had fully returned to her. If only he shared her faith in God.

Taking his hand, she led him past the shanties that clung to each other and to the hillside. When they reached the clubhouse, they found Salvador with a room full of children. Not wanting to interrupt, Ellen paused in the doorway with Erik behind her.

The children stood. "*Hola*," they shouted in unison. "*Bienvenido*. Wel-come."

Ellen turned to look at Erik. "Did they know we were coming?"

He shrugged his shoulders but his grin eliminated any doubt.

Salvador strode to greet them and hugged Ellen and then shook Erik's hand. "Come in, please. You must see what the children have done with the supplies you sent. You don't know what a difference it has made in their lives."

He pulled them into the room where colorful paintings of flowers and animals hung on every wall. "We are selecting paintings for an exhibition. I am letting the children decide which ones should be included."

"That's wonderful!" Ellen clapped her hands together. "Where will you hold it?"

"Manuel has arranged it with a school in your city— Minneapolis. Some school children there are painting similar subjects—the flowers and animals of their country."

"Really? I wonder why he has not mentioned that to me. I'd like to help."

"Yes, so would I," Erik said. "It could help to raise awareness of the needs here."

The children sported wide smiles and clean clothes that fit, thanks to the donations from Neilson Enterprises, Ellen knew. She searched the room until she spotted Donato. Even he had his hair combed and wore new tennis shoes. She went to him and crouched in front of him. "How are you, Donato?"

He didn't speak, but he held her gaze instead of looking away. She felt Erik's hand on her back. "So this is Donato? It's nice to meet you, son." He held out his hand. Donato peered up at him and then reached out his hand and allowed Erik to grasp it.

Erik squatted beside Ellen. "Donato, did Salvador tell you about the trip?"

Salvador had stepped up behind them and translated the question. Donato nodded his head once but kept his eyes on Ellen.

She wrinkled her forehead. Donato couldn't go anywhere. If he went to an orphanage or if someone adopted him, she might never see him again. "What trip? Where is he going?"

Erik stood up and helped her rise. Then he turned her to face him. He grasped her shoulders tenderly. "I know it's our first vacation in several years, but I thought you might like to bring Donato with us for a few days."

She stopped breathing. She must be hearing things. "With us? You and me? Now?"

He took her hands and his eyes met hers. "These last few months, you've talked about Donato so much. It seemed logical to bring him along. I wanted to surprise you."

She hugged Erik and knelt to look Donato in the face. "Would you like to take a trip with us, Donato?"

He remained stiff at first but then seemed to melt as he wrapped one arm around her shoulders and one around Erik's leg.

As they huddled together, she became aware that the children were singing in English. She wiped her face, stood up, and took Donato's hand. Erik grabbed his other hand, and they watched as Salvador directed.

"Yes, Jesus loves me," they sang. And she heard a small voice next to her whisper, "The Bible tells me so."

She and Erik both looked down at Donato. Not only did he say the words, but he wore a smile for the first time since she had met him. Just a small upturn of his lips, but a spark of hope nonetheless.

Two days later, she and Erik held Donato's hands as they

toured the new construction underway in the workers' housing compound at Indiana Plantation. He had promised this would be the only day related to business during the trip.

Manuel led them to a half-finished building where one man placed concrete blocks while another added mortar. He had spent much of his time since his promotion ensuring that the Guatemala plantations met Neilson standards. "This will be the new school. We have located a teacher who will move here as soon as all is ready. I would like, if you do not object, to invite children from the village to come here, too. We will have enough room."

Erik peered through the open doorway. "Of course. Fine idea."

"I want you to see the medical clinic." Manuel led the way to the next building. "You know that mission doctors and nurses come once a week, and a dentist visits every month."

He held the door for them to enter the small but clean concrete block building. A small woman wearing a white lab coat turned from the storage cabinet. She had skin slightly darker than Manuel's, black hair like Ellen's, and a graceful manner. Her dark eyes shimmered with an inner radiance that extended to her beaming face.

Manuel stepped up beside her and put his hand on her back. "I would like you to meet Ana Lopez Hernandez. She is a physician's assistant, and she runs an excellent clinic."

"God brought me here." Ana smiled and offered a hand to Erik. "I am privileged to serve these people."

As they talked, her affection for Manuel, and his for her, became obvious. Ellen made a mental note to ask him about Ana later.

He took them to see the housing units. Erik had told her how Neilson Enterprises had improved living conditions in the past year. Manuel had added more buildings for housing as well as bathroom facilities and a laundry room. Their little group stopped to watch a dozen exuberant children who were enjoying a new playground that rivaled any in the States.

Donato tugged at Ellen's hand. She looked down and saw his dark eyes had formed large circles filled with longing. "Yes, Donato," she said in Spanish. "You may go play with them."

He released her hand and took a couple of steps toward the red monkey bars. Then he stopped. He looked back at her. She moved forward and put her hand on his shoulder. Together they walked up to the other children, who stopped what they were doing and watched them approach.

"*Hola*," she called. "This is Donato. May he join you?"

One boy about Donato's size jumped up from the bottom of the slide where he had been waiting. Manuel spoke to him in the Mayan dialect, then turned to Donato. "His name is Juan. He will show you around, Donato."

Juan led Donato to the slide and showed him how to climb the ladder. Moments later, Donato flew down the slick surface, his eyes wide and his mouth open. He slid off the end and landed on the sand. When he got up and ran around to climb the ladder again, Ellen laughed with relief.

"Manuel, you've done a wonderful job here." Erik clapped him on the back. "I believe my father would be proud of this place. And our pesticide-free bananas are gaining traction in the marketplace. That agency you recommended has done a great job with the ad campaign."

"I knew they would, sir."

"There is one issue you'll need to address, though."

"Yes, sir. What is it?"

"You need to find a replacement for your clinic manager."

Manuel frowned. "What's wrong with Ana?"

"Don't you think she should move to Minneapolis?" Erik

grinned. "When you marry her?"

Manuel shook his head. "I—I haven't asked her yet."

Ellen laughed and hugged him. "What are you waiting for? She's crazy about you."

Two days later, after visiting the ocean and a volcano, they took Donato back to the shanty where he lived with elderly *Tante* Maria. Ellen squeezed him and did not want to let him go. She had fallen in love with the shy little boy who reminded her of her own small self. He returned her embrace with a fierce strength that surprised her.

Erik placed his hand on her back and rubbed. "This will not be forever, you know."

She looked up at him through her tears. "You mean we can come back to see him again?"

He laughed. "Yes, of course, we will. And, if you would like—"

She pulled away from Donato and stood. "What are you trying to say, Erik?"

Erik reached up, and with his thumb, wiped a tear from her cheek. "I always thought we would have our own children, but somehow that doesn't seem important anymore. There are so many kids who need a home."

She remembered how she had prayed that she would get pregnant after reading in the Bible about the barren woman. The desire to have a family remained, hidden deep in her heart.

"I've talked to the authorities," Erik continued. "If you want to, I think that we can arrange to adopt him. The government's beginning to loosen up on international adoptions. It will take some time to work through the paperwork, and it won't be easy, but I believe in a year or so …"

As the meaning of his words became clear, she could not hold back the tears. Tears of joy, not of sorrow. Perhaps God would answer the prayer for her own infant someday, but for now, she knew she could love Donato as much as if she had carried him in her womb.

"Oh, Erik." She threw her arms around his neck and kissed him. "I would love to!" She pulled back. "Are you sure?"

"Yes, I'm sure. You will make a wonderful mother, and I'll do the best I can to be a good father. Donato needs us."

With tears flowing down her face, she bent down and gathered Donato into another embrace. She murmured to him, telling him they would come back to get him, to take him home with them.

"You know," Erik said, "I've seen how you've changed over the last few months. You've been happier and more confident, less worried about everything. It's because of your faith in Jesus, isn't it?"

She released Donato, raised herself to look at Erik, and nodded. "He helps me to live day by day instead of regretting the past or fearing the future."

"Bringing this little boy into our lives will be a challenge." Erik placed his hand on Donato's shoulder, and his smile bridged the gap where the child stood between them. "I believe I'm going to need God's help. Will you teach me about your faith?"

Her heart leapt at those words she never expected to hear. With Donato still between them, Erik leaned toward her and brushed his lips against hers. Donato giggled as she reached her hand to Erik's neck and held on tight.

The End

"For Such a Moment"
Discussion Questions

1. Ellen seems to "have it all"—beauty, talent, a wealthy husband, a job she loves. Yet she lacks the assurance of security that she desires. Why? Have you ever felt that one thing was missing from your life that would give you lasting happiness?

2. Manuel and Ellen lived in similar circumstances as children. Ellen went to the United States and enjoyed a "typical" American life, while Manuel never did. What was the difference that gave Manuel peace while Ellen became bitter towards God?

3. What motivated Erik to become like his father? When might trying to please someone else become a danger?

4. Compare the similarities and differences between Ellen, Erik, and Warren.

5. We see Warren as greedy and deceitful. What do you think may have shaped his behavior? Does he have any redeeming qualities? Is there reason to believe he could ever change?

6. Ellen believed that revealing her past to Erik could cause her to lose the comfortable life she enjoyed, but not informing him could mean people would continue to be poisoned. Have you ever had to step out of your comfort zone, like Ellen did, in order to be obedient to something God asked you to do? How did you feel afterwards?

7. In the biblical story of Esther, Esther's cousin tells her, "Who knows? Maybe it was for a moment like this that you came to be part of the royal family." How does Esther's story apply to Ellen's situation? Have you encountered a situation where God placed you in a specific place at a specific time for a specific purpose?

8. What evidence did God give Ellen that He loved her and had a plan for her life? Can you identify specific evidence or situations that show you that He has a plan for your life?

9. This book is part of the "Mended Vessels" series. In what ways was Ellen "broken" and how did she become a "mended vessel"? How has God taken any broken pieces of your life and mended them, allowing you to become useful for His kingdom?

Esther's Story

Adapted from the Book of Esther

Who would have expected an orphan girl living in a foreign land to become queen?

Certainly not me.

I just wanted to marry a nice Jewish boy and live a peaceful life with lots of sons, hopefully returning someday to Jerusalem, the home of our ancestors.

Instead, I found myself captured and brought to the Persian palace against my will, along with many other girls about my age. For a year, the other prisoners and I had luxuries we had never known. We were treated to daily spa treatments, special foods, and professional makeovers. We had our hair styled by the royal beautician and we selected jewelry from Jared's. The country's top designers created our gowns. We learned palace etiquette and practiced the runway walk. We studied Persian history, current events, and the art of conversation, and learned to speak the language without an accent.

Hegai, the man who supervised our training, took a special interest in me and saw that I received extra benefits, including nicer quarters and several servants of my own.

The stakes were high. At the end of the year, each young woman would spend a night with the King. The one who pleased him most would reign as queen for as long as she lived. The others would be relegated to a life of luxurious boredom in the harem. Some might occasionally be called for again if the king desired.

The treasures of the palace presented a huge temptation for all of us. I prayed daily to Yahweh that I would not succumb to the competitiveness and jealousy I saw in the others. For most of the women, being queen would fulfill a fantasy they'd had since childhood. However, the crown did not particularly appeal to me, especially when I recalled how King Xerxes had so callously disposed of the previous queen.

My older cousin Mordecai, who cared for me after my parents died, had taught me about the God of Abraham and Isaac, the God of our people. The prophet Moses asked, "What does the Lord your God ask of you but to fear the Lord your God, to walk in obedience to him, to love him, to serve the Lord your God with all your heart and with all your soul?"

Knowing that Yahweh ruled over kings and princes, and could arrange my life to suit his purposes, I concluded that He had chosen to allow me to come to the palace. Since He had put me in this situation, I chose to follow His leading. I devoted myself to the lessons we were being taught so that I could fulfill my duties with excellence, as if I were serving the Lord God Himself.

When my turn came to go to Xerxes, I could feel God smiling as I walked across the palace gardens. A soft breeze brushed my face with the fragrance of roses and pomegranates. Blades of grass tickled my feet, shod in golden sandals adorned with amethysts and turquoise. Birds called out to me, as if they were saying, "Be strong. Be of good courage, Esther."

Though it seemed my knees would give out and land me on the floor in front of the king, I managed to perform the perfect curtsy I had practiced. I must have pleased him, because a few days later, Xerxes announced that he had chosen me to be his queen.

A royal marriage comes with unique challenges, but Xerxes developed some affection for me, and I for him. We enjoyed several happy years, and he shared with me his dreams for the future and concerns for the kingdom. We learned to trust each other.

Then the trouble started. Since my people had been exiles for a hundred years, many of the Persians looked down on us. Mordecai had told me to keep my Jewish heritage a secret to avoid any problems. But one man named Haman—my husband's number one adviser—held an especially deep hatred for Jews.

Haman also desired power and honor that should have been reserved for Xerxes. Mordecai, who worshiped only Yahweh, refused to bow down when Haman passed. That infuriated Haman. When he learned Mordecai was a Jew, he began to plot a way to destroy not only Mordecai, but all of our people living under Persian rule.

That schemer convinced my husband to sign a proclamation that would destroy the Jews within a year. On a day determined by casting lots, the Persian people would be allowed to kill all the Jews. The Jewish people would have no way to defend themselves. Mordecai urged me to speak to the king about this injustice.

But I had not been called before Xerxes for more than a month. "Mordecai, my dear cousin, if I ask to speak to the king and he refuses me, I could be put to death." I grasped his hands. "You warned me to keep my Jewish heritage a secret. Surely you would not ask me to risk my life now."

His eyes filled with tears. "Esther, if you do not go before the king, Yahweh will find another way to save His people. But do not think that your life will be spared when this decree is carried out."

"I cannot do it." I pulled away from him and crossed to the window, staring over the compound walls to the city beyond. "Do you forget what happened to Queen Vashti when she displeased Xerxes?"

"No, I have not forgotten. It grieves me to ask you this, my dear. But perhaps our Lord God has brought you to your position for such a moment as this."

I could not refuse. I asked Mordecai to gather the Jews in the city to fast and pray while I did the same. Three days later, I went to the king, and he granted me an audience. I invited him and Haman to a banquet in my chambers.

I took great care to arrange an elaborate feast. My servants arranged my hair and dressed me in a gown that Xerxes had admired. When the two men arrived, my knees felt as shaky as the first time I had appeared before the king. I prayed that Yahweh would again give me the courage I needed.

At the end of the banquet, Xerxes promised me whatever I wanted, up to half his kingdom. In my spirit I felt the time was not yet right to tell him, so I invited both men to another banquet the next evening. I spent all day preparing and praying. When we had finished eating, my husband relaxed on the cushions and again offered to give me whatever I asked.

I bowed my head. "Please, your majesty, spare my life and save my people. For someone has connived to destroy us, to slaughter every one of us."

Xerxes sat erect. "You are my queen. How could this be possible?" His face reddened. "Tell me who has done this, and where he is."

"He is here," I said. "This vile man, Haman." Then I told the king my story. He listened, becoming more distressed as he grasped my meaning. He jumped to his feet and stormed out to the garden.

As I talked, Haman had grown more and more miserable in appearance. He must have suspected what the king would do, for he remained at the table. He threw himself on me, begging for mercy. Just then, Xerxes returned. "How dare you molest the queen?" He pulled the man off me and ordered his guards to lock up Haman.

Xerxes took me in his arms. "Are you hurt, my dear? I should not have left you alone with him. Please forgive me." He pressed my head to his chest and stroked my hair.

"I am unharmed." My clogged throat would not allow me to say more, so I nestled against my strong husband and drew comfort from him.

Xerxes ordered my enemy to be hanged on the very gallows that Haman had built for Mordecai. In his place, Xerxes made Mordecai his top adviser and gave him his signet ring. My cousin used his position to speak up for our people and he worked to improve the welfare of Jews throughout the land.

Since the proclamation providing for our destruction bore the king's seal, it could not be repealed. But at Mordecai's suggestion, my husband issued another proclamation allowing our people to arm ourselves. When the day of the expected genocide came, the Jewish people throughout Persia were prepared, and prevailed against those who would have annihilated us.

We celebrate the Feast of Purim each year to remember how Yahweh brought a Jewish orphan to the throne of a foreign country so that He could use her to save His people. I praise the Lord God that He put me in that place for that moment, to fulfill His purposes.

About the Author

Marie Wells Coutu, a debut novelist, has written for business, government, and nonprofit organizations, including the Billy Graham Evangelistic Association for the past fourteen years. The author or editor of five published nonfiction books and hundreds of newspaper and magazine articles, she has edited devotionals and other books published by the Billy Graham Evangelistic Association. She manages an inspirational website, mended-vessels.com, where she and others blog, review books, and offer inspiration and encouragement.

She has been a finalist in the 2009 ACFW Genesis Contest, 2010 Women of Faith Writing Contest, and placed as a Bronze Medalist in the 2011 and 2012 Frasier Awards sponsored by My Book Therapy.

A graduate of the 2005 and 2008 She Speaks conferences sponsored by Proverbs 31 Ministries, she has spoken to church, ministry, and non-religious groups ranging in size from twenty to three hundred. She presents dramatic readings to church groups, and has been interviewed for newspapers, radio, and television.

She holds BA and MA degrees in journalism from Murray

State University (Kentucky), and taught journalism and mass communications at St. Cloud State University (Minnesota). She and her husband live in South Carolina and have two children and three grandchildren.

Marie is a member of American Christian Fiction Writers, and served as president of the local chapter, Carolina Christian Writers. She has held various leadership roles for government communicators' associations and the local historical commission.

You can find Marie on the Web:

www.Mended-Vessels.com
www.MarieWellsCoutu.com
Marie Wells Coutu Facebook
Twitter: @MWCoutu

Look for other books

published by

www.WriteIntegrity.com

and

Pix-N-Pens Publishing

www.PixNPens.com